the
man
I loved
before

the man I loved before

Georgina Cutler

Black&White

Black&White

First published in the UK in 2025 by Black & White Publishing
An imprint of Bonnier Books UK
5th Floor, HYLO, 103–105 Bunhill Row,
London, EC1Y 8LZ

Owned by Bonnier Books
Sveavägen 56, Stockholm, Sweden

Hardback ISBN: 978-1-78530-794-2
eBook ISBN: 978-1-78530-795-9

A CIP catalogue record for this book is available from the British Library.

Cover design by Bonnier Books Art Dept
Typeset by IDSUK (Data Connection) Ltd
Printed and bound in Great Britain by Clays Ltd, Elcograf S.p.A

1 3 5 7 9 10 8 6 4 2

Black & White Publishing is an imprint of Bonnier Books UK
www.bonnierbooks.co.uk

For Marc
My Joe. My Luca.
My everything

1

There were many things Joe did that confirmed he was the one. Painstakingly picking out all the red M&Ms for me whenever we went to the cinema. Always leaving the light on for me in the hall if I came home late from a night out, a clingfilm-wrapped plate of something waiting in the microwave. The way he'd reach for me subconsciously in his sleep, pulling me tight against him as though unwilling to be apart from me for a single second. And how he always, *always*, let me have the last spring roll.

'You're just seeing what you want to see,' Joe declared, his chopsticks hovering territorially over the one remaining spring roll. *My* spring roll.

You wouldn't dare, my narrowed eyes screamed silently across the dining table.

Oh, I would, his cornflower-blue irises winked back at me behind their tortoiseshell frames.

'Joseph Andrew Carter, I'm telling you, I know what I saw,' I insisted, brandishing my weapon of choice. A prawn cracker.

'So, let me see if I've got this right.' Chopsticks lowered, Joe leaned back in his chair, hands behind his head,

1

elbows splayed. He had that look on his face. That annoying, I'm-just-humouring-you-but-I-know-I'm-right look where the corner of his mouth hitched and his right eyebrow shot so far up his forehead it disappeared into his hair line. 'Ryan Reynolds was in front of you in the queue at Mr Hau's? As in THE Ryan Reynolds?'

'Green Lantern himself.'

'Did you speak to him?'

'Well, no—'

'See his face?'

'His back was to me, but I'd know the back of that head anywhere.' I swooned with the confidence of a woman who could quote *The Proposal* word for word. 'And that voice.' I shuddered, something inside me melting like butter on hot toast. 'Never have the words *Set Menu A* sounded so sexy.'

'Aha!' Joe mic-dropped his chopsticks, a look of smug satisfaction spreading across his face. 'Even if we overlook the impossibility of Ryan Reynolds knowing that Hove exists, let alone having a reason to be here, and then the added one-in-a-million chance of him fancying a Chinese from our local, I think we both know he's not a Set Menu A kind of guy. Had you said the holy grail that is Set Menu D on the other hand, with its prawn dumplings and deluxe appetiser sharing platter, you might have persuaded me.'

'You're just jealous because he's on my list,' I huffed, going to fetch the plates from the kitchen. The plates that every Friday Joe placed on the table and we duly ignored, choosing to eat straight from the containers before stacking the clean plates back in the cupboard, ready for the process to be repeated the following week. It was part of our routine. A routine that started with me picking up our usual order from Mr Hau's on my way home from work. When I closed the front door of our flat behind me at 6:30 p.m., my shoes would join the pile of mismatched lefts and rights that formed a small mountain in the corner of our hallway, my handbag and jacket dumped on the bench beside them, the latter normally sliding down onto the floor where it would remain until Joe rescued it later.

'I thought that was Brad Pitt?' Joe frowned, a look of surprise flashing across his face at the unexpected addition to my celebrity hall pass list.

'Yes – Brad Pitt, that guy from the Italian cooking channel, and Ryan Reynolds.'

I made a show of setting the plates down with a dramatic clatter, sliding a wine glass across to Joe's side of the table, not removing my fingers from the stem until he looked up. Setting the table, albeit a pointless exercise, was Joe's job. I picked up the food, he set the table. It was like an unwritten rule.

'Ryan would never forget to set the table,' I said pointedly, pouring us both a generous glass of wine.

'Ah, but would he willingly offer up the last spring roll to his gorgeous fiancée? Now if that doesn't scream true love, I don't know what does.'

'You always did know the way to my heart,' I grinned, popping the surrendered spring roll in my mouth with a triumphant smile. 'I knew there was a reason I agreed to marry you.'

'Really? Just the one?' Joe chuckled, his eyes twinkling mischievously across the table at me. I took a long sip of wine, twiddling my engagement ring round and round my finger as I made a show of racking my brains.

'Hmm, you also make an excellent spag bol.'

'Go on.'

'You always hold my hand when we cross the road.'

'This is true.'

'And you bring me ice cream whenever I'm a raging hormonal nightmare.'

'Your words, not mine, but you're right, I am literally *the* perfect man. Maybe I do stand a chance with Emma Watson?' Joe's gaze drifted to some faraway place as if picturing their date, before settling back on me, grin spreading at my raised eyebrows. 'Nah, she's got nothing on you, my love,' he concluded, his eyes suddenly serious as they locked with mine, the intensity of his scrutiny making my body tingle with desire in at least four different places. My heart gave a little flutter.

I grinned back at him. 'Is the right answer.'

I left Joe to clear up whilst I padded through to the bedroom in search of comfy clothes. It's never too early for PJs in my opinion, although that stomach-sinking feeling when the doorbell goes at 5:30 p.m. and you find yourself having to justify your faux-fur John Lewis onesie complete with bunny rabbit ears to the Evri delivery guy can almost make you regret it. Almost.

I breathed a sigh of relief as I unhooked my bra, everything that had been unwillingly held in all day finally allowed to relax and be where it naturally wanted to be. Men would never put up with this shit.

PJs on, I collapsed onto the bed just as my phone started vibrating on the bedside table. I twisted to read the caller ID. Mum. My favourite picture of us on her 60th birthday last year was flashing up on the screen: her sat on a wrought-iron garden chair in the late July sunshine, me with my arms around her shoulders, both of us grinning at Joe behind the camera. I glanced at the clock. 7:15 p.m. I contemplated not answering it.

'You going to get that?' Joe's voice floated in from the kitchen. 'You know she'll just keep calling otherwise.'

Ergh, he was right. I loved my mum, but she'd recently developed a rather annoying habit of phoning repeatedly until I answered. She had some serious stamina.

'Hi, Mum,' I yawned, stealing one of the pillows from Joe's side and stuffing it behind my back.

'Oh, hi love, sorry, did I wake you?' She sounded relieved that I'd answered, but also a bit concerned, as if I'd already failed some sort of mother-daughter test with my lacklustre greeting.

'No, just getting into bed.'

'Oh—'

Silence.

'I thought you might have plans, it being Friday night and all?'

'It's been a long week, Mum,' I sighed, trying not to let the disappointment in her voice grate on me. 'I just fancied a quiet one in with a takeaway.'

'I do hope they're not pushing you too hard at work? Derek's in the pub tonight, I could nip over and have a discreet word with him if you like?'

'Work's fine, Mum,' I reassured her quickly. Discreet and my mother were not words ever uttered in the same sentence.

'Righto, well, that's good, love. And, umm . . . how's everything else?'

'Fine, all fine.'

More silence. I could hear her mouth opening and closing, as though she wanted to say something more but wasn't quite sure how.

'Maybe I could pop round tomorrow and we can have a proper catch-up? I could bring those doughnuts you love so much?'

'Umm, I'm not too sure what my plans are this weekend, Mum.'

'Oh, all right. Well, just give me a bell if you change your mind. We're doing family dinner at the pub on Sunday, after the lunch rush has finished. Everyone will be there, it would be lovely to see you?'

The eagerness in her voice lodged a lump in my throat.

'Sure, I'll try to make it.'

I heard a door swing open and a rowdy jeer sounded in the background.

'Better go, love, I left your brother manning the bar and it's a full house tonight.' I pictured the jostling crowds swarming around the bar of Mum's pub like bees to honey. The ruddy-faced farmers, the tie-stuffed-in-pocket, fresh-off-the-train commuters, the barely legal teenagers teetering unsteadily in their high heels. The air abuzz with the excitement of an entire weekend stretching before them.

I slid further down the bed.

'OK, bye, Mum.'

'I love you, sweetheart.'

'Love you too,' I mumbled, before collapsing face-first into the mound of pillows. My phone vibrated with a message, but I didn't need to look at it to know it was from Mum. A love heart emoji, or some cheesy gif of a kitten sending a virtual hug. She'd been sending a lot of gifs recently.

'Are you wearing my clothes again, woman?'

Joe had appeared in the doorway of the bedroom, leaning rather sexily against the doorframe. What was it about men in doorways? I glanced down at my pyjamas. One of Joe's faded Tough Mudder t-shirts that used to be black but was now more of a sad grey colour, the logo cracked and scratchy, with a hole in the right armpit; and a pair of his old, checked boxer shorts.

'What can I say, they look better on me than you,' I smirked, fluttering my eyelashes unashamedly.

'They certainly do.' His voice was rough, sexy. The way his eyes lingered on where the too-big t-shirt had slipped to one side, exposing my bare shoulder, making me ache for him. A grin spread devilishly across his face, exposing the dimples in his cheeks. Oh, I knew that look. 'Maybe your clothes will look better on me?'

'Where are you going?' I frowned suspiciously as he closed the doors to my glorified cupboard of a walk-in wardrobe behind him. After several minutes, one of the doors was flung open to reveal Joe's bare, hairy leg extending playfully behind it like a burlesque dancer starting their opening number. I hugged my knees to my chest, giggling as Joe hooked a second stocking-clad leg around the edge of the door, sliding it up and down as he *da-dahed* what I could only assume was supposed to be the *Cabaret* theme tune. Black-silk-gloved fingers strummed teasingly around the doorframe before the other door was thrown dramatically open to reveal Joe in all his glory. He'd somehow managed to entice one of my wrap skirts around his waist, a dangerous amount of pale thigh peeking out from between the gap where the two sides refused to meet. My black t-shirt bra strained across his chest, the clasp threatening to ping free at any moment, and the ridiculously oversized floppy hat with my name around the brim that Instagram had influenced me to buy wobbled precariously on his head as he flung the end of my red tartan scarf theatrically over one shoulder, strutting around the bedroom like a model at Fashion Week.

'What do we think?' he asked, stopping at the end of the bed to pose, one leg performing a half-lunge atop the ottoman.

I shrieked with laughter as the skirt, which had been valiantly holding on for dear life until this point, finally admitted defeat and dropped with a sigh to the carpet.

'Ryan Reynolds has got nothing on me, baby,' Joe winked, puffing his chest out like a prize gorilla, in an uncharacteristic show of masculinity that he instantly came to regret when a sharp snap confirmed the inevitable.

'Oww!' The bra clasp had finally given up the good fight, whipping Joe around the face as it pinged free. We both looked at each other for a second, lips quivering, and then erupted into fits of giggles.

'You're right,' I hiccupped, gasping for air as the tears streamed uncontrollably down my face. 'Only you could pull that look off.'

'It's really working for me, right?' Joe turned to admire himself in the full-length mirror, his bra-related injury quickly forgotten as he flexed and posed, twiddling the end of the scarf coquettishly in one hand.

'Work it, baby,' I cheered, whooping with delight as Joe started slowly removing each layer of clothing that hadn't already deserted him. He threw his shoulders back, letting the scarf drop to the floor before flicking it in my direction with his toes. He stalked towards the bed, the promise of something hot and delicious swirling in his eyes as he slipped beneath the sheets.

'Get the light, Joe,' I mumbled, snuggling over towards his side of the bed until I felt the subtle dip of the mattress that had moulded to his shape after all these years.

'Hmmm?'

'The light.'

'It's your turn.'

'No, you were the last one into bed!'

A resounding snore vibrated beside me and I turned to see Joe pretending to be asleep, mouth open, head slumped in what looked like a very uncomfortable position. Oscar-winning performance it was not.

'Fine,' I huffed, breaking the silent stand-off we had most nights. Flinging the duvet back, I stomped over towards the light switch, glaring accusingly at the matching bedside table lamps still in their dust-topped, unopened boxes in the corner of the room. 'You know, maybe one of these days you'll finally get round to wiring those lamps we bought five months ago,' I said pointedly, flicking the switch and plunging the room into darkness.

'Honey, if you wanted a handyman, you should have gone with Brad Pitt.'

'There's still time,' I maintained, sliding back into bed and pulling the covers right up to my chin with a shiver. I sensed him move closer. Could almost feel the tickle of his breath against the nape of my neck.

'You know,' he breathed, his voice barely more than a whisper in my ear, 'I can think of something even better than you in my clothes.'

'What's that?'

'You out of them.'

My toes curled in anticipation, my body moving with a will of its own as it surrendered, rolling over to face Joe's side of the bed.

'I thought you'd never ask.'

2

On 6th February 2008, precisely two days before my 13th birthday, I fell in love.

It wasn't some cute boy-meets-girl story. Fate didn't partner us up to play Romeo and Juliet in the school play. Fingers didn't accidentally touch as we both reached for the last chocolate sponge with lumpy skin-topped custard at lunch time. In fact, the very first words that Joseph Carter said to me that day, or indeed ever, were *you do know everyone can see your knickers, right?*

It was a Wednesday. I remember it so vividly it's like it was yesterday. Double English Lit had just finished. The main locker-lined corridor was heaving with students, the air vibrating with excitable chatter as if we hadn't just been sat next to those very people for the past hour. At first, it was just a few double takes. Heads snapping back and forth at an unnatural speed. Two girls whispering together in a doorway, one pointing me out to her friend. I smiled delightedly to myself, thinking they were admiring my new butterfly hairclips. I'd practically begged Mum for *Top of the Pops* magazine that weekend, purely so I could be the proud new owner of six sparkly clips that Kimberley from Girls Aloud had been seen wearing the week before.

'You do know everyone can see your knickers, right?' came a matter-of-fact voice to my right.

I closed my locker door a fraction to reveal Joseph Carter's spectacle-clad face behind it. He had a camera slung around his neck, something I quickly learnt he never went anywhere without. It was a vintage Kodak with a pillar-box-red leather strap, a model that still used film even though digital cameras were very much all the rage. Despite having been at the same school for almost two years, I'd never really noticed Joe. He wasn't the most popular kid in school, but then he wasn't unpopular either. He was that guy who was friends with everyone, somehow managing to deftly traverse the horribly cliché cliques that dictated secondary school life for the rest of us. Which table we sat on at lunch. Who we hung out with. What so-called specialism we'd been pigeonholed into, because God forbid you were a Maths-loving rugby player who played the French horn.

'Huh?'

'Your skirt,' he said calmly, removing the strawberry lace he was chewing from his mouth and waving it at my waist region. 'It's stuck under your backpack.'

'What?!' My cheeks flushed with a level of embarrassment only a 13-year-old girl can possess as I spun quickly on the spot, head over one shoulder like a dog chasing its tail. My hand scrabbled at the back of my skirt, pulling the hem out from where it had bunched beneath my backpack, exposing my 80-denier-clad bottom. A group of girls sniggered to my left. I willed the ground to swallow me whole.

'I once spent an entire day last year with my flies undone. Half the school saw my Spiderman underpants – which I was only wearing because they were the one clean pair in my drawer that morning,' he added hastily. 'I was known as Spidey Pants for a week. Wish someone had told me.' He shrugged, his eyes wide and kind behind his glasses. 'Strawberry lace?'

I looked down at my shoes in panic, thinking he meant my shoelaces had somehow turned into giant strawberries or something equally mortifying. Joe just laughed, presuming I was joking, dimples cutting deep into his cheeks as he thrust the open bag of fluorescent red laces under my nose.

Back in the present, I closed my eyes, remembering how the sickly-sweet scent of artificial sugar had instantly made my mouth water. And how I'd felt as we'd walked side by side down the corridor together, the pointing fingers and muffled scoffs suddenly irrelevant. As though with Joe by my side, nothing else mattered. I had no idea then, on 6th February 2008, who he was. Who he would become to me. The man who liked to torture me by saying things like *do you need more thrush cream, babe* at maximum volume in the supermarket just to watch my cheeks bloom. The man I shared a joint bank account with, which sailed into its overdraft the last week of every month. And the man I would drop everything for in a heartbeat.

'Are we getting up at any point today?' Joe's voice was muffled, distant-sounding. As though he were speaking to me through a wall. My eyes snapped open, landing on his side of the bed – empty – both pillowcases plump and smooth. He must be in the kitchen already. He always was an early riser. I could see the natural light, which flooded in through the big sash windows of the flat every morning, glowing invitingly around the bedroom door, as though it too were trying to entice me out of bed. I rolled my eyes but made no move to get up. My phone buzzed suddenly on the bedside table, making me jump. Who the hell was calling at – huh, it was 10:30 already? – still, it was the weekend. I ignored it, pulling the duvet up higher around my ears until it stopped. I breathed a sigh of relief, only for it to start up again. Short, aggressive buzzes with varying times in between. Text messages. Lots of them.

'For God's sake, Mother,' I growled, anticipating the multitude of paw-waving kittens and dramatic sunrise Good Morning gifs that no doubt awaited me. But as I rolled over, I watched my phone vibrate closer and closer to the edge until, eventually, it dropped onto the rug below. I peered over the side of the bed, squinting to read the phone display.

Brunch today?

I had THE worst date last night with that guy from Hinge. Unhinged *more like!*

It was from Jacob. My best friend. Well, one of them. Jacob and his twin sister Alice were used to sharing things. Genomes. Clothes. Even romantic interests, if

14

you count David Horrigan who Jacob hooked up with last year at Brighton Pride. Alice does not, because as she likes to remind us, declaring he was her boyfriend for three days when she was six does not constitute a relationship. But status as my best friend was an accolade they'd happily shared since we met aged five in the playground of Brunswick Primary School. My phone pinged again.

I need to vent. Preferably with waffles.

And again.

And bacon. Lots of bacon.

And again.

Is it too early for mimosas?

'Jenny, the need for caffeine is reaching an almost fatal level out here. I might keel over at any moment.'

Christ, why were all the men in my life so bloody dramatic?

'Keep your pants on, I'm coming,' I grumbled, flinging the duvet back and dragging myself out of bed. Fuck, it was cold. I shrugged my biggest, cosiest knitted jumper on over Joe's old t-shirt, sniffed my way through various articles of clothing draped over the ottoman and eventually settled on my mom jeans which, if you overlooked the suspicious-looking stain near the crotch (was that ketchup? Please tell me that was ketchup?!), were the cleanest item to be found. I left my jumper untucked, the oversized hem hiding the stain from view. Problem solved.

'Coming!' I trilled, odd socks sliding across the bare wooden floorboards of the dining room as I shoved my phone in the back pocket of my jeans. It vibrated again and I made a mental note to text Jacob en route. My nose wrinkled. *Ergh, what was that smell?*

I frowned accusingly at the still open, half-full Chinese containers that littered the dining table. Having neither the energy nor the time to get into a domestic about household chores, I rescued my coat from the floor, slung my bag over one shoulder and, turning my back on the mess, followed Joe out the door, the pungent waft of stale sweet and sour following me down the communal staircase as it slammed shut behind us.

We took a left as we exited our building, walking on autopilot along the promenade as we had done a thousand times before. The location was what had sold us on the flat five years ago. Yes, the lift was permanently out of order, the decorative Victorian cornicing in the entrance hall was crumbling, and the creaky floorboards had a suspiciously shaped bleach stain at the foot of the spiral staircase. But the building was right opposite the sea, and that vast, uninterrupted horizon of blue made my heart stutter whenever I stepped outside, nothing but a tiny patch of carefully manicured lawn and a rusty run of turquoise railings separating us and the ocean. It never failed to take my breath away, whether it was bright and winking like a sapphire, or tinged with grey, as it was today, the smell of vinegar and brine ever present in the air.

The March weather was brutal, wind biting at every bare inch of skin around my neck, the cuffs of my wrists, the bones of my ankles, as dark clouds swirled threateningly above us. I turned the collar of my coat up high around my neck as we walked, pulling it close as the tails flapped wildly around my shins.

'You should have brought a coat,' I scolded, frowning at Joe's shoulders hunched around his earlobes, his jumper billowing around the arms like a parachute ready to take off. But he just turned and smiled at me, a kind of knowing look in his eyes as if he would rather freeze to death than admit that I was right.

We were greeted by the welcoming jangle of the bell above the door as we hurried into the warmth of Drew's Brews, our favourite coffee shop. It was small. Only big enough for four tiny hairpin-legged tables and a chaotic assortment of mismatched chairs. The exposed brick walls were lined with old books, battered board games and chipped plant pots occupying every little ledge and crevice. We liked that they served coffee in proper ceramic mugs, no-one demanding to know our names so they could spell them incorrectly on flimsy cardboard cups. Most people got their coffees to go, in and out before the bell had even stopped its merry jingle, but Joe and I liked to sit and watch the world go by.

'Usual spot?' Joe asked, his feet already steering him towards our favourite table in the back right-hand corner. The one with one leg shorter than the rest. I nodded silently, smiling after him as I queued behind a tired-looking woman with a baby carrier strapped to her chest.

'Here we are,' the barista announced, handing the woman a large steaming takeaway cup. Coffee. Black, judging by the smell of it. The woman took it eagerly, closing her eyes as she breathed in the restorative caffeine fumes. She gave the barista a grateful smile, her eyes already a fraction brighter, and then bobbed her way out of the shop, wrapping her coat tightly around the sleeping baby as the door closed behind her.

'What can I get you?'

I turned to see the ruddy-faced barista smiling across at me.

'One coffee, black, and one oat milk hazelnut mocha with extra whipped cream, please.' Our normal order rolled off my tongue like an ice cube on a summer's day. One of the first things I noticed about Joe, when we met at the tender age of 13, was that he enjoyed ridiculously flavoured drinks. Strawberry milkshakes with a mountain of whipped cream. Radioactive slushies made by combining every possible flavour on offer. As we got older, these progressed into toffee nut lattes with syrup so sweet it made your teeth hurt, and brightly coloured cocktails complete with garish umbrella and a sparkler, or two. I quickly came to realise that it was a sign of something else he enjoyed. Life. It was why I loved him. Well, one of the reasons.

'Take away?'

'Sorry?' I blinked, dragging myself back to the coffee shop and the expectant face of the barista staring back at me.

'The drinks? To take away?'

18

'No, drink in.'

She paused, her eyes performing a quick scan of the coffee shop before inclining her head in the direction of the card reader. I tapped my Apple watch against the front, and it gave a cheerful chirp as though it knew caffeine was on the way.

Joe was sat in his usual seat, facing the front of the shop, shoulders hunched as he inspected the photos he'd just taken in the tiny viewfinder on his camera, like he'd done a million times before in that very spot. As a photographer, and one of those lucky individuals who'd managed to turn their hobby into a career, Joe never left the house without his camera. It was the third person in our relationship. Every time he stepped outside was, to him, an opportunity to capture the beauty he saw in the world.

'Jenny? Jenny Thompson?'

A rush of cold air swirled around my ankles, making me shiver, or maybe it was the sound of that familiar high-pitched voice. The barista banged the used coffee grounds of the sleep-deprived mother's double shot nosily into the dispenser below, and I tried to pretend that I hadn't heard her. No such luck. A leather-gloved hand gave my shoulder a brisk tap, and I had no choice but to turn around.

'It *is* you, I thought so. I'd recognise that mop of red hair anywhere!' *Mop, seriously?* There were a few places I'd like to tell her to shove her bloody mop. Grace McCory – my former childhood friend (sadly not as loyal as either Jacob or Alice) turned arch-nemesis, who'd just decided on the first day of secondary school

19

that I was 'so last year' and proceeded to make the rest of my school years a living hell – had an unrivalled ability for making anything sound like a sugar-coated insult. A hard, sickly-sweet shell with a bitter centre.

'Grace, how lovely to see you,' I lied.

'Gosh, I haven't seen you since . . .' Grace's voice trailed off, her face twisting into an odd, pained expression that could be attempted sympathy or a severe bout of constipation. The Botox made it impossible to tell. She stared unblinking at me, as if expecting me to finish her sentence. I buried my fist deep into the pocket of my coat, clenching so tightly it felt as though my nails were piercing the skin. We stayed locked in our awkward, silent stand-off until the hiss of the milk frother forced Grace to blink, the spell broken. '. . . Well, in a very long time,' she concluded with a pitying look. 'How are you doing with everything? You look – great. Truly, great.' The obvious pause as she ran her eyes from my *mop* down to my Converse and back up again, said otherwise.

'I, on the other hand, look an absolute state,' she pouted, her perfectly manicured fingers brushing some imaginary dirt from her lululemon leggings. 'We just moved and the place is a right fixer-upper; I mean, it doesn't even have underfloor heating. Can you imagine?! I'll miss our cute little townhouse, but since Arabella came along, we just need more space.' Thanks to her @athomewiththemccorys interior design account on Instagram, I – along with her 50k other followers – knew that her *little townhouse* was a palatial four-bedroom, double-height-ceilinged, detached period property on the outskirts of town that wouldn't look out of place on the cover of *Architectural Digest*. There was a pause, which she was clearly expecting me to fill with sympathy, but when none came her smile tightened. 'Are you here alone?'

'No, I'm here with—' but when I turned automatically to gesture in Joe's direction, I saw the table was vacant. Both chairs tucked neatly underneath. 'Must have just nipped to the bathroom,' I explained, waving my hand casually in the direction of our table.

Grace nodded slowly, an irritating noise coming from the back of her throat.

'Jenny.'

'Hmm?'

'You know, a friend of mine runs this fantastic group in a little studio near Hove Park. You should try it some time, it would do you the world of good.' Her head tilted to one side, her perfectly blow-dried bangs falling neatly around her face, which was now contorted into another baffling expression where her eyes bulged from their sockets, her bottom lip sticking out in a pout. Oh God, was it pity? Did she feel sorry for me? Whatever it was, it made me miss the insults. I bit my tongue, holding back the *I would rather stick pins in my eyes* response that was so eager to come out.

'One black coffee and one oat milk hazelnut mocha with extra whipped cream.'

'Yes! That's me!' I shouted eagerly, even though I was literally stood right next to the startled-looking barista. She placed two oversized mugs on the counter in front of me before taking a small step back. Fair enough. I grabbed both cups and quickly retreated to our table, before I found myself accidentally panic-accepting an invitation to some heart attack-inducing spin class or whatever fitness fad was in vogue right now.

'Lovely to see you,' I called over my shoulder at Grace, only letting my fake-ass smile slip when I was safely sat with my back to her. I placed Joe's cup down in front of his empty chair, cradling my own in both hands. Two sips of coffee later and the welcome tinkle of the bell above the door had me breathing a sigh of relief, my shoulders visibly lowering an inch or two. I risked a quick glance over my shoulder, relieved to see the coffee shop was now a Grace-free zone.

When I turned back, Joe was sat opposite me. As though he'd never left.

'What took you so long?'

He arched an eyebrow. 'You timing me now?'

'Some knight in shining armour you are, leaving me to fend off Grace McCory by myself.'

'I had no doubt you'd emerge victorious.'

'It was a close call, she almost talked me into coming along to some hot naked yoga class or something,' I shuddered, my face suitably appalled by the idea as I took another sip of coffee, closing my eyes as I felt its warmth spread through me.

'Hot naked yoga? Now that sounds like something I could get on board with,' Joe wiggled his eyebrows suggestively. 'Has she left already? If I go now, I might still be able to catch her, sign us both up . . .'

He was peering eagerly around me, halfway to a standing position as though he fully intended to chase Grace down the street and book into the next class

22

then and there, when my death stare stopped him in his tracks. A grin quivered at the corner of his mouth as he slowly lowered himself down again, my scowl only relenting when his bum was firmly back on his seat. He eyed me across the table, something wicked twinkling behind his glasses.

'So, just to be clear, that's a firm no on the hot naked yoga?'

3

When people ask me what I do in that small talk, comment-on-the-weather way us Brits do, I tell them I'm a journalist. Or rather I tell them I'm a journalist and then cringe slightly, my face scrunching inwards, my shoulders shrugging apologetically. I don't know whether it's because I'm afraid of the look of mistrust that often follows this admission, or the fact that I'm calling it *journalism* when I spent the best part of last week writing an article entitled *Serial shop-lifting seagull, Ralph, wanted by Sainsbury's Local for £200 of stolen sandwiches*. Not exactly the hard-hitting reporting I envisioned I'd be doing when I started at the *Brighton Tribune* 10 years ago.

There was a time – long, long ago – when I semi-enjoyed my job. I never jumped out of bed on Monday morning or came home feeling I'd changed the world, but starting out as a lowly intern, there was still that fizzing excitement of possibility, a naive belief that the world was my oyster, that I could make a difference. Ten years, two pitiful pay increases (which, considering inflation, meant I was being paid less now than when I started) and one too many articles about prize-winning vegetables later, and that spark had been well and truly stamped out, pissed on and smothered into oblivion.

16:52.

I'd been sat staring at the clock in the top right-hand corner of my computer screen for nine minutes, moving my mouse pointlessly around my desk so that my Teams status didn't switch to inactive.

16:54.

Six minutes until I could escape the nauseatingly fishy-smelling office. Beryl, the office manager who had overly inflated ideas about her administrative responsibilities, thought it was socially acceptable to reheat her monkfish curry in the office kitchen (an instantly fireable offence in my opinion), and was making me miss the usual musk of damp, mouldy carpet. 'Kitchen' was probably an overly generous description. A kettle, one impossibly small fridge and a sauce-splattered microwave balanced precariously atop the windowsill does not a kitchen make, however much the laminated KITCHEN sign Blu-Tacked to the window tried to convince us otherwise.

16:56.

I twirled my engagement ring slowly around my finger, a habit that had me smiling at the thought of getting home to Joe. Of curling up on the sofa together with a glass of wine, me warming my never-not-cold toes on that bit of exposed skin between Joe's waistband and his jumper, much to his displeasure.

16:59.

I got to my feet a little too quickly, my office chair skidding backwards as though it too were desperate to escape, and I had to grab the headrest to stop it colliding into an unsuspecting Beryl. (Although considering the whole fish incident, it was far less than she deserved.) As I turned, a man stood before me. He was what my mum would call portly, his one-inch-too-short beige chinos straining across his protruding stomach, greying hair combed forcibly over to the right to hide the fact he was going bald. My boss. Derek Kingston.

'How's that story coming along, Jenny?' he asked, aggressively clearing his throat as though trying to dispel a particularly stubborn piece of phlegm from the back of his tonsils.

'Fine.'

Well, it will be fine. Once I actually start it.

'Just fine? This is one of the biggest legal cases Hove has seen in years, Jenny; it'll set precedent for years to come. I've reserved Friday's front page for you, so I'm hoping for a little more than *fine*,' Derek puffed, rocking up and down on the balls of his feet in that way he did that made it look like he was thrusting his pelvic region in your direction.

17:01.

For fuck's sake. I was not paid enough to stay a minute longer in this place than contractually necessary. I just wanted to get home to Joe.

'If it's not too much for you, that is? I mean, if it's too much pressure, what with everything else going on . . .' He was looking over my shoulder as he back-tracked, and I turned to see Beryl giving him a shrewd look. Beryl had many hats. HR hat. Office Manager hat. General Busybody hat. Her actual hand-knitted, oversized, bobble-topped hat. Something told me she was wearing the first of those right now.

'Great, it's going great,' I assured him, making a point of shoving things in my bag. Keys. Water bottle. Stapler. The 'legal case' in question was 66-year-old Mr Beckles of 12 Wisteria Drive and 79-year-old Mr Gorringe of 14 Wisteria Drive's ongoing dispute over who owned the 14cm-wide strip of gravel separating their two proper-ties. A pointless battle that had cost them both tens of thousands of pounds in legal fees, and me one pair of per-fectly good ballet pumps that were now soaked beyond repair after standing for hours in the rain outside the grey, concrete monstrosity that was Hove Crown Court.

'Fantastic! On my desk by midday tomorrow,' Derek bellowed, glancing pointedly at his watch as I put on my jacket. As though leaving work on time was worse than skiving off early.

'Got to run, Derek, *woman's appointment*,' I mouthed in a dramatic whisper when he showed no sign of moving.

'Oh . . . yes, of course, righto. Good luck! Break a leg and all that. What's that, Roger? Yes, *coming!*' He raised a hand in acknowledgement, walking purposefully in the

27

opposite direction as though he'd just been summoned. Clearly no one had told him Roger was off sick today. I pressed my lips together, stifling a smile as I hurried down the corridor. Jacob was leaning against the exit. As a reluctant five-foot-seven (and a half) male, Jacob's hair added at least an extra inch – sometimes two – and today looked like a new record, his gravity-defying quiff curling like a scoop of soft-serve ice cream as he hid his smile in the ridiculously cavernous turtleneck of his jumper.

'Another woman's appointment, is it?' he sniggered, guessing I'd just played my over-utilised trump card. 'What's that, the third one this month?'

'Fourth actually,' I shrugged. 'Anyway, since when is it a crime to leave work on time?'

'You're asking the wrong person. I'm rarely here after 4 p.m., in fact I'm surprised I've not burst into flames by now . . .' Jacob gave himself a quick once-over as though checking for scorch marks on his beloved cream cashmere.

Like me, Jacob also worked at the *Brighton Tribune*. He was our resident photojournalist but, unlike me, viewed our contracted hours of 9–5 more as a loose guideline than an actual rule. Luckily for him, though, he was a man and therefore immune from passive-aggressive digs from Derek.

'Woah, where do you think you're going?' Jacob asked, looping his arm through mine as I made to turn left and commence my usual route home.

'Umm, home?'

'Oh no, we're going to the pub tonight, remember?'

I had a vague memory of a calendar reminder to that effect pinging up on my phone earlier and my ignoring it. The first of Mum's live music nights she was hosting at the pub. Her latest initiative to support local artists and hopefully drum up some more business during the midweek lull.

'Is that tonight? Look, Jacob, I'm exhausted, it's been a long week . . .'

'It's only Tuesday.'

'I'm just not feeling that great, honestly, I think I ate something dodgy at lunch.'

'You seemed fine when you were scoffing down seconds of Lucy's birthday cake an hour ago.'

'I'm just—'

'Out of excuses?'

I scowled at him, hating that he knew me so well.

'Come on, Jenny, you've bailed on the last three drinks we've organised *and* that bottomless brunch place I practically had to sell a kidney to get a reservation for last month.'

A lump formed in my throat that I couldn't swallow. He was right. I had been flaky recently.

'Come on, just one drink,' Jacob cooed. 'Alice switched shifts and everything.' As a junior doctor four years into a highly competitive six-year specialist training programme to become a Cardiothoracic Surgeon, time off during sociable hours was a rarity for Alice. The fact that she was spending said time off with us rather than going home to sleep, another rarity, made my heart squeeze a little for my other best friend.

'Fine, but just one.'

'Another round!'

29

My brother, Matt, raised an amused smile from behind the bar as I wobbled precariously on the rungs of my stool, holding my empty wine glass aloft. My mum, on the other hand, was sporting her concerned mother hen look that, if the crowd surrounding the bar wasn't three people deep, meant she would have been over here like a shot. I had to hand it to her, I'd never seen it so busy on a Tuesday night. Every table was occupied, a crowd of people stood nursing pint glasses and tapping feet against the flagstone floor in time with the guy strumming his guitar in the far corner, his voice deep and sultry. I tried to focus on the lyrics. Something about being each other's sunshine and kissing in the rain. I quickly tuned back out, reaching for my wine glass before remembering it was empty.

'For someone who hasn't been out in months, you sure are making up for lost time.' Jacob eyed the three empty wine glasses I'd consumed whilst waiting for Alice, balancing the paper umbrella from his Sex on the Beach behind one ear. He was exaggerating, of course. It hadn't been that long. Had it?

'I'm just thirsty. These nuts are super salty.' I popped another peanut in my mouth, but I could feel the warm, comforting buzz of tipsiness wrapping itself around me like a blanket.

'Hey, I hear you. Nothing worse than an overly salted nut.'

'Speaking of salty nuts, how was your date the other night?'

Jacob gave a small shudder, either at my choice of segue or in recollection of said date. Seeing as Jacob was Mr Innuendo, my money was on the later.

'That bad?'

'Well, other than the fact he showed up half an hour late, called me *sweetcheeks*, and apparently had never heard of a napkin, because I spent most of the evening staring at various bits of food caught in his beard, it was fine.'

'At least this one didn't bring his mum,' I shrugged, remembering the infamous evening in question when Jacob had had to sit through a Spanish-inquisition-style grilling from his Tinder date's mother.

'The fact *that's* the positive we can take from this says everything about my dating life,' Jacob guffawed, doing that thing where he tried to pretend being single in his thirties didn't bother him. 'Honestly, you're so much better off, trust me!'

My fingers tightened a fraction on the edge of the table, an uncomfortable weight pressing hard against my chest.

'Better off.' I repeated his words slowly. They felt strange and bitter in my mouth. Maybe it was the whole drinking on an empty stomach thing kicking in.

'Shit, Jenny, I didn't mean—' but Jacob was interrupted before he could finish his sentence.

'I'm here! I'm here!' We heard Alice before we saw her. All five foot two of her concealed by the jostling crowd until she eventually broke through a tiny gap and appeared by our table. 'Sorry, I'm soooo late! Stentless heart valve implementation.' She threw Jacob and me a look that suggested she knew we'd understand, even though we both had zero clue what a stentless heart valve implementation was. 'Oh my god, I can't believe you're actually here!' she squealed, dropping her coat and bag to the floor and wrapping her tiny arms around me. She smelt of disinfectant and her favourite brand of dry shampoo. 'I mean, Jacob texted me saying he managed to drag you here, but I didn't believe it.'

'It's really not been *that* long,' I insisted, pretending I didn't see the exchange between Jacob and Alice that said otherwise.

Alice nodded towards the glass-strewn table. 'Looks like I've got some catching up to do.'

'Another round,' Matt announced as if on cue, appearing with a drink-laden tray balanced in one hand. 'On the house, in honour of my sister gracing us with her presence this fine evening.'

'Not you too,' I mumbled sulkily, helping myself to the large glass of chilled Chardonnay.

'Have I mentioned how much I *love* the fact that your mum owns a pub?' Jacob grinned, his eyes lighting up at the sight of another garishly bright cocktail.

'Only three times since we got here.' I rolled my eyes.

'And that she books sexy, tortured-looking musicians with *very* capable-looking hands.'

A gap had appeared in the crowd and I followed Jacob's lustful gaze to where the singer was perched on one of the leather-studded bar stools in the corner. His fingers were strumming the strings of his guitar, an unruly mass of jet-black curls concealing most of his face. He was handsome in that obvious kind of way that meant, statistically, he was 90% likely to also be an asshole. Broad shoulders. Chiselled jaw. An air of confidence that meant he could make eye contact with just about anyone – like he was with me right now, those impossibly dark eyes trained unashamedly on mine. Musicians.

'Speaking of Mum, she asked me to ask you how you're doing. Apparently, you're not replying to her texts?' Matt winced with the pained reluctance of someone passing along a message they really didn't want to give.

'I'm fine.' The words, ready to go on the tip of my tongue, tumbled readily out of my mouth. 'She texts me a million times a day; shoot me if I don't respond to every single one.' I scowled, hating the sharp, overly defensive edge to my voice. '*Sorry*,' I mouthed at Matt, who just placed a big, bear-like hand on my shoulder with unexpected tenderness, the briefest shake of his head that said *don't worry about it*.

'It's good to see you,' he whispered in my ear. He was a man of few words, my brother, but the squeeze of my shoulder said so much. It was only when Matt's shirt started to blur as I watched him walk away, the colours bleeding into each other, that I realised my eyes were watering. God, I wasn't becoming that annoying person who cried every time she had a drink, was I?

'Got to pee,' I muttered, slipping quietly out from behind our table before either Alice or Jacob could see. The bathroom was deserted and I braced my hands either side of the basin, the ceramic smooth and cool beneath my skin. I leaned over, splashing cold water on the back of my neck as I tried to calm the blotchy red patch slowly spreading across my chest, creeping up my throat like an ink stain. My face was paler than normal, dull even, with a greying undertone that matched the bags under my eyes. Maybe it was time to call it a night?

An image of Joe and I snuggled up in bed, watching old episodes of *Friends* as we passed a tub of Ben & Jerry's back and forth between us swam into my mind. It looked so perfect. I nodded decisively to myself in the mirror, spinning on my heel as I headed for the door. But as I exited the bathroom, my left foot tripped over something (probably my right foot), sending me stumbling forwards.

'Woah, easy there.'

A big, strong arm looped itself around my waist, body-slamming me against the torso it was attached to, to prevent my fall.

'You OK?'

I looked up, coming nose to nose with the singer with the capable hands. Jacob's words, not mine, although seeing as they did just save me from going arse over tit, the evidence thus far seemed to support his hypothesis. I was suddenly very conscious that said hands were still flat against the small of my back, the hem of my top riding up beneath his grip.

'Fine, thanks,' I said, clearing my throat a little too loudly as I took two steps backwards. His head tilted to one side as he started to push the door to the men's bathroom open, eyes glinting in the dimly lit corridor.

'Make sure you tie that shoelace now.' I looked down, clocking the trailing shoelace responsible for my clumsiness. Well, maybe the four glasses of wine had also had a little something to do with it. 'Wouldn't want you falling for anyone else.' He winked, an amused curl to his lips, before the door swung shut behind him. I rolled my eyes, wondering how many women he'd used that one on.

As I made my way back through the crowd, my gaze fell on a young couple. They were sat at a tiny table in the corner, edging towards each other like two magnets, him inching his stool closer, her ducking her head coquettishly as she leaned into him. He reached out, tucking a piece of hair behind her ear, a single finger caressing the side of her cheek. They were sat at mine and Joe's table. Our heart-enclosed initials, carved into the underside with my protractor 15 years ago, declared it so.

This way we'll always be together. Me and you. Jenny and Joe. Always and forever.

An unwelcome heaviness pressed against the pit of my stomach, the wine threatening to make a reappearance. Yep, definitely time to go.

4

'What breaking news awaits us this week, do you reckon?' Jacob mused, plonking himself down next to me in the staffroom. I say staffroom. Again, like a lot of things at the *Brighton Tribune*, it was quite an over-generous description for what was essentially a semi-circle of ten plastic chairs in the worst-smelling corner of the office. I took the polystyrene cup of coffee Jacob handed me with a weak smile, the first sip doing little to alleviate the pounding headache that had been present all morning. It was like the better version of myself – the smug one who knew that fifth glass of wine was a bad idea – was sitting on her high horse with a giant wooden mallet, bashing it repeatedly against my skull.

'Can't be worse than the Asbo from last week,' I yawned, smiling at the thought of poor Rory, the local cockerel, who finally ruffled one too many feathers with his early-morning siren calls and was served a noise abatement notice by Brighton & Hove City Council.

'Order, order,' Derek bellowed, rapping his knuckles on the back of his clipboard as he perched one butt cheek on the edge of poor Sally's desk. He was sporting a particularly hideous salmon shirt today, paired with an aggressively yellow tie. I had to squint just to look at him. 'Everyone's favourite time of the week – new assignment day!' He paused, as though expecting an enthusiastic cheer, but all he got was a loud slurp of tea from copyeditor Rahul. 'Right, Jenny and Jacob, I need you over in West Blatchington this morning, some music therapy group operating out of the community centre is under threat of closure. Oh, and I almost forgot – Jenny, you're down to interview a Mr Hatfield next Friday at 10 a.m. He's convinced he's seeing his dead wife's face in the clouds.'

I spluttered a mouthful of coffee back into my cup, only narrowing avoiding spraying it in Derek's face. Shame.

'I stand corrected,' I coughed quietly to myself.

'Wasn't Rahul going to cover that one, Derek?' Jacob was trying to communicate something to Derek via his bulging eyeballs, but I was too focused on dabbing at the coffee running down my chin to notice.

'Why would I send Rahul? He's already covering the village fete on Friday, poor man can't be in two places at once, Jacob,' Derek chided.

'It's fine,' I mouthed silently to Jacob, who'd just opened his mouth to argue otherwise. My stomach churned as I downed what was left of my coffee, last night's wine threatening to make a reappearance as my grip tightened on the edge of my chair.

'Right, Sally,' Derek continued, not missing a beat as he ran one finger down his clipboard. 'You're covering the town council meeting this afternoon, and it's your lucky day. Wheelie bins are on the agenda!'

'Are you sure this is the right place?'

It was late March, the omnipresent clouds not having parted for a single second to reveal even a *glimmer* of sunshine these past few months, so sunglasses were entirely unnecessary, bordering on ridiculous, but today they were essential for my continued survival. I lowered my Ray-Bans a fraction to survey the – well, it could only be described as an oversized garden shed, thanks to its bottle-green corrugated iron facade. Someone had tried to brighten the place up, with a hanging flower basket dangling on a rusty chain to one side of the flaking wooden door, the vibrant blooms a stark contrast to the otherwise gloomy building. I took a few exploratory steps up the cracked, weed-riddled path before an assault of sounds stopped me in my tracks. A low warble, followed by a nails-on-a-chalkboard style screech that only a brass instrument can produce, floated out of the open window. The rhythmic pounding of a bass drum made the poorly fitted door shudder slightly on its hinges. And a familiar piano melody tinkled over the top of the chaos.

'Sounds like the right place,' Jacob smiled, hoisting his camera bag further up his shoulder. The door gave a sad, pained wail as he held it open for me with a dramatic sweep of his arm.

The community centre was just one big room with a raised, stage-like platform at the far end, a foot or so off the ground. The floor was that awful faux-varnished wood that you get in village halls, and it smelt a bit like an old church. Musty and a tad damp. A bunch of kids were sat in a circle on the floor, captivated by the short, bearded man wearing a burgundy cardigan in the centre who was demonstrating different musical instruments. A boy who looked about seven or eight was bashing a xylophone with one hand, while another clung firmly to the trousered leg of a woman sat with a smattering of other adults on the chairs that lined the edge of the room. Another group of children were crowded around a piano on the other side of the room, belting out the lyrics to the *Lion King*'s 'I Just Can't Wait to Be King' at the top of their lungs. One little girl sat atop the piano, her flashing trainers dangling just above the pianist's fingers, the multicoloured beads on the ends of her braids click-clacking along to the rhythm.

'Which one's yours?'

I turned to see a man who must have been at least six foot five, wearing the kind of paint-splattered cargo trousers and heavy-soled boots that told me he was a tradesman, towering over me.

'Excuse me?'

'That one's mine – Kiki,' he smiled proudly, revealing a set of gleaming white teeth as he pointed in the direction of the little girl with the flashing trainers.

'Oh, I don't have a child.' The man's brow furrowed, giving me a quick look up and down as though trying to determine if I were a threat. 'I'm here with the *Brighton Tribune*. We're doing a feature on the community centre,' I added quickly, keen to reassure him I wasn't some creep that lingered outside playgrounds or snuck into village halls without being invited. I dug in the back pocket of my jeans, flashing him my work badge as though I were a cop in the NYPD.

'And I'm Jacob, photographer.' Jacob raised his trusty Canon EOS R5 with one hand, his own personal form of ID.

'Terry,' Kiki's dad smiled warmly.

'Do you mind if I—?' Jacob held up his camera, nodding over at little Kiki.

'Nah, go for it, mate.'

'Have you and Kiki been coming here long, Terry?' I asked as Jacob wandered off, camera glued to his face.

'Coming up to a year now,' Terry sighed. 'We started coming after my wife passed.'

My pen jarred audibly against my notebook, a big, ugly line splitting the page in two.

'I'm so sorry,' I whispered, forcing the words out from behind the lump in my throat. Terry smiled kindly, but I could sense the pain he carried, a shadow passing momentarily across his vision like a cloud in front of the sun.

I followed his gaze to where his daughter was smiling shyly down at the broad-shouldered pianist with his back to us. I felt a string tug somewhere deep inside of me as I clocked her pink tutu skirt, her purple- and yellow-striped tights. She was so young. Too young to have suffered a loss so great. But life was cruel. It didn't care if you were six or sixty, had twenty things still to tick off your bucket list, or planned to marry the love of your life in six months' time. The string pulled tighter.

'Luca always says he just teaches music, but he does so much more than that. Honestly, places like this are a lifeline for communities like ours; it's criminal that the council have pulled their funding. I can't walk down the street for bumping into a million of those ridiculous eco scooters that people just dump willy-nilly and yet they don't have enough left to support places like this?' He sucked air sharply between his teeth, his hands thrust deep into two of the many pockets that adorned his trousers. He let out a deep breath and turned to me, a little abashed. 'Sorry, didn't mean to go off like that.'

I smiled at him. 'Please, don't apologise. You're absolutely right. That's why I'm here, after all.'

'Ah, speak of the devil.' Terry raised his chin at someone behind me and I turned to see the piano now occupied by a ginger-haired boy with glasses who was carefully pressing each key in turn, delighted with every new note he produced. The stool's previous occupant was striding towards us. There was something about him that felt familiar: the broad shoulders, the single dark curl falling just so across his brow, the soft crease in the middle of his chin a stark contrast to his sharply chiselled jaw. He was wearing black jeans and a denim shirt, the cuffs of which were rolled up to expose his forearms.

'Jenny, is it? From the *Tribune*?' His right hand extended as he approached and I noticed his index finger was stained with black ink, the tips hard and calloused against the back of my hand as he enveloped it between both of his. 'Thank you so much for coming. I'm Luca. Luca Patel.'

His eyes held mine, a tiny *v* appearing in the space where his eyebrows almost joined that made me wonder whether we'd met before.

'Jenny Thompson.' I smiled, the intensity of his gaze making the back of my neck prickle with heat. 'So, you're in charge round here?'

'Well, Ivan helps, too.' Luca pointed over towards the cardigan-wearing man trying to encourage a boy to use his drumstick to hit the drum, not the child sat next to him.

'Ah, you're just being modest. Luca runs the show,' Terry piped up, punching Luca playfully on the shoulder.

'Yeah, well, I'm not doing that great a job, considering the council just cut our funding,' Luca sighed, raking his fingers through his hair 'Something to do with government cutbacks or some bullshit, but that funding was our lifeline. Without it I'm not sure how much longer we can stay open.' My pen stilled as I watched him looking about the room, his eyes lingering on each child's face in turn. It was evident how much he cared. He shook his head fiercely, as though eliminating some awful scenario his brain had cooked up from either ear. 'Anyway, that's why we're putting on a fundraiser in a few months. It's an opportunity for all the kids to perform, but also, hopefully, for us to raise some much-needed funds.'

'That's a fantastic idea. Do you have a date? I'll be sure to mention it in the article.'

'28th May. It's the main reason I called the *Tribune*. Thought an article in the paper might help sell some tickets, raise enough money that we can keep the doors open for another year.'

'Oh, I think we can do a little more than that,' I said, feeling a renewed sense of purpose pumping through me for the first time since I could remember, beating its own tiny drum. Determined to be heard.

'I've got the money shot,' came Jacob's voice behind me, and I turned to see him jiggling his camera triumphantly in the air. He did a double take when his eyes landed on Luca, head dipping to one side and then the other. He clicked his fingers, recognition dawning on his face. 'Hey, weren't you the guy playing at the Old Bell last night?'

Aha, so that's where I recognised him from. The musician.

Luca blinked, clearly thrown by the question. 'Um, yeah. You were there?'

'When are we *not* there, more like?' Jacob scoffed, giving me a nudge-nudge-wink-wink-style hip bump.

'My mum owns the place,' I added, keen to clarify that we weren't raging alcoholics.

'Cool.' Luca's blank look confirmed he had no memory of me or our brief encounter outside the toilets. Probably for the best. Drunkenly colliding with a stranger pre-8 p.m. on a Tuesday didn't exactly scream *I'm a serious professional journalist.*

'Right, well, I think we've got everything we need.' I stabbed the top of my pen against my notebook with a sharp click. 'We'll be in touch,' I added with a smile, turning for the exit before Luca's memory had a chance to become less hazy.

'I can come up if you want? We could order Dominoes and watch old episodes of *Bake Off*?'

Jacob's cajoling tone made my hand still on the door handle of his beat-up VW Polo. Like most traditions, I couldn't remember exactly how it had started, but somewhere along the way Wednesday nights had become me and Jacob and Joe (and Alice, when she wasn't on shift) sardined on the sofa, pizza boxes juddering on our laps as we shook with laughter at Mary Berry's passing comment about a contestant's nut size. But it had been a while. Come to think of it, I couldn't remember the last time all three of us were together . . .

'Maybe next week?' I countered, forcing a smile through the wave of tiredness that swept over me. Jacob nodded, his lips pursed in that way that told me there was something else he wanted to say.

'You know—' he added quickly as I opened the door, one foot on the pavement, '—I can cover that interview for you on Friday, if you want? It's no bother.'

'Why would you do that?'

Jacob gave me a look. One I couldn't fully comprehend, but if I wasn't mistaken landed somewhere between concern and pity. An icy wind whipped down the street, making me shiver.

'Jenny—' Jacob started, but I was already out of the car, suddenly desperate to get inside.

'I'll see you tomorrow!' I waved over my shoulder, breaking into a semi-jog towards the communal front door. I heaved it open, throwing a longing look at the faded Out of Order sign hung across the elevator doors, and began the long ascent to the top floor. I had to stop outside Mrs Norris' door on the 3rd floor to catch my breath, removing my coat and tying it around my waist.

I physically dragged myself up the final set of stairs, using the banister to aid my climb as though I were summiting the peak of Mount Everest. The second stair from the top creaked loudly beneath my shoe, making me jump even though it had been that way ever since we'd moved in. Our own personal security system, Joe used to joke, and I smiled at the thought of him glancing up from the sofa, alerted to my arrival even before the jangle of keys could give me away. I was so engrossed digging through the contents of my handbag to find said keys – mmm, half-eaten Twix, yes please – that I didn't notice the piece of paper taped to the door until I was staring right at it. I tried to focus on the tiny, typed letters but they floated aimlessly around the page, toying with me as they scrambled into an incomprehensible jumble. I squinted, my eyes zeroing in on the giant red capital letters at the top of the page.

EVICTION NOTICE

Those two words were like a punch in the gut and I doubled over, afraid I was going to be sick, the stale Twix that had seemed so appealing thirty seconds ago now like a lump of coal in my mouth. My brain was in overdrive, a thousand questions all bouncing around demanding immediate answers.

Eviction? I mean, I know the rent is a little late – OK, a lot late – and this isn't the first time, but they can't evict us. Can they? I mean, where the hell will we go? This is my home. Our home that we built together. Joe and me. They must have the wrong address. Yes, that's it. It's probably intended for that couple with the cat that moved in downstairs a few months ago. I'll phone in the morning and sort this all out.

I nodded to myself, snatching the paper angrily from the door, a ripped corner clinging stubbornly to the wood as I crumpled the rest in my fist. Letting myself into the flat and closing the door behind me, I flicked the deadbolt across with a satisfying *clunk*, sliding the chain in place for good measure – as though I was afraid someone was going to barge in right that second and demand I leave.

The flat was dark and silent, an eerie rectangle of light on the floor courtesy of the half-moon shining in through the bay window, illuminating the place just enough for me to confirm it was empty, Joe's spot on the right-hand side of the sofa – visibly moulded to his shape after all these years – unoccupied. The clocks went forward this weekend, the debate Joe and I always had over whether we gained or lost an hour due its annual rematch. But the light he'd normally leave on for me when I got home from work was off. I flicked the switch, blinking as my eyes fell on the pile of unopened post that had begun as a neat-ish stack on the bench by the door and, at some point, had spilled over onto the floor. A few red-stamped envelopes peeked out from amongst the sea of white letters.

LATE PAYMENT

FINAL NOTICE

LATE PAYMENT

My heart began to race, the eviction notice burning in the palm of my hand as though intent on reminding me of its existence, forcing me to connect the dots. But the picture that emerged made me feel sick to my stomach. No, this couldn't be happening.

I dropped the ball of paper to the floor, watching it roll under the bench and out of sight. If only the panicked thoughts that had taken root in my brain – demanding answers to questions I didn't even want to think about – could disappear so easily. I marched into the kitchen, a sinking feeling in the pit of my stomach as I spotted the overflowing recycling bin. The game of Tetris I'd been playing for the past few weeks was clearly over, the empty milk cartons and cereal packets I'd been carefully balancing atop the bin now littering the floor. My eyes fell wearily on the bin collection timetable stuck to the fridge door, trying to make sense of the complicated colour-coded system. Joe always did the bins. Giving up, I scraped my hair up into a messy bun, opening all the kitchen cabinets with a clatter and transferring their contents onto the countertop.

'Everything all right?'

Joe had appeared in the doorway to the bedroom, leaning casually against the doorframe as he assessed the scene before him with a modicum of amusement.

'Mhmm,' I mumbled with a brisk nod of the head, focused on organising the ten different types of flour we had into military-like formation.

'Yeah, I'm not buying it. You're doing that thing you do.'

'What thing?'

'You know, the thing where you organise pointless stuff when you're stressed.'

'That's not what I'm doing,' I huffed, blowing a stray hair out of my face.

'Really? So, Wednesday night is the perfect time to be alphabetising the canned goods?'

I thought my resulting silence and the way I slammed the cupboard door shut would be answer enough, but apparently not.

'I know I should probably know this, but did I do something wrong? 'Cause I'm getting the vibe that I did?'

I ignored him, grinding my teeth as I busied myself with pulling random cans out of the cupboard. Anything but look in his direction, into those eyes of his. Because then I knew there'd be no holding it together anymore.

'Or maybe it's just something you *think* I did?'

I closed my eyes slowly, grip tightening around a can of baked beans.

'No, it was definitely me,' Joe backtracked quickly, holding his hands up in surrender. 'I did it. I was wrong. It was a stupid, awful, terrible thing to do; please don't make me sleep in the bathtub again.'

He walked towards me, head cocked as he tried to get my attention with that lopsided smile of his. The one that made my insides melt like ice cream on a summer's day. But I was too focused on trying to decipher the sell-by date on a can of minestrone soup to notice. The fact it was faded to the point that I was struggling to read it was probably all the information I needed to know, but I continued to squint at the numbers all the same.

'Come on, Jenny, I'm sorry. With all my heart. I shouldn't have done it. Thought it? Said it?' He was down on his knees now, hands clasped dramatically against his heart. I could feel my palms starting to sweat, my heart beating too fast behind my ribcage as my chest heaved up and down with the effort. Was that a one or a seven? Surely that didn't say 2013?! Although 2073 seemed even more worrisome somehow. Taking my chances, I shoved it back in the cupboard, slowly twisting the can until the label faced outwards.

'Jenny, babe, help me out here,' Joe pleaded with a chuckle, performing a series of fake dodges either side as he battled to get in my line of vision. 'I can't apologise if I don't know what I did wrong. If I even *did* do anything wrong, that is, I mean seriously, what could be so bad that . . .'

'*You died, Joe!*'

The words echoed around the walls of the kitchen again and again, each time more painful than the last. It was the first time I'd said them out loud, heavy and unwilling as they finally broke free. I sank to the floor, my knees no longer strong enough to hold me up – the weight of the world, of my world, simply too great to bear. A dent appeared between Joe's eyebrows and he opened his mouth as though to say something, but then shut it again. What was there to say? Instead, he fiddled awkwardly with a loose thread at the hem of his fisherman's jumper. The same jumper he'd been wearing for the past 162 days. The same navy jumper, the same overly loved Chelsea boots with the left heel that was almost completely worn down, the same pair of jeans. His favourite ones that hung low and loose around his hips. The denim so worn that they were soft to the touch.

The same outfit he'd been wearing that day. The day of the accident. The day my whole world fell apart.

It was also the day that *this* Joe first appeared. He was there, waiting for me in his usual spot on the sofa, when I eventually made my way home from the hospital. Broken and alone.

'Hey you,' he'd smiled, that dimple-topped, crooked smile that warmed me to my very core. 'Did you pick up some of those chocolate Hobnobs?'

I'd blinked. Hard. Several times. But every time, Joe was there. Sat in his dented spot on the sofa, his left leg jiggling up and down in that way that used to drive me crazy.

'Jenny?'

'Hmm?'

'The Hobnobs?' Joe had repeated, looking right at me this time. Those eyes, those perfect-colour-of-raindrops eyes. 'Oh God, you didn't get Garibaldis again, did you? Look, we might have to seriously rethink this whole marriage thing if you've come back with those abominations again.'

A bubble of laughter had escaped my lips. It sounded so foreign as it echoed around the living room, almost as though it belonged to someone else. Someone I used to know. I didn't question it. In fact, I don't think I even hesitated before walking over and taking my place beside him. Questioning required careful, rational thought and careful, rational thought would most likely cause this walking, talking, leg-twitching version of Joe to disappear. And that simply wasn't an option. Perhaps it was a dream. A hallucination. A sign that I'd finally gone completely bonkers.

I didn't care. As long as I didn't have to live in a world without Joe.

And for 162 days, I hadn't. Which is how I came to be sat on the kitchen floor, surrounded by canned goods, talking to my dead fiancé. We were as close as two human beings could be without touching, if I just tilted my head a fraction to the right it could rest on his shoulder—

My head snapped upwards when it met nothing but air, as though jolting awake from a dream. A sob exploded out of me, tears streaming down my face as I felt the deep, gaping hole that had ripped its way through my heart five months ago tear a little bit wider. Something was digging into the fabric of my trousers and while I welcomed the discomfort – anything to distract from the crippling heartache that was threatening to tear me in two – I reached down and pulled a now-very-squashed packet of Garibaldis out from under me. I turned it over in my hands, watching my tears land with a plop on the plastic packaging, right next to the sell-by date.

February 2024. They, like Joe, had also expired.

5

'Well, I think this is going to be great,' Alice announced brightly, puffing her fringe away from where it had stuck to her forehead as she dropped the final box to the floor.

'How exactly is this great?' I croaked, my voice hoarse.

They were the first words I'd spoken all day. I'd said nothing when Alice and Jacob had arrived at my front door thirty minutes after receiving the latest in a long stream of incomprehensible voice notes, arms filled with packing supplies and freshly baked cinnamon rolls from Drew's. Not a word as I curled into a ball on the sofa, watching silently as they packed mine and Joe's things into boxes, dismantling what was left of our life together piece by piece. I really needed Joe today. But I knew he wouldn't show. He never did whenever people that knew him were around. Another fact that I tried my best not to question as I highly doubted I'd like the answer.

'Is it the fact that I'm 30 years old and still haven't managed to get on the housing ladder? Heck, I don't even own a bloody ladder! Or that I've no choice but to move back in with my mum? Or that mine and Joe's life together has been reduced to nothing more than a few stupid boxes?' I kicked the nearest box for good measure.

It was a lot sturdier than it looked and I bit my cheek to keep from crying out in pain.

'It's a new chapter,' Alice rephrased carefully, taking a seat next to me on the bed. The springs creaked in protest, the child-sized single bed also voicing how unhappy it was about this situation.

'I don't want to start a new chapter. I liked the old one,' I mumbled childishly. An awkward silence descended over the room, the kind that comes after talking about something difficult where no one wants to be the first to speak for fear of saying the wrong thing.

'Personally, it's the Peter Andre poster that's doing it for me,' Jacob finally said from where he was stood in the doorway, pointing up at the faded 'Mysterious Girl' poster above my bed where a shirtless, soaking-wet Peter Andre was giving us the blue steels. Jacob erupted into song, belting out the lyrics to 'Mysterious Girl' at the top of his voice as he performed some form of stomach-rolling/hip-thrusting move towards us. A reluctant smile progressed into a grin as he hoisted one foot on the bed, the other on the floor as he straddled both Alice and me, gyrating like a seasoned *Magic Mike* performer.

'Ewww, get your crotch out of my face!' Alice squealed, disgusted, swatting him away like a fly.

'Surprisingly, not the first time someone's said that to me,' Jacob snickered, collapsing on what little unoccupied space remained on the paper-thin duvet. The bed groaned.

'You know we'd totally have you at ours if we could, right?' Alice leaned her neat pixie crop on my shoulder. 'It's just there's barely enough room for the two of us as it is, you'd quite literally have to sleep in the bathtub – and even that's half-sized.'

'Of course, don't be silly.' Although sleeping in Alice and Jacob's ridiculously tiny bathtub in their ridiculously tiny, ridiculously overpriced flat that they'd bought together six months ago – technically a one-bedroom, but with an additional sofa bed taking up most of the open plan lounge/kitchen/dining room/hallway – seemed marginally less tragic than moving back into my child-hood bedroom. It was like a time warp in here. The same quilted bedspread, the same cracked-spined *Harry Potter* books lined up on the windowsill, the same *Top of the Pops* posters stuck to the walls, their age-curled edges and outdated fashions the only hint of just how much time had passed since I'd last called the flat above the pub home. It was as if nothing had changed. My hands balled into duvet-filled fists at the thought, because nothing could be further from the truth. *Everything* had changed. That was the problem.

'How's it all going in here?'

After loitering in the hall for the past half an hour, Mum had finally appeared in the doorway. She was sporting a long blonde fishtail braid over one shoulder. Last week it had been a Debbie Harry-style bob. Next week my money was on an 80s Cher-era mullet. Never afraid to try something new, my mother. I saw her eyes linger briefly on my hole-ridden tracksuit bottoms that I'd been wearing since – well, I couldn't remember ever not wearing them at this stage – and Joe's stain-ridden Yale sweatshirt that fell just above my knees. I had zero intention of ever washing it, of replacing Joe's scent with generic cotton-fresh laundry detergent. But, if I was being honest with myself, his scent had faded long ago.

Mum pressed her lips together, swallowing the words she so clearly wanted to say and instead opting for, 'Can I get anyone a cuppa?'

'Thanks, Mrs T, but I'd better get going,' Alice said, glancing at her watch. It was 5:30 p.m. She was due back at the hospital again in half an hour. She stood up, smoothing the back of her already immaculate hair before hesitating. 'Unless you need me to stay—'

'No, you go,' I said quickly, trying to arrange my face into something vaguely reassuring. 'Honestly, you've done more than enough already. You both have,' I added, my voice thick with gratitude at the sight of my two best friends who'd dropped everything to be there for me. Again.

'Cup of tea, Jacob? Or I could open a bottle of rosé?'

'Now you're speaking my language, Mrs T!' Jacob clapped both his hands together, jumping to his feet and heading straight down the hall towards the tiny galley kitchen as though the bottle of rosé in the fridge door were some sort of homing beacon. I'm not sure why Alice and Jacob called Mum *Mrs* T. She'd never been married. Never even had a serious relationship after the man who was mine and Matt's father – in the biological sense of the word only – had left before I was even born. And yet they'd called her Mrs T for as long as I could remember. The idea of a grown woman, and a mother at that, not being married was apparently not an option in a five-year-old's mind.

'I'll be right there,' I called after them, forcing a smile when Mum turned back with a concerned look on her face. My shoulders caved as soon as they were out of sight, slipping like the mask I'd being trying so hard to keep in place all day. It didn't matter how many glasses of wine I drank, how many times I managed to shower and put on clean(ish) clothes, or how many things I wrote I was grateful for in that stupid mindfulness app Mum had recommended. It didn't get any easier. Any of it.

'Blimey, who's that absolute hunk?'

My breath caught in my throat at the sound of Joe's voice, that familiar baritone I'd recognise in a thousand different lifetimes making my heart skip a beat. I sat bolt upright on the bed, hardly daring to believe it, but there he was. Sat on the duvet beside me, as though he'd been there this whole time.

'That is one seriously lucky girl, is all I'm saying,' he added, eyes twinkling mischievously as he nodded towards the heart-shaped picture frame on the bedside table. Sixteen-year-old Joe and me beaming in the pub car park. Me in my cherry-red satin prom dress. Joe in his ill-fitting, off-black suit and spiky gelled hair. He had his arms around me from behind, my hands over his as I smiled up at him over my left shoulder. We looked happy.

'You're here.' I breathed a sigh of relief, a genuine smile gracing my face for the first time all day as I let go of the crippling fear that had taken over me ever since I'd closed the door to our flat for the final time. The fear that I'd never see Joe again. That these visions – whatever you wanted to call them – would stop.

'Of course I'm here.' He sounded mildly offended that I'd thought otherwise. 'When do I miss an opportunity to see your darling mother?'

For once, his unwavering humour grated on me slightly, the fact that he had the luxury of sitting there and joking around while I was freefalling in a never-ending spiral. I shifted awkwardly on the bed, the squeaky springs giving away my discomfort.

'Hey,' Joe said, softer this time, his hand reaching out across the bedspread. The tiny scar still visible on his little finger, the skin all pink and puckered from when he'd slipped and fallen off a groyne on Hove beach.

'I really needed you today,' I whispered, my eyes fixed firmly in my lap before inevitably finding his, like a magnet drawn towards its partner. There was no fighting it. It was chemical. Undeniable.

'I know,' he said simply, a troubled frown darkening his brow. 'But just because you can't see me doesn't mean I'm not with you, Jenny. You can't get rid of me that easy,' he added in a teasing voice, trying to lighten the mood once again. I gave a weak smile this time, more at the irony of it all than at Joe's poor attempt at humour.

'I just miss them,' I sighed, running my forefinger over the two smiling faces in the photograph, a streak of dust coming with it. 'I miss us.'

'You coming, Jenny?

Mum had appeared in the doorway, a hint of a frown just visible beneath her clip-in fringe. *Shit, how long had she been standing there?* My eyes flicked guiltily to my right, but the bedspread was empty where Joe had previously sat.

I was alone.

'It has to be in here somewhere. It just has to.'

'Have you tried the box labelled *Kitchen*?' Mum asked for the fourth time.

'Of course I have,' I snapped, upending the contents of yet another box onto the already overflowing bed.

'Well, I'm sure it'll turn up, love. Why don't I make you a cuppa in your *Harry Potter* mug? You know, the one that changes colour when you put the hot water in? That was always your favourite—'

'I don't want another mug, I want *that* mug. I drink my coffee out of *that* mug every morning,' I insisted between clenched teeth, growing increasingly panicked in my search for said mug. It was the *Star Wars* one with the small hairline crack down one side. Joe's favourite. He drank everything out of that mug. Water. His teeth-achingly sweet coffee. Even wine. I knew I was being ridiculous. It was just a mug after all. But I couldn't bear the thought of losing yet another part of him. However small and insignificant that part might be.

'I must have left it at the flat,' I declared, slapping both hands against my thighs in resignation. We stood in silence for a minute, my ragged breathing suddenly very obvious in the otherwise silent room as I took in the mess before me. It looked like a tornado had passed through, empty cardboard boxes flung everywhere, their contents now three inches deep on the floor.

'Sweetheart,' Mum said gently, pausing in a way that told me she was about to say something I didn't want to hear. 'Do you think maybe this is about something other than the mug?'

'What? Of course it's about the mug. I just told you I can't find it. What else could it be about?' I caught sight of my reflection in the mirror on the back of the door, trying not to look too startled by the crazed-looking, sleep-deprived, hair-sticking-in-every-direction-it-shouldn't woman staring back at me. 'I'll just go past the flat on my way to work and get it,' I told myself, the frantic-looking woman in the mirror nodding her approval at my plan back at me.

'Jenny, love, I know it's difficult letting go. That flat was an important chapter of your life, of—' she hesitated, clearly wondering whether she should say his name, '— Joe's and your life together, and nothing can take away those memories. But perhaps everything that's happened these past few days is the universe's way of telling you to leave the mug behind? To move on?'

'Move on?' I spat, the words hot and fiery in my mouth. 'Move on from what, Mum? From Joe?' I could feel the tears burning behind my eyes at the thought of a time when I'd no longer yearn for Joe every second of every day. Rooting through the mountain of belongings on the bed in search of socially acceptable clothing, I gave up trying to find socks, and shoved my bare feet into trainers, not bothering to tie the laces. 'Well, I'm sorry I'm not moving on fast enough for you, Mum.'

'No, that's not what I—'

'I've got to go,' I said briskly, rescuing my handbag from beneath a pile of Joe's stuff and brushing past her. I knew I was avoiding, but I couldn't hear this right now. To be reminded that I had to move on, but not forget entirely. To be strong, but also gentle with myself. To live, but not let the memories die. Everything was a pre-carious balancing act. One false move, and the scales could tip to the point of no return and there'd be no going back. Grief yet another pre-determined timeline that I was failing miserably to follow. It was exhausting just thinking about it, and the truth was I had no desire to do any of those things. I just wanted to find Joe's mug.

'Why. Won't. You. Open?' I growled aggressively at the door, jiggling my key in the lock for the tenth time to no avail. It was less than 24 hours since I'd moved out; they couldn't possibly have changed the locks already – could they? Come to think of it, the bright, gleaming metal surround was noticeably shinier than before. Like, *new* shiny. This fuelled my rage further and I jammed my key in once again, willing it to open.

'*Aha!*'

My moment of triumph was short lived as the door swung inwards and I toppled ungracefully forward, realising as I did so that my key had not opened the door after all, but that the latter had in fact been wrenched open by the black t-shirt-wearing, mildly irritated-looking man who I was currently falling face-first towards.

'What the—?'

Thankfully, he chose to prioritise preventing us both from ending up in a heap on the floor over finishing his sentence. His left hand caught my right forearm, his less accurate right hand performing an incredibly awkward (and slightly painful) boob grab before managing to slide to the safety of my shoulder. My cheek slammed hard against the man's pectoral region. I staggered backwards, feeling like I'd just run headfirst into a brick wall, and ricocheting painfully off the doorframe as I went. A searing pain shot up my arm as I opened my mouth to give this hard-chested stranger residing in *my* flat a piece of my mind. Squatters was the very last thing I needed.

Only it wasn't a stranger.

'It's you?'

Luca stared back at me with that same quizzical look he'd given me at the community centre. Head lopsided, tongue poking out the corner of his mouth, eyes narrowing as though he were trying to place me. Of course he was *that* guy. The one who didn't remember the woman he'd spent the best part of an hour speaking to a mere two days before. I bet if I'd been wearing a short skirt and knee-high boots he'd have remembered me. A sour taste built up in my mouth at the sight of him stood there, the doorway too narrow to accommodate his broad shoulders so he was forced to turn sideways. It looked wrong. It *was* wrong.

'What the hell are you doing here?' I spluttered accusingly, my brain working overtime to try to comprehend this weird turn of events. Luca frowned, glancing briefly over his shoulder as though to check I wasn't talking to someone else.

'I'm Jenny,' I said simply, as if that explained everything.

Luca just blinked at me, his face blank. OK, seriously? Was I really that forgettable?

'From the *Tribune*?' I added.

'Right, yes, of course.' A flicker of recognition sparked behind his eyes and he gave a little laugh, as if my name was somehow amusing to him. 'Well, Jenny from the *Tribune*, do you mind explaining why you're trying to break into my flat? Is this to do with the article?'

61

My stomach lurched. 'Your flat?'

'Yes, my flat.'

The way he stood there, his bare feet looking so comfortable on the wooden floorboards – my wooden floorboards – made my teeth grind.

'I'll have you know that until 22 hours ago, this was very much *my* flat.'

'Great. I'm glad we've established that you no longer live here. Although that does bring us back around to the whole breaking and entering thing.'

'I wasn't breaking in. I have a key.' I jangled my keys in front of his face as if to prove my point. That annoying head slant told me he already knew said key did not work. 'And I didn't realise someone had moved in already, otherwise I wouldn't have—'

'—wouldn't have committed a felony by attempting the worst case of breaking and entering I've ever seen?' Luca finished for me. Ergh, he was one of those men that thought it was his God-given right to interrupt a woman. See, I knew it – no guy can have cheekbones like that and not be an asshole. I glared at his stupid smile, the one making his dark-brown eyes sparkle with tiny flecks of gold. He was actually enjoying this. 'Tell me, have you committed any other crimes recently? You know, just so I can give the police a thorough report. Theft? Carjacking? Child abduction?'

'I'm seriously considering murder right now, if that counts?' I forced through gritted teeth. He just laughed, his bicep flexing as he reached up to ruffle the back of his hair, which was long enough that it teased the base of his neck.

'Well, on that note it's been a pleasure, Jenny, but if you'll excuse me—'

I wedged my foot in the gap between the door and the frame, preventing him from closing it.

'Seriously?' Luca raised a questioning eyebrow. He gave me a quick once-over, his eyes flitting from my squashed Converse to my face and back again with the speed of a seasoned pro. His expression shifted from one of amusement to that of uncertainty. Clearly my crazy bed hair and questionable outfit combo of crumpled white shirt, which I suddenly realised was buttoned up wrong, and black workout leggings was not giving out calm, mentally stable vibes.

'I want my mug.'

'Excuse me?'

'My mug,' I repeated firmly, trying to ignore the fact that I was 99% certain I'd broken my baby toe. 'Star Wars mug. Quite faded. Crack down one side?'

Luca just stared at me as though I'd admitted I wanted to personally commandeer the Millennium Falcon and fly it to a galaxy far, far away. When I showed no signs of moving, he ran his fingers through his hair again with an impatient sigh. Like I was ruining his day. Relinquishing his weight on the door he turned, padding barefoot into the kitchen without so much as a backwards glance. I nudged the door further open with my shoe, my eyes roaming hungrily over the familiar details.

Part of me felt relieved it was all still there – the fraying wicker bench by the front door that Joe would stub his toe on every day without fail; the faded circle on the floorboards where our beloved cheese plant, Big Kev, had lived for years, gradually demanding more and more space; the black scuff marks on the wall where Joe used to lean his bike. Proof that our time here together was real. That it had happened. But that comforting familiarity was shattered by the unfamiliar pair of black Nike trainers kicked carelessly to one side, the guitar case leaning against the wall, a pizza box from that place down the road sitting in Joe's spot on the sofa, the dip in the cushion making the box tilt precariously. I bit the inside of my cheek, tears of a thousand emotions pooling in my eyes at the idea of someone else's stuff where ours used to be.

I blinked quickly as I heard Luca returning.

'Is this what you mean?'

He was holding Joe's mug in one hand. It had been used. The ring of dried coffee residue at the bottom told me as much.

'You drank out of it?!' I snatched the mug from his outstretched fingers, hugging it possessively to my chest.

'Err, yeah? It's a mug, what else was I supposed to do with it?'

'It wasn't yours to use,' I hissed angrily, my cheeks burning with irritation.

'Well, excuse me for thinking that something left in *my* flat when I moved in was fair game,' he snapped back, his eyes flashing with a similar anger. 'Take it, I'm more of a *Star Trek* guy anyway.'

'Of course you are,' I snorted, hitching my bag further up my shoulder. That explained so much.

'As much as I'd love to stand here and enlighten you as to all the reasons *Star Trek* is superior, some of us have jobs to get to.' Luca looked deliberately at his watch as he spoke, then took an intentional step forward, forcing me out into the hall.

'I have a job too,' I added pettily, even though he already knew as much. For some reason I wanted to stress that I had at least a modicum of my shit together. But he'd already closed the door in my face.

6

'OK, that's it,' Mum announced mid-way through the following week, snapping shut the library book she'd been pretending to read with a crisp flourish. 'I can't just sit by and watch this anymore.'

'Watch what?' I frowned, absentmindedly stirring my coffee as I continued staring at the spot in front of the fridge that, until Mum's arrival twenty minutes ago, Joe had been occupying. The two of us, dancing in the dim glow from the open fridge door, bodies almost but not quite touching as we swayed together, his hand hovering over mine, my head over his shoulder, oblivious to the repetitive beeping of the open fridge door.

'This. You.' She gestured in my direction, her hand falling with a frustrated smack on the trouser leg of her dungarees. They were bright yellow denim with little embroidered flowers spilling out the top of the pockets. If positivity had a designated uniform, that would be it.

'What are you talking about?' I sighed, a wave of tiredness sweeping over me even though it was only 8 a.m. I'd stayed up too late talking to Joe, hushed whispers under the duvet so Mum wouldn't hear, like when we were teenagers.

'Trust me when I say this comes from a place of love, sweetheart, but you look . . . well, terrible,' she admitted, placing her warm hand over mine as though that might soften the blow. I'm not sure if it was the shirt I'd been wearing for three days straight or the diabolical state of my roots that made her physically wince, but her mouth and eyes puckered tightly at the seams. 'By the looks of it you're barely sleeping, I don't even want to know the last time you showered, and you spend all your time holed up in your bedroom. It's not healthy.'

I fidgeted in my seat, the creaking wicker giving away my discomfort as I struggled to find the words to tell her this was it. This was my best. Every day I got up, I washed (sometimes), I put on clothes as if I cared what I looked like, I tried to breathe, to live, even though I had absolutely zero desire to do so.

'This isn't living, Jenny,' Mum added softly when I failed to respond. 'It's existing at most and, to be honest, you're barely doing that. Honestly, it pains me to see you like this. Alice and Jacob are worried about you too; they said you barely see them these days?'

I scowled into my lap, misplaced anger bubbling up inside of me at the thought of the three of them conspiring behind my back. I could see the look of concern on Mum's face, her forehead wrinkled with worry and I reminded myself it was coming, as she said, from a place of love. But it did little to comfort me. If anything, it just reminded me what that felt like – that unconditional, I'd-do-anything-for-you love – and my heart squeezed with memories of the past.

'I'm fine, Mum,' I said, plastering a smile on my face but it clearly looked about as fake as it felt.

'Jenny—' Mum paused in a way that made me stiffen, '—you know, deep down, this isn't what Joe would want. He'd want you to be happy, to find your joy again. Whoever *this* is—' she said, gesturing at me, '—it isn't you. It isn't my Jenny.'

I felt a familiar knot tighten in my stomach the way it always did whenever someone mentioned Joe. The legs of my chair jarred harshly against the linoleum floor as I made to leave, but Mum's hand on my thigh stopped me.

'Please, Mum, I can't do this,' I whispered, a quivering ball of emotions lodged in the back of my throat, threatening to detonate at any moment. My eyes met hers for the first time since she'd sat down twenty minutes ago, a look of silent understanding passing between us as she simply nodded, her grip loosening.

'You need to break this cycle, Jenny, try something new.'

I hid my face in Joe's coffee mug, not having the heart to tell her that I'd had enough change in my life recently, and 'something new' was the last thing I wanted. 'I'm going to a spin class at the gym tonight, you should come!' Her eyes lit up at the idea.

'The last time I set foot in a gym was three years ago and it was purely to use their showers when our hot water wasn't working.'

'You need to leave this house, Jennifer,' Mum said firmly, apparently not taking no for an answer. She swiped my still half-full cup of coffee away, replacing it with a banana and a brisk *hmm* of satisfaction, as though a phallic-shaped fruit was the answer to all my problems. 'Besides, you might surprise yourself and actually enjoy it.'

'*This. Is. Hell!*' I panted, barely scraping together enough oxygen to get the words out and immediately wishing I'd preserved the energy. My thighs were burning as they pistoned up and down, valiantly trying to keep up with the annoyingly perky spin instructor at the front of the class who was wearing dangerously short shorts and looked like he'd barely broken a sweat.

'Looking good out there, gang. OK, we're going to pick up the pace now in three . . . two . . . one . . . let's go!'

I groaned as the instructor stood up on the pedals, watching with dread as twenty Lycra-clad bottoms lifted off their saddles around me in perfect time to the chorus of Whitney Houston's 'I Wanna Dance with Somebody'. I turned to my right, watching in disbelief as my some-how still-grinning mother gave me a double thumbs up, legs spinning almost as fast as the neon-coloured wheels.

'Work that core, ladies, work it. Come on, finish strong. Here we go! How are we doing on that leader board? Yaaaaaas, Courtney, I see you riding high at the top there.'

The brunette in front of me with an impossibly long ponytail and a full face of make-up beamed proudly around the room as though intent on letting everyone know that was her. While Mum had somehow main-tained a perfect middle-of-the-pack ranking the whole class, I was firmly in last place, three points below some other poor sucker called Vivienne who, like me, was trailing woefully behind everyone else.

'Good job, Brenda, keep it up. You're killing it, Michelle. Jennifer. Yes, you, Jennifer – back row, third from the left, you can't hide from me.'

Fuck, he'd seen me. I'd been taking a much-needed break, doubled over on my handlebars, heaving in great gulps of air.

'Come on, Jennifer!' the instructor barked, yelling into his Britney-style headset like an army drill sergeant. 'Work it, Jennifer, don't give up on me now. Today's the day you meet the best version of yourself. Today's the day you look in that mirror and visualise the change you want to see.'

I lifted my head, finding my reflection in the intimidating wall of mirrors in front of me. My face was bright red, bordering on the same shade as Courtney's sports bra, my cheeks blowing outwards like an aggressive pufferfish. Sweat had plastered my hair slick against my forehead, my once light-grey t-shirt now decorated with ever-expanding dark patches under both arms and between my boobs. If *this* was the best version of myself, I was in even deeper shit than I realised.

'Nice work, Vivienne, another point on the board! That new hip is really working,' bellowed the instructor, throwing a thumbs up in the direction of a woman at the end of my row. I turned to offer her a look of solidarity, my fellow sufferer at the bottom of the leader board. But when I saw the grey hair, the dentures, the bifocals with the delicate pearl chain, I quickly turned back to the front. *That was Vivienne?!* She was old enough to be my grandmother!

'*Ahhhhh!*' The heavy bass of the music vibrating through the dimly lit room drowned out my scream as I heaved myself up off the handlebars, somehow convincing my legs to keep on turning. I couldn't let myself be beaten by octogenarian Vivienne and her new hip.

'Yes, Jennifer. Loving your attitude, never give up, girl. Keep pushing for ten . . . nine . . . eight . . .'

My legs were burning. As in, they felt like they were on actual fire. But still I kept pedalling, some misplaced fear of failure preventing me from giving up. I turned to my right, catching a glimpse of Vivienne who was looking morosely up at the scoreboard as I moved to within a point of her. She turned and caught my gaze, her eyes narrowing behind her inch-thick spectacles. Oh, it was so on.

'. . . seven . . . six . . . five . . . four . . .'

I dropped my head back down, watching beads of sweat trickle off my nose, everything between my legs throbbing from being bashed repeatedly against the rock-hard saddle.

'. . . three . . . two . . . one . . . *woooo!*'

'YESSSS!' I shrieked, punching both hands in the air as I looked up at the giant TV screen. Two whole points from the bottom, and more importantly, not last. I turned and gave Vivienne a smug smile but she was already heading for the exit, leaning heavily on her walking stick in a way that took the shine off my victory somewhat. Christ, how tragic was my life that I viewed beating a little old lady with a dodgy hip and a free bus pass as an achievement?

I winced as I hoisted my left leg over the saddle, worrying that I'd done permanent damage to my vagina as I swivelled to face sideways, my legs dangling freely for one glorious minute as I watched the instructor hop nimbly off his bike and dab himself unnecessarily with the world's smallest towel.

'How great was that?' Mum grinned, her face sporting a healthy glow.

'So great,' I wheezed, not having the heart to tell her I felt ten times worse than when I arrived. I hobbled gingerly after her, walking as though I still had something in between my legs – and not in a good way.

My phone rang as I was crossing the tiny car park at the back of the *Brighton Tribune* after work. I wouldn't go as far as to say there was a pep in my step at the thought of curling up on the sofa with Joe watching old *Star Wars* episodes – Mum was working the late shift tonight so we'd have the flat to ourselves – but my feet didn't drag in the same way they had when I'd arrived at 9 a.m. that morning.

'Yes? Hello?' I asked impatiently, balancing the phone between my shoulder and ear as I fished my car keys out my bag.

'Is that Miss Thompson?'

'Yep, speaking.' I was in the driver's seat now, handbag dumped in the passenger footwell.

'Miss Thompson, this is Craig Lester calling from Rogers, Pinkman & White.'

There was an expectant pause, as though he assumed I knew who he was talking about. My thumb hovered over the End Call button, convinced it was yet another person trying to tell me I'd been in an accident that wasn't my fault.

'Mr Carter's life insurance providers,' he clarified. I froze, the Twix bar I'd been attempting to tear into with my teeth slipping from my fingers into the dreaded chasm between the driver's seat and the handbrake that had claimed countless hair bobbles, a McDonald's chicken nugget and several Jelly Babies over the years, never to be seen again. 'I've been trying to get hold of you quite urgently, Miss Thompson. As I'm sure you're aware from our written correspondence, Mr Carter listed you as the sole beneficiary of his life insurance policy. A cheque was issued a few weeks ago now, but I can see here it's yet to be cashed?'

I heard Craig's tone go up at the end. A question, expecting an answer. But the thought of some bored, middle-aged man in a too-tight suit punching numbers into his computer to determine what figure Joe's life was worth made me physically sick. I clamped my lips tightly together.

'Hello? Miss Thompson?'

'Yes, I'm here,' I whispered, my voice fractured.

'The cheque, Miss Thompson. Have you received it?' Craig pressed. 'The address it was issued to is Flat 6, 4 Kings Gardens, BN3 4NP?'

'That's my old address.'

'It's the address we've got on file for you, Miss Thompson.' Craig sighed impatiently, as though I was the one somehow inconveniencing him.

'Well, I can just give you my new address now.'

'Any change in residential address must be verified, a process that can take up to 28 working days, Miss Thompson. Do you have a bill or bank statement with

73

your new address on that we can use for verification purposes?'

'Err, no, not exactly. You see I'm staying with my mother right now. Temporarily, of course.'

'Of course.' Something about Craig's tone made my cheeks flush with heat.

'Well, Miss Thompson, without proof of residence I cannot very well send another cheque to an unauthorised address, I'm sure you understand.'

'No, Craig, I don't bloody understand,' I barked down the phone, rage bubbling up inside of me. I didn't even want the bloody cheque. All the letters they'd sent me over the past few months still sat unopened at the bottom of one of my moving boxes, and those are just the ones my neighbours left outside my door when the contents of my woefully ignored pigeonhole downstairs repeatedly spilled out onto the floor below. The very thought that I'd benefit financially from Joe's death made me want to throw up, but the fact that asshole Craig was now refusing to send me said cheque that I had no intention of cashing, for the sole reason that I was living with my mother, pushed me over the edge.

'You know what, Craig,' I snapped, cutting him off midway through what sounded like him reading the company handbook to me, 'I'll just get the sodding cheque myself!'

The communal front door was unlocked, as it always was, and I let myself in, ignoring the PLEASE LOCK THE FRONT DOOR BEHIND YOU sign courtesy of Mr Higgins from Flat 1 that no one ever adhered to.

I wandered over to the wooden pigeonholes, my jaw clenching when I saw that mine and Joe's nametag on the top row had been replaced by one that read LUCA PATEL in capital letters. A quick inspection revealed there were no letters addressed to me, just the latest issue of *Rolling Stone* magazine and an envelope from British Gas. Of course it wasn't down here. Of course not. The universe was not that kind to me.

I was out of breath by the time I reached the top floor, my thighs – which had not been the same since that spin class – burning from the climb. I rapped sharply on the door, standing as tall as my quivering legs would allow. As soon as I heard the lock snap back, I launched right in, not wanting to give him an opportunity to no doubt say something incredibly annoying.

'Look, believe it or not, you're quite possibly the *last* person in the world I want to see right now, but I've come for a letter and I'm not leaving until – oh!'

My mouth opened and closed like a goldfish, stunned into silence by the person staring back at me. It wasn't Luca. It was a woman, wearing a black t-shirt. His, judging by the way it fell halfway down her bare legs. Her jet-black hair was piled atop her head in a messy bun, several long tendrils escaping down her back as she blinked wide-eyed at me.

'Canihelpyouuu?' A mouthful of foamy toothpaste and the toothbrush wedged between her teeth made it impossible to understand what she was saying.

'Umm, I'm looking for . . . Luca?'

The woman held up a finger, disappearing momentarily from view as she dashed in the direction of the kitchen.

My eyes fell on a pair of red-soled high heels just inside the door, one on its side, as though their owner had been in a rush to take them off. The sound of running water and someone gargling echoed through the flat before the t-shirt-clad, barefoot woman reappeared.

'Sorry about that,' she grinned, wiping a stray smear of toothpaste residue from her bottom lip. 'You said you're a friend of Luca's?'

'Err, no. I wouldn't say we're friends,' I said firmly, my trainers crunching against the door mat as I shifted from foot to foot. 'I used to live here.'

'Ah, *you're* the old tenant!' she said in a way that confirmed Luca had already mentioned me. The unwavering smile on her face told me she was either incredibly polite, or Luca miraculously hadn't used words like stalker, criminal or unhinged when describing our previous run-in. My money was on the former.

'That's me.'

'Nice to meet you. I'm Jasmine.' She flashed me her pearly whites again, her dark-brown eyes shimmering with a genuine warmth.

'Jenny,' I smiled back, immediately taking to her. With her long, slim legs and enviably symmetrical eyebrows, she was undeniably beautiful. And nice. Too nice to be with someone like Luca, that was for sure.

'Well, Jenny, Luca's just in the shower, but you're welcome to come inside and wait? I would say he won't be long, but in my experience that would probably be a lie. What men get up to for so long in the bathroom is beyond me.' She pushed the front door open a little wider, enough that I could see through to the lounge and the worn sofa that spoke of a million evenings together snuggled up on the lumpy cushions. The empty bottle of wine in the middle of the paper-strewn coffee table, two glasses on the floor, right next to a pair of black, lacy . . . *oh!*

'It's OK, I'll just come back another time,' I said quickly, having no desire to see evidence that would confirm Luca and his way-too-good-for-him girlfriend had had sex in my former flat. Ergh, I hope they hadn't done it on the sofa. Maybe they hadn't made it that far? There'd been many a night when Joe and I had stumbled through the front door, Joe's hips pinning my body against the wall as our hands were everywhere all at once, shirt buttons scattering across the floor in our haste to have nothing between us. I eyed the hastily discarded high heels again with a suspicious eye. 'I was just looking for a letter that might have been sent here by mistake, but it can wait . . .'

'Wait a second, I think there was something – yes, here it is!' Jasmine reached over, producing a sizeable, elastic-band-clad bundle of letters from the hallway table. 'There's some for you, and then one for a Mr Joe Carter?' She squinted uncertainly at the typeface on the front of the envelope, the pain of my nails digging into the soft skin of my palm a welcome distraction from the ache already sweeping through me.

I took the bundle of white and brown manila envelopes from her without saying anything. But I wasn't prepared to see him, dimples and all, smiling up at me from the bottom-right corner of the flyer for his photography exhibition. The one he'd worked so hard on, and that I'd agreed with the gallery should go ahead posthumously.

The one I'd yet to attend. My thumb brushed gently over his face, each typed letter of Joe's name on the glossy flyer like a dagger to the heart. I turned abruptly, hurrying down the stairs without so much as a *thank you* or *goodbye* so that she wouldn't see the tears that had already started to fall.

I'd been sat staring at the envelope for over an hour, turning it over and over in my hands. At some point, the sun had set. It was now pitch-black outside, the lights from the pub car park illuminating the white rectangle in my lap. I ran my fingers over the raised lettering of the Rogers, Pinkman & White company stamp in the top right-hand corner. The envelope was thick, expensive, not the cheap £1 job lot from the corner shop. Everything about it already screamed money.

'Not getting any younger over here.'

I turned and gave Joe a look. He was in the passenger seat, head turned against the headrest as he glanced amusedly in my direction.

'Aren't you even the least bit curious?' he asked when I continued staring silently into my lap.

'Why would I be curious?'

'About how much I'm worth.'

I winced, my breath sucking sharply between my teeth as a pain shot through my chest like broken glass. My fingers were gripping the edge of the envelope so hard that it was starting to crumple, the once-smooth paper as furrowed and creased as my brow.

'Well, *I'm* curious,' Joe continued, undeterred by my silence. 'Personally, I'm going to be disappointed if it's anything less than £100k. I mean look at me, I'm an absolute specimen.'

'Will you just – stop!' I pleaded, my voice a lot louder than I'd intended as it echoed around the car. We sat in silence for a moment, the faint hum of activity from inside the pub growing momentarily louder as the door swung open and two men came out, disappearing off down the street.

'Sorry,' Joe said after a while, the joking nonchalance act firmly dropped. His right hand reached out across the centre console, palm face up by means of an invitation, like he always used to do on long drives. My left hand reached out automatically and, as I closed my eyes, I swear I could feel the warmth of his hand in mine, our fingers neatly interlocking as though they were made for that very purpose. 'I'm sorry I've left you to deal with all this, Jenny. I guess I just want to know that you'll be OK, that you'll be – comfortable, you know?'

I smiled weakly. That was so Joe. Always making sure everyone else was looked after, without any thought for himself.

'It makes no difference how much it is,' I insisted, slipping my finger beneath the flap of the envelope and tearing a jagged line across the top. 'It's not like I'm going to cash it.'

'Hey, it's yours to do whatever you want with – cash it, don't cash it, use it as a coaster for all I care. It's up to you . . . holy cow, that's a lot of zeros!' Joe let out a low whistle as I stared at the cheque in front of me. So, this was it. The amount that Joe's life was supposedly worth. It was a lot of money. More than I could earn in ten years on my current salary. But it wasn't enough. Joe's life was worth so much more than any number they could write on a stupid cheque. Tears of frustration prickled on my lash line, hot and fiery as my hand tightened into a fist around the paper. My other hand lingered on the door handle. I was stalling, putting off going inside because I knew as soon as I set foot in the pub Joe would disappear, at least until I was in the solitude of my bedroom, and the prospect of even a few minutes without him by my side made every inch of me ache.

'You got this,' Joe said with a level of confidence I'd never possessed.

I watched the yellow flashing lights illuminate the empty passenger seat as I finally exited the car, clicking the lock button on my key fob. It was a Thursday night, which meant the pub was fairly quiet, a few regulars perched on the leather-studded bar stools, a couple trying their hands at darts in the corner. But that was it. There wasn't even anyone behind the bar. Perhaps they'd gone to change a keg. I didn't pause to question it, slipping gratefully around the unmanned bar and down the narrow hallway that led to the flat. I was two steps up when the door opposite the staircase opened, a great roaring cheer prompting me to turn around. Mum was stood in the doorway, a great beaming smile on her face, her cheeks flushed in that way that told me she'd had a glass of wine. Or two. But when she saw me, her smile faded almost as quickly as she pulled the door shut behind her.

'Jenny. You're home early, love. I thought you were going round to Jacob's tonight?' She was talking a bit too fast, her hand still firmly grasping the door handle behind her back.

'Ah, no, something else came up.' I shrugged, having neither the energy nor the desire to get into the whole life insurance thing right now. 'What's going on in there?'

'Where?'

'The function room you just came out of?'

'Oh, nothing.' She ruffled her fingers roughly through her freshly dyed hair, something shimmering in the dim hallway lighting. Was that confetti?

'Mum, we need more champagne!' came Matt's muffled voice. A panicked look flashed across Mum's face as her eyes flipped frantically between me and the door, her grip on the doorknob tightening. 'And not that cheap prosecco. The good stuff you keep in the cellar for special occasions. It's not every day your son gets engaged!' The door swung inwards, almost taking Mum with it, to reveal a grinning Matt stood with his arms raised as the small crowd behind him gave a whooping cheer. The *Congratulations* bunting that Mum rolled out for every passed driving test and exam results day since we were little hung between two picture frames on the back wall. A giant ring-shaped balloon floated aimlessly in the corner.

'You're engaged?' I croaked.

The look on Matt's face told me that he hadn't been expecting me, either. His shoulders shimmered with the same confetti that adorned Mum's centre parting.

'Ah, yeah,' he mumbled, rubbing the back of his head uncomfortably. Both he and Mum were looking at me like I was a bomb about to explode. I guess I couldn't blame them: inside, it felt as if one already had.

'Cheer up, it's not a death sentence,' I laughed, punching him jovially on the shoulder. I hoped the smile I'd plastered on my face looked more convincing than it felt. Matt grinned, his shoulders relaxing an inch or two as he pulled me in for a one-armed hug. 'Congrats, Matt, I'm so happy for you. For both of you,' I whispered into the fabric of his shirt, holding on for a second longer than necessary as I blinked away my tears. I spied Alyssa, Matt's long-term girlfriend, laughing with a group of friends in the room behind, her left hand outstretched as they all ooh-ed and aah-ed over the ring glinting on her finger. That was me not too long ago. In that very room, with Joe, celebrating our own engagement. The fake promise of a lifetime together stretching out before us.

'I'm, umm, just going to get changed, and then I'll join you,' I said, clearing my throat as we broke apart, the smile firmly back in place.

'Are you sure?' Matt asked, exchanging another look with Mum. 'You don't have to—'

'Yep, be right down,' I called over my shoulder, already halfway up the stairs, my grip tightening around the strap of my handbag. I ran along the hallway, not stopping until I was in my room, the door firmly shut behind me. Only then did I let the tears fall. Big, ugly, heavy sobs that shook my whole body as I slid down the back of the door, collapsing in a heap on the carpet.

'You're still wearing your ring?' I turned to see Joe sat cross-legged beside me, watching me twirl the platinum band round and round my finger.

'I'm not ready to take it off just yet,' I sniffed, hugging my knees to my chest and rocking gently back and forth. Who was I kidding? I'd never be ready.

'What can I do?' Joe pleaded softly, the sadness in his eyes sending another waterfall of tears cascading down my face. Everything else seemed to disappear: the insurance envelope peeking out the top of my overturned handbag; the faded *Top of the Pops* posters of 90s boy bands; the piles of moving boxes. It was just him and me. Side by side. How we were always meant to be.

I smiled, weakly. 'You're already doing it.'

7

'Which one did you say it was again, Mr Hatfield?' I asked, squinting up at the sky and the vast array of white billowy clouds above us. None of which even vaguely resembled a human face.

'Just there,' 87-year-old Mr Hatfield said, pointing his walking stick shakily up at a squished oblong-shaped blob in front of us. 'Spitting image of my Doris, I tell you. Here, look.' He reached into the pocket of his corduroy trousers, producing a black-and-white, slightly crumpled photograph of a young woman with perfectly pinned hair and a pussy-bow blouse. My heart swelled at the thought of Mr Hatfield carrying a photograph of his recently deceased wife around with him, wanting to keep her close wherever he went. Jacob tilted his head from one side to the other, eyes squinting as they flicked from the photograph up to the sky and back again.

'The day after the funeral, I was just sitting out here with my afternoon cup of tea and a fig roll, like we always used to do, and there she was. Been there every day since. Watching over me, she is, my Doris.' Mr Hatfield beamed proudly, holding one hand up against the weak spring sunshine as he stared adoringly at the sky. I followed his gaze, scanning the random mass of white lacy clouds, like tiny puffs of candyfloss in an otherwise pale-blue sky. But there was no face. I knew that. Judging by Jacob's dubious expression, he knew that. And deep down, I think even Mr Hatfield knew that. But so great was his love for his wife of 52 years that he was willing her into places where she was not, categorically refusing to live in a world where she didn't exist in some capacity. Even if it was in the form of a cloud. I swallowed, twizzling my engagement ring round and round my finger as I tried to ignore the voice inside my head. The one saying *but isn't that exactly what you're doing?*

'Do you see her? Do you see my Doris?' Mr Hatfield asked eagerly, his eyes wide behind his NHS-issued frames. I recognised the joy on his face, the way he seemed to light up from within. It was the same feeling I had whenever I was with Joe. I forced a smile, trying to clear the lump lodged at the back of my throat, but it wouldn't budge.

'Yes, I see her,' I croaked, blinking back the tears that were threatening to fall. 'Jacob is just going to take a picture for the paper, OK?'

Jacob frowned.

'But I don't see—'

'Just take the damn picture,' I hissed, suddenly wanting to be anywhere but here. 'Well, I think I've got everything I need,' I said quickly, throwing Jacob a knowing look before turning and walking as fast as I could back through the bungalow, trying not to make eye contact with the many smiling iterations of Mr Hatfield and his wife that lined the wallpapered hallway. Outside, I placed one hand against my car door, the other braced against my thigh as

I gulped down great mouthfuls of air, my heart stuttering like an engine trying to jump-start into life.

'Hey, are you OK?' Jacob wheezed, out of breath from his short jog to the car. He must be worried. I'd never seen Jacob run for anything in his life, except to catch the bride's bouquet at a wedding two years ago. He also rugby-tackled two ladies out of the way to do so, a detail he adamantly denies to this day.

'I'm fine. Just needed some air,' I assured him, raising my hand at a slipper-clad Mr Hatfield, who was waving enthusiastically at us from his front doorstep.

'You don't look OK. In fact, you look kind of . . . green.'

'You get the pictures?' I asked, ignoring his previous statement.

'I mean, I got *pictures*. Hundreds actually. None of them feature dear old Doris though, whichever way you look at them.'

'Can't you work your magic in Photoshop or something?'

'What, add in a pearl necklace and some pin curls?' Jacob guffawed.

'Yes, if that will make the difference. Who are we to tell Mr Hatfield it's not real? He can see it, he can see Doris up there every day watching over him, so that makes it real, and I for one am not going to take that away from him.' My heart was beating so loudly I swear I could hear it pounding against my rib cage. *Da-dum. Da-dum. Da-dum.*

'All right, I'll see what I can do,' Jacob conceded, holding his hands up when he realised I was being serious. He took another step towards me. 'Are you sure you're OK? That can't have been easy—'

'It's fine,' I said quickly, cutting him off. 'I'm fine.' I wasn't sure who I was trying to convince more, Jacob or myself. Although judging by Jacob's blank stare I was failing at both. I climbed into my car before he could question me any further. I felt guilty keeping Joe a secret from him and Alice. It weighed heavy like a stone in the pit of my stomach. We told each other everything. That's the way it had always been. But this was different. Part of me worried about what they'd say. But the other part was even more afraid that telling someone, saying it out loud, would be like popping a bubble. Joe here one second, and gone the next.

'Jenny, look.'

I turned to see Joe sat in the passenger seat, left elbow resting against the window, right hand pointing up at the clouds through the sunroof.

'That one looks just like my penis!'

'Nooo, he did not just say that!'

I hid my face in my mug of hot chocolate, shoulders shaking with laughter as I watched Joe's wide-eyed, open-mouthed expression of horror beside me. He'd been slowly edging further and further forwards in his seat as the drama intensified, and was now sat on the very edge of Mum's patchwork-quilt-topped sofa. Now, though, he shifted backwards, feet kicking off from the floor, face hidden behind splayed fingers as we watched one of the grooms admit that if he was sexually attracted to his new wife, he wouldn't have kissed someone else. As if it was somehow her fault.

We were three episodes into a *Married at First Sight Australia* marathon and Joe was fully invested. He'd reeled off his usual *I don't watch reality TV* spiel for a good five minutes as I was making the hot chocolates, and as usual I ignored him. It was a game we liked to play, where he insisted he didn't like *trashy reality TV* as he called it, and I didn't raise an eyebrow when he inevitably suggested watching *just one more episode* when the teaser credits started rolling.

'Geez, if married life is this full of drama, I'd say we dodged a bullet.'

I stared resolutely ahead at the TV, refusing to take the bait. Joe puffed his cheeks out dramatically.

'Yeah, just seems like *really* hard work.'

'Oh, and you're not?' I scoffed, shooting a fiery look towards his end of the sofa. 'It's the men in this that are all psychos. Except that farmer guy, I guess, but then he's just weird. That's all us women have to choose from – psycho, or weird.' I juggled both hands in front of me like a scale, weighing up which was the lesser of two evils.

'And which category do I fall into?' Joe pondered, twisting himself around so that his full attention was on me – my decision apparently far more interesting than the argument currently playing out on the TV. I looked up at him from beneath my eyelashes.

'Honey, we both know you're a massive weirdo.'

'Takes one to know one, my dear.'

Crash.

I jumped, sloshing the dregs of my no-longer-*hot* hot chocolate down the front of my t-shirt. Well, Joe's t-shirt. One of his old ones that I liked to wear to bed, the material soft and familiar against my skin.

'*Ow, what the*—?' came the muffled protests of who- ever had just tried to let themselves into the flat. I'd taken to locking the door whenever I was alone, not wanting Mum or Matt to silently appear and find me talking to Joe. The few seconds it would take them to wiggle their key in the lock was all the warning I needed to avoid a *very* awkward conversation I did not want to have.

Rat-a-tat-tat.

'Jenny, it's me. Open up,' came Alice's voice through the door.

I pressed the mute button on the remote, turning towards Joe with a conspiratorial finger to my lips. Maybe they'd think we weren't home. That *I* wasn't home. But my stomach did that weird flip-flop thing when I saw the scratchy patchwork quilt was empty. The material pulled taut in a way that seemed to scream *no one was sitting here, you are alone*. My heart sank.

'Jenny, we know you're in there. Your mum said you haven't left the flat all day.'

I rolled my eyes with a sigh, trying to fix my face into something that resembled less of a smacked arse as I opened the door. Alice and Jacob were crammed into the narrow stairwell, Jacob two stairs below Alice, who was busy rubbing her shoulder with a pained look on her face.

'What are you guys doing here?' I added a smile to try and soften the accusatory tone of my voice. I saw

Alice's gaze linger over my t-shirt, her lips pressed tightly together as though she were physically trying to restrain herself from passing comment.

'You didn't think we'd forget what day it was, did you?' Alice raised a palm to her chest in mock offence, her dimpled smile somewhat ruining the act.

Today was 19th April. The day *The Simpsons* first appeared on TV. The day the American Revolution started. But most importantly, it was the day Joe was born. The day he would have turned 30. A calendar reminder had pinged up on my phone at 8 a.m. this morning – complete with accompanying party hat emoji and two clinking champagne flutes that once upon a happier time I'd spent way too long selecting – like a punch to the stomach. I hadn't forgotten, of course, but time passes differently for the heartbroken. It moves to a different rhythm, dragging and skipping backwards like a broken record, forcing you to relive the past on repeat, making you believe that moving forward is impossible.

'We brought the essentials!' Jacob brandished a bottle of rosé in one hand and two tubs of Ben & Jerry's in the other. My heart swelled for my best friends, beyond grateful to them for showing up and not allowing me to endure this day alone; but also twinged with sadness at the thought of no longer spending it with Joe. This constant feeling of being torn between the past and the present was exhausting, and either way I felt like I was missing out.

'Can we come in?' Alice frowned questioningly at the still half-closed door, my fingers firmly gripping the handle. I hesitated for a second, only a second, before pulling it wide open.

'Sure, yes, come in.'

'Did we hear you talking to someone just now?' Jacob asked, disappearing into the kitchen and coming back with three wine glasses and three spoons.

'What? No, must have been the TV,' I said, gesturing vaguely in the direction of the muted television and immediately wishing I hadn't. Thankfully one look was all it took for Jacob to recognise his favourite show, his attention swiftly diverted.

'Oh my god, have you seen the episode yet where Tracey lobs a prawn at Harrison during the dinner party?' Jacob squealed with delight, plonking himself down in Joe's spot and peeling the lid off one of the tubs of ice-cream. Alice, on the other hand, was not so easily distracted.

'Do you have company?' she asked, inclining her head towards the two mugs on the coffee table. My eyes flitted to Joe's hot chocolate, only just realising that I must have made him one too out of habit. It was still full, a cold skin wrinkled across the top.

'Nope.' My gaze roamed guiltily around the room, like I was half expecting Joe to appear at any moment. I stared at the empty doorway until I saw Alice watching me, her eyes narrowed.

'OK, what is going on here, Jenny?'

'What do you mean?' I asked innocently, busying myself with some unnecessary plumping of the sofa cushions.

'Something is up. You've had this mysterious, sneaking-around act going on for months now,' she said, flapping her hand in my general direction as though proving her point. 'Have you met someone new and you're afraid to tell us, is that it?'

'*What?!* Of course not!' I spluttered, furious at the implication that Joe was somehow replaceable.

'It's OK if you have, Jenny. In fact, it's perfectly natural,' Alice insisted, her voice doing that soft, cajoling thing people do when trying to convince you of something. *Natural?* There was nothing natural about the prospect of me dating someone who wasn't Joe. About thinking that I could find even a fraction of what he and I'd had together with someone else. In fact, it was almost – laughable. A giggle escaped between my lips before I could stop it, and I watched as Alice and Jacob shared a concerned look. Alice nodded her head in my direction, giving Jacob a stern eyeballing until he turned off the TV.

'Jenny, you know you can tell us anything, right? We're not going to judge,' he said encouragingly. 'Unless you're dating someone who doesn't like Beyoncé, in which case I cannot be held responsible for my actions.' I knew he was joking, trying to lighten the awkward atmosphere in the room, but anger flooded through my veins, hot and fiery.

'I am *not* seeing anyone,' I insisted through clenched teeth, but as I spoke, all the fight seemed to drain out of me and I slumped on the sofa next to Jacob. I was exhausted. Tired of feeling like I was living a double life. Of carrying this huge secret around with me, the weight of it growing heavier every day. Would it be so bad if I told them?

Yes, it would. They'll probably check you straight into the psychiatric ward.

But they were my best friends. Surely they'd understand?

Understand that you've gone completely crackers.

I screwed my eyes up, trying to block out the unhelp-fully sassy voice of reason currently perched atop her high horse in my head.

'OK, maybe I have been seeing someone,' I admitted quietly, my fingers twisting themselves into an anxious tangle in my lap.

'I knew it! See, I told you, Jacob, didn't I tell you?' Alice squealed, giving Jacob an *I-told-you-so* smack across the shoulder.

'I was the one who suggested it in the first place,' Jacob tutted, jabbing his ice-cream spoon accusingly at his sister before going in for another helping of Cookie Dough. 'So come on then, what's his name?'

I was going to need some liquid courage for this. I reached over, grabbing the bottle of rosé and giving silent thanks for Jacob's penchant for screw tops as I flicked the lid off and proceeded to glug several mouthfuls straight from the bottle. The crisp flavours of summer fruits and peach blossom exploded in my mouth, the room-temperature wine gliding a little too easily down my throat.

OK, deep breath.

'It's Joe.'

The seconds ticked by. Mum's grandfather clock in the hall, which we'd inherited from the previous land-lord, marked each uncomfortable second as the silence stretched on. Jacob spoke first.

'Huh. I'm not trying to be a Debbie Downer here or anything, but could you not have picked someone with a different name? Bradley. Theodore. Ordinarily I would immediately veto a Boris for obvious reasons—' he threw us an *am-I-right* eyebrow, '—but in this case, I'd make an exception.'

'Yeah, I'm not sure that's super healthy, Jenny,' Alice said slowly, hesitating over every word as though unsure of my reaction. *Christ, if you think that's unhealthy, just wait until you hear I've been talking to my dead fiancé for the past five months!* I fidgeted awkwardly on the sofa, my stomach twisting in similar knots to those I was currently tying into the tasselled hem of the blanket.

'It's not a different Joe.' I cringed as I listened to the words coming out of my mouth. Even I could hear how crazy it sounded.

'What do you mean, it's not a different Joe?' Jacob frowned, his confused expression a mirror image of his sister's. Bloody hell, how were they not getting this?!

'I've been seeing Joe. As in *my* Joe,' I stressed slowly, wanting to make it crystal clear as I knew there'd be no way I could go through this twice. Jacob dropped his spoon, the metal rattling against the glass-topped coffee table as his mouth hung open. His expression would be comical if it weren't in response to my possible confession of insanity. Alice just blinked at me. Repeatedly. Her eyes scanned my face as though trying to process what I'd just said. Shit, this was worse than I thought.

'OK,' she said slowly, coming over to perch on the armrest. She took both of my hands in hers, waiting me out until I was forced to look up into those giant green eyes of hers. They were full of sympathy and understanding, and just a hint of sadness that made my stomach turn over. 'This is a totally natural response to bereavement, Jenny, it's nothing to worry about. Studies have shown that over 80% of elderly people experience hallucinations associated with their deceased partner for up to several weeks after their passing, their perception yet to catch up with the reality of their death. We call them grief hallucinations,' she explained calmly, full doctor mode initiated.

'Yeah, well, how about five months?'

Alice's eyes narrowed a fraction. 'You've been *seeing* Joe this whole time?' She swallowed audibly, a crease appearing on her normally wrinkle-free forehead.

'Since the funeral,' I admitted, my cheeks burning.

'Are they just visual hallucinations or auditory?'

'Both.'

'Have you been having migraines? Any flickering in your vision?'

I shook my head silently.

'What about trouble sleeping?'

'I mean, no more than usual.' I shrugged, watching Alice bite her lip as she mentally ran through numerous textbooks and research studies in her head, searching for the correct diagnosis.

'Hang on, rewind a second. Are you saying that—'

'God, keep up Jacob. She's been seeing visions of Joe, OK?' Alice snapped impatiently.

'But that's just it, they don't feel like visions,' I insisted, looking at both of them in turn. 'He *is* Joe. He walks like Joe, makes the same bad jokes as Joe, even does that annoying head tilt thing Joe always did whenever he knew he was right about something.' Jacob nodded as though he knew exactly what I meant. 'And I know how crazy this sounds – trust me, I do – but it even *feels* like Joe. I mean, not physically, obviously, but I can't describe it. It just feels right.' I could feel Alice staring at me, analysing every little move I made.

'Is he here right now?' she asked, her eyes trained on my face whilst Jacob's roamed hopefully about the room.

'He was, before you guys arrived,' I admitted with a sigh. 'He disappears when I'm around anyone that knew him.' Alice nodded, as if I'd just ticked one of the boxes on her mental checklist and I winced, realising how pathetic I sounded. Like a little girl trying to explain how her imaginary friend conveniently only appeared when they were alone.

'So, that's why you've been so flaky these past few months?' Jacob asked, putting two and two together. I nodded meekly, embarrassed by my own admission. That I'd chosen to spend time with my dead fiancé over my best friends. We all sat in silence for a minute, the weight of what I'd just admitted hanging over us until Jacob broke the ice.

'Well, that's good. I was starting to think it was a whole Sarah Jessica-Parker/Kim Cattrall situation and you'd just gone off us!'

'I can call in a favour at work and get you an appointment with Dr Thomas on Monday,' Alice announced, springing into action and pulling out her phone. 'He's one of the best psychiatrists in the country.'

'A psychiatrist? So, you think I'm crazy?' My voice was sharp, defensive.

'Of course not,' Alice said quickly, her thumbs pausing their furious typing to throw me a reassuring look. 'But hallucinations are a psychological symptom, Jenny. After an initial assessment, Dr Thomas will be able to put together a treatment plan for you to help stop the visions.'

I fiddled with my fingers some more, my eyes falling once again on Joe's *Star Wars* mug.

'What if I don't want them to stop?' I whispered, almost afraid to admit it. But it was the truth. The very thought of not seeing Joe again, real or otherwise, was enough to make me want to curl up into a ball and never emerge. Jacob's hand came to rest on my jittering knee.

'Jenny, you know that it's not real, right? Joe's gone.' His words were gentle, careful, as though he were afraid of saying the wrong thing.

'I know that,' I snapped, getting to my feet and pacing about the room. And I did know. Deep, deep down. In a place I didn't allow myself to think about very often, because I feared what might happen if I did. That I'd wake up one day and Joe would just be – gone. I turned sharply, cursing as the loose oversized hem of Joe's t-shirt caught against Jacob's wine glass, spilling the contents over the floor.

'I'll get it!' Jacob jumped to his feet, disappearing into the kitchen in search of a towel and a much-needed breather from the tension-filled room.

'Mum doesn't know,' I confessed, in a *please don't tell her* kind of voice as I completed yet another lap around the coffee table.

'Obviously I won't tell her,' Alice snorted, in answer to my unspoken plea, her tone uncharacteristically flustered. 'She's already worried enough about you as it is, without throwing this into the mix.'

Guilt knotted my stomach, tugging at my heart-strings. I watched Alice pick at the skin around her thumb, her anxious tic that was normally reserved for the morning of exams or the day Taylor Swift tickets were released.

'Have you been to Joe's exhibition yet?'

I paused my pacing, her question throwing me off guard. What did that have to do with anything?

'I thought as much,' Alice continued, without even waiting for my answer. 'Jacob and I went the other week,' she admitted, her eyes briefly flitting to her lap as though trying to hide her own sadness from me. 'It was—' she let out a breath, a full kaleidoscope of emotion flashing across her face, unzipping a slow smile from one corner of her mouth to the other, '—you should go, Jenny. I think it would really help you.'

'Err, Jenny, what is this?' Jacob's voice floated through from the kitchen.

'Just help yourself to anything that's in the fridge,' I called back, grateful for the change in conversation. 'I think there's a batch of Mum's sausage rolls in the tin on top of the—'

'One step ahead of you, sister.' Jacob appeared in the doorway, battered McVitie's tin wedged firmly under one arm. 'But I was talking about this.'

I stopped pacing and eyed the crumpled rectangle of paper Jacob was waving about with his non-sausage-roll-filled hand. It had caught me off guard the other night, stuck smack bang in the middle of the fridge door between Mum's Venice and Mallorca holiday magnets, demanding my attention when all I wanted was some milk. The insurance cheque. I'd crumpled it into a tiny ball, throwing it in the bin in the hope I'd never have to see it again. Clearly the universe had other ideas.

'It's nothing.'

Jacob guffawed. 'I wouldn't call £100,000 nothing.'

Alice's head snapped up from her phone and she skipped over towards Jacob, plucking the cheque straight out of his hands.

'Hey!'

'Jenny, what the fuck is this?' Alice gawped, her eyes boggling as they took in all the zeros.

I fidgeted awkwardly with the hem of Joe's t-shirt. 'It's Joe's insurance payout,' I mumbled, ashamed to admit that I'd financially benefitted from Joe's death.

'Why is it all crumpled? And *what* is that smell?' Alice's nose scrunched with revulsion as she inspected the piece of paper dangling between her thumb and forefinger, intent on touching as little of the soiled cheque as humanly possible.

I shrugged noncommittally. 'I just haven't got round to cashing it yet.' Telling them I'd literally thrown £100,000 in the bin probably wouldn't help with the whole proving-I-wasn't-crazy argument.

'*Yet*. So, you are going to cash it, then?' Alice asked, her eyes narrowed.

'Yes.'

No.

'It's £100,000, Jenny!' Jacob spluttered, about as unconvinced by my lie as I was.

'Yes, thank you, Jacob!' I yelled, a little louder than intended. 'Thank you for reminding me just how much

Joe's life is apparently worth, because that's all I think about when I look at that damn cheque.'

I shovelled a giant spoonful of ice cream into my mouth, hoping the brain freeze would distract from the crushing weight in my chest, then threw myself down on the sofa, burying my face in a cushion. I felt the sofa dip to my left as Alice sat next to me, and then substantially more on my right when Jacob joined her.

'Jenny, don't you think that the visions and the not cashing the cheque are just ways for you to avoid acknowledging that Joe's gone?'

My fingers tightened their grip on the cushion. Alice was annoyingly right as per usual, saying the very thing I refused to admit to myself.

'That money doesn't represent what Joe's life was worth, Jenny, it doesn't even come close,' Jacob sniffed, his voice shaky with emotion. 'But it does represent Joe's desire for you to live your life. You know that's what he'd want, right? What we all want.'

My insides felt gooey, like the room-temperature tub of ice cream perspiring on the coffee table.

'I'm scared,' I mumbled incoherently into the cushion.

'Scared of what?' Alice pressed gently. I knew what she was doing. She was prising open the lid that I'd duct-taped closed, encouraging me to confront everything I was feeling head on for once – and now that lid was ajar, there was no stopping the words as they tumbled out.

'*Everything!* I'm scared to move on. But I'm also scared of being left behind. Of talking about Joe. Of not talking about Joe. Of forgetting things. Of waking up and Joe not being the very first thing I think about in the morning. Of what my life will be like without him in it. I'm afraid of never feeling happy again. And I'm scared that, if by some miracle I do, if that makes me a terrible person.'

'You're right, it will be scary,' Alice said matter-of-factly. 'And hard. And painful as hell. And there'll be so many days when you'll want to give up.'

'Is this supposed to be a pep talk, because it's really shit,' I sniffed.

'So shit,' Jacob agreed, shaking his head in disbelief at his sister. Alice ignored him.

'But we're going to be here with you every step of the way until eventually there'll come a day when you wake up and feel slightly better than the day before. And I promise you that day will come. And that you'll have another. And another. But you're never going to be able to move forward, Jenny, if you're still living in the past.'

A tear slid down my face. I couldn't speak. Instead, I leaned my head against Alice's shoulder, squeezing Jacob's hand so hard I saw him wince.

How, though?

How do you let go of the love of your life?

8

'Do you think Beryl's salad will go with Rahul's chicken noodle thing?'

I was crouched by the communal work fridge, performing the delicate task of skimming off my unsuspecting colleagues' Tupperware just enough so I didn't starve but not so much that it would arouse suspicion. It was a fine art that I had sadly perfected in the days leading up to payday these past few months.

'Do you know how many meal deals you could buy with £100k?' Jacob retorted smartly, looking horrified as I gingerly prised the lid off one of Beryl's neatly stacked bento boxes and sniffed. I recoiled, retching violently when the intense smell of egg that had clearly been added to said container whilst still warm knocked me backwards. Literally. Arse well and truly on the floor. 'I would offer to buy you one, but seeing as you're a bajillionaire who's freely choosing to eat Beryl's quite frankly lethal egg salad rather than buy her own lunch, I have no sympathy.' He bit into a piece of seaweed-wrapped Tesco sushi with a smug smile. I grabbed a second roll from the tiny black plastic tray and shoved it, as pointedly as I could, in my mouth before he could stop me, almost choking in the process. It was tuna. I didn't even like tuna.

'That's called karma, my friend,' Jacob told me, looking pleased and not at all concerned by my aggressive coughing fit. 'Some would argue what you're doing is the definition of insanity. Maybe Alice is right, maybe you are crazy.' He nudged me jovially with his elbow just to make sure I knew he was joking. I rolled my eyes.

'She's already texted me seven times today – three to confirm the appointment I told her I'm not going to, and the other four with suggestions on how to stop hallucinations.' My phone lit up with an incoming WhatsApp as I nibbled a piece of cold, congealed chicken. 'Make that eight,' I corrected, pushing my phone across the table so that Jacob could read the latest message.

'No alcohol,' he read, before snorting with laughter. 'As if! Now she's the crazy one.' We both ate in silence for a while, Jacob's eyes roaming randomly about the break room as though searching for something. I gave a small smile.

'He's not here, Jacob.'

'I know,' he said quickly, although he sounded a little disappointed. 'I just – does he ever ask about me?' His voice caught a little and it made me look up. He was staring at me across the table, eyes big and wide and full of hope. My heart ached and I was reminded that I wasn't the only one who lost someone that day. That I wasn't the only one missing Joe.

'All the time,' I lied.

His face lit up. 'Really?'

'Yeah, it's kind of annoying, actually.'

'Well, I always was his favourite,' he teased, mock-tossing his imaginary waist-length hair over one shoulder.

We both looked up as Rahul, the long-suffering copyeditor at the *Brighton Tribune* who looked exactly the same as he did ten years ago (Velcro Reeboks and all), shuffled into the break room. Again, the break room was not a room as such. As with everywhere at the *Brighton Tribune,* it was just another corner of the same open plan office where someone had shoved an impossibly small table that could only seat two people but which had four mismatched chairs crammed around it. Rahul clicked the sides of his lunchbox and inspected the contents with a sigh.

'The wife's got me on some bloody diet again,' Rahul tutted, miserably watching his half-full Tupperware rotating round and round in the microwave. 'Keeps giving me smaller and smaller portions, thinking I won't notice. Honestly, the woman's trying to starve me!'

Jacob almost choked on a California roll, eyes streaming with water as he tried to contain his laughter. I smiled tightly at Rahul, waiting until the microwave pinged and he turned around before I shovelled what was left of his missing lunch into my mouth. If there's no evidence, there's no crime, right? He trudged back out of the room again with his steaming container, muttering under his breath.

'Poor Rahul's wife is going to get it in the ear tonight,' Jacob sniggered, throwing me a judgemental look. I ignored him, reaching for my phone as it let out a series of aggressive buzzes, one after the other, inching closer to the edge of the table.

'More doctor's orders?' Jacob guessed.

'Worse. Alyssa's hen do group chat,' I groaned.

As if the bride, groom, clinking champagne glasses, wedding ring, chapel and love heart emojis in the group title weren't bad enough, the maid of honour calling everyone 'girlies' definitely was. With Matt and Alyssa not wanting to wait, and deciding on a summer wedding in just three short months, the self-confessed bride squad had wasted no time planning the hen. I'd never wanted to remove myself from a group more in my life, and would have if it weren't for the fact I knew WhatsApp would publicly shame me with its *Jenny has left the group* statement.

'Ooh, fun!'

My face suggested it was the opposite of fun. 'I have zero desire to spend a night surrounded by a gaggle of screaming women I don't know, drinking out of penis straws and pretending to have a good time.'

'Speak for yourself. I can't remember the last time I had a penis in my mouth.' Jacob's face was deadpan as he stared wistfully into space. I smacked him playfully on the arm.

'Still no luck on the dating front, then?'

'*Nada*. Had a date the other night – if you can call it that when it lasted less than an hour. The guy actually ordered me a *skinny* margarita!'

I sucked my breath audibly between my teeth. 'He didn't?'

'Yep. Honestly, I don't know what I did in a past life to deserve the shitshow that is my dating life. I must have been a mass-murdering psychopath.'

'Or a spin instructor,' I countered with a wry smile.

'Or someone who wore those trousers that zip off at the knee.' Jacob visibly shuddered, before his eyes bulged at something over my left shoulder. 'Incoming,' he warned, but it was too late.

'Ah, Jenny, just the person I was looking for!'

I shrunk further down in my chair in the hope of becoming invisible.

'It was supposed to be in my inbox on Monday and what day is it today, Jenny?' Derek chided, his faux-leather belt squeaking slightly in protest as he thrust his pelvic region forward, hands clasped behind his back. *Christ, did he actually expect me to answer?*

'*Tuesday!*' Derek trilled when I failed to respond. 'Today is *Tuesday*, Jenny. Ergo, after Monday.'

'Right.' I nodded dumbly, as if this was the first time that fact had been brought to my attention.

'Looks like someone is out of the running for Employee of the Month. *Again.*'

I stuck my bottom lip out in fake disappointment, trying to pretend I gave a crap about the makeshift A4 certificate that Derek printed out every month, while he crouched down, his sizeable rear end skimming the back of my chair as he rooted around in the fridge. He squinted at the instructions written in looping, feminine script on the Post-it note attached to the lid of his Tupperware before popping it in the microwave and turning to face me with a sigh.

'Look, Jenny, it's been almost six months.' He paused, clearly expecting me to meet his gaze or nod my head, some acknowledgement that I knew what he was talking about. But every muscle in my body was too busy tensing in response to him somehow turning Joe into this big, awkward elephant sat in the middle of the room. 'You barely say a word in staff meetings, I can't remember the last time you turned in a piece of work on time, and even when you are here, you're not *really* here. There's only so long I can keep making allowances for you, Jenny.'

I shifted in my seat, fingernails digging into the soft, fleshy palm of my hands. When? When had he *made allowances* for me? When he called me the morning of Joe's funeral to assure me there was absolutely no rush, but when did I think I'd be back to work? Or when he assigned me that cycling accident my first week back? Or Mr Hatfield last week?

Derek sighed again. Like he had the weight of the fucking world on his shoulders when, in actual fact, his biggest dilemma today was whether he should eat his KitKat Chunky now, or save it for his three-time tea-time, as he liked to call it.

'We're short-staffed as it is, Jenny, I need you firing on all cylinders or else—'

I could feel moisture starting to gather on my top lip, my palms clammy against the fabric of my jeans as I thought of possible endings to that sentence. Of not just being a single 30-year-old living with her mum, but a single, *unemployed* 30-year-old living with her mum. Of falling yet another rung lower than I already was on the ladder that is life. A pathetic image of me in a crumpled heap at the bottom of a wooden ladder floated into my head. Rock bloody bottom.

'Sorry, Derek, I'll get it to you by end of day. I promise it won't happen again,' I said firmly, cringing at the desperation in my voice. How had it come to this? Begging for a job that I hated. But I *couldn't* lose anything else right now. Even if it was this shitty excuse for a job.

'Jenny's just been so busy working on this pitch, Derek,' Jacob interjected, coming to my rescue. I desperately latched on to the lifeline he'd thrown me.

'Yes, exactly! Major story, hard-hitting stuff.' I was babbling now, words falling out all over the place.

Jacob rolled his eyes at me. Too far? 'Hard-hitting' was Derek's new buzzword. Last week it had been synergy. God knows what delight awaited us next week.

'Oh yes, what is this story, then?' he probed, jabbing a straw through a carton of chocolate milk and taking a loud slurp.

'Oh, it's, umm—'

I wracked my brains, trying to think of something, anything . . .

'It's, err—'

'The community centre,' Jacob finished for me.

Derek frowned. 'I thought you already did a piece on that last week?'

'Mhmm, I did.' I nodded slowly, shooting Jacob a warning look over the table. The last thing I needed right now was to spend more time in the presence of Luca Patel.

'It was the most popular article on the website last week,' Derek mused quietly to himself, stroking his non-existent jawline with his finger and thumb in a way that made my stomach heave with nausea. 'And they've had their funding cut, haven't they? Must be in serious danger of closing?' His eyes shone with the delight of a child being given a 99 on a hot summer's day, no thought or care to the repercussions if the community centre did actually close. I bit my tongue, swallowing the words that would 100% get me fired.

'No, you're right, Derek, as always. Total waste of time,' I backtracked, trying to pander to his already oversized ego. Anything to avoid having to be in the same postcode as Luca Patel.

'OK, you've twisted my arm,' Derek conceded, flat-out ignoring what I'd just said. My jaw clenched some more. 'Have an outline on my desk by the end of the day,' he barked, squeezing himself into the chair next to me and shovelling a forkful of lasagne into his mouth. A globule of tomatoey mince dropped down his shirt, another landing on my notebook. Just when I thought this day couldn't get any worse.

'So, are you going to knock any time soon or did we just come to admire the cornicing?'

Joe was leaning against the wall at the top of the stairs, one ankle slung over the other as he stared amusedly at me. My watch informed me I'd been stood in front of Luca's front door for twelve agonising minutes now. The very fact that somewhere along the way I'd started referring to it as *Luca's* front door only fuelled my rage further.

'I mean it is technically his front door now, seeing as he lives here.'

I scowled at him, hating it when he read my mind. 'Whose side are you on?'

Joe chuckled. He was clearly enjoying this.

'Never thought I'd see the day that Jenny Thompson was afraid of a man.'

'Please. I am *not* afraid of Luca Patel,' I scoffed, my scowl deepening.

'Whatever you say, baby.' A smile played on his lips, his dimples cutting two endearing divots into his cheeks. My eyes narrowed. I knew what he was doing. He was goading me.

'Buk buk buk buk ba-gawk!' Joe squawked, hands buried in his armpits as he flapped both elbows like an overgrown chicken.

'OK, OK,' I huffed, taking a step towards the front door. But the door swung inwards before I even had a chance to knock. A floppy-haired teenage boy stood blinking back at me in the doorway.

'Really, this guy? What are you so afraid of? That he's going to tell everyone not to sit next to you at school?' Joe teased, clocking the kid's Marvel t-shirt and neon Air Jordans.

'That's not him,' I hissed over my left shoulder, although apparently not subtly enough, as I watched the boy's expression shift from one of confusion to evident concern at the strange lady talking to herself.

'Harry, you forgot your sheet music again. How are you going to practise if you don't have your – you've got to be kidding me.' Luca appeared behind the boy, his ink-stained fingers clutching several sheets of paper, and his face doing some weird scrunched-up thing that made it look like he was sucking a lemon.

'I've come to talk to you,' I said. Obviously.

Luca sighed, already sounding exasperated. 'Well, it's a relief to hear you're not here to break in – *again*.'

Joe sucked his breath in between his teeth. 'Ooh, burn, Jenny.'

I took a deep breath, wishing for once that Joe was not here right now. A sentiment that poor Harry clearly shared as he grabbed the sheet music from Luca's hand, shoved it carelessly into his backpack and made a speedy exit down the staircase.

'I didn't know you taught private lessons too.' I didn't bother to hide the tone of surprise from my voice.

'Pays the bills.' He shrugged, his shoulders filling the width of the doorway as he leaned against the architrave. 'Besides, there's a lot you don't know about me.'

I snorted. 'I highly doubt that.'

'It might be hard to believe, but there's a lot more to me than just my good looks and obvious charm.' He wiggled his eyebrows suggestively, his mouth curving into a frustratingly symmetrical smile as he clocked my discomfort.

'God, this guy's positively dreamy.' Joe fake swooned to my right. Momentarily forgetting where I was, my head snapped to face him.

'*You are not helping!*' I hissed angrily.

I turned back to see Luca frowning at me. This in itself was not unusual. It was his facial expression for 99% of our interactions. It was the apprehensive flitting of his eyes to my right, where Joe was stood, that was a cause for concern. I gulped.

'That's not helping,' I repeated, this time staring unwaveringly at Luca as though he'd been the intended recipient of said statement all along. His brow smoothed;

any previous doubt washed away with a smug smile of satisfaction. He took a step closer. He smelt of coffee – earthy and strong – and shower gel, that musky sandal-wood scent you just know comes in a blue bottle.

'Am I making you uncomfortable, Thompson?'

'Nauseous is the word I'd use,' I said indignantly, but my cheeks burned. I could *feel* his smile. The way it made my insides squirm. It annoyed me that he thought *he* was the source of my discomfort. Not my dead fiancé stood four inches to my right. 'Look, I've come to talk to you about something.'

'So you keep saying,' Luca drawled. He was humour-ing me, which just riled me up even more. I took a deep breath, counting to ten before I trusted myself to respond.

'My boss wants me to do a bigger feature on the community centre – keep the public updated on your fundraising efforts, interview some of the parents, maybe even the staff?'

Luca's eyes narrowed, that one strand of hair that cork-screwed at the end falling just so across his left eyebrow. He was clearly as conflicted as I was. Desperate to do anything he could to protect the future of the community centre, to make a difference to those children's lives, but equally would rather walk across hot coals than spend a single second in my company. *Well, the feeling was mutual, matey.*

'So, I'll need to come by the community centre again?' I added, looking impatiently at my watch rather than his face, as if I had someplace else to be.

His cupid's bow quirked. 'How . . . convenient.'

That flicker of amusement dancing behind his eyes made my teeth grind. It annoyed me that he thought he

112

knew what was happening here, when he didn't have a fucking clue. But it bothered me even more that I cared. That he got under my skin so easily, leaving it prickling.

'Trust me, it was *not* my idea.'

He leaned closer, shielding one side of his mouth with his hand as he whispered, 'I'll pretend I believe you.'

God, he was incorrigible. I rolled my eyes, throwing Joe a warning look as he snorted with laughter beside me. When I turned back, Luca's expression was fixed, his lips slightly parted.

'What?' I frowned, my arms crossed defensively.

'Why are you doing this?'

'What do you mean?'

'Helping me. You hate me.'

'True,' I admitted, with a level of sarcasm that hid more complex emotions. Emotions like fear of what might happen if I lost my job. Whether I'd finally crumble into a million pieces like a game of Jenga, the one remaining constant in my life being pulled out from under me enough to send the already swaying tower crashing down. Game over.

The fingers of my right hand found my engagement ring, twisting the cool, platinum band round and round, forcing myself not to look in Joe's direction. 'I know this is probably a foreign concept, but this isn't actually about *you*.' I smiled with mock sweetness.

'1-0 to Miss Thompson,' Joe intoned, licking his finger and drawing a 1 on an imaginary scoreboard.

'You're right,' Luca said stiffly. I blinked, taken aback by him agreeing with me. 'It's about *you* tragically looking for any excuse to spend time with *me*. It's not your fault, really. I'm told I'm next to impossible to resist.' He winked at me, eyes sparkling with amusement.

'And the underdog comes from behind to even the scoreboard at 1-1.' Joe tittered, his voice rising and falling like an overexcited sports commentator.

'Forget it, I knew this was a waste of time. I'll tell my boss he made a mistake—' I turned on my heel, purposefully whacking Luca with my handbag as I hoisted it onto my shoulder. I was four steps down the worn carpeted staircase when he caved.

'Fine!'

I paused, my back to him. 'Fine, what?'

Luca sighed impatiently. 'You know what.'

'I honestly don't know what you mean,' I said innocently, descending another one, two, three steps.

'Are you really going to make me say it?'

I turned, fingertips drumming against the banister.

'Fine. Yes, I would like your help. I *need* your help. There, are you happy?' His hands smacked against the sides of his jeans in frustration, jaw clenched with discomfort at having to ask for it. I took a mental picture in my head.

'Ecstatic,' I grinned triumphantly, before continuing down the stairs.

2-1 to me.

9

Sometimes it just hits me. Actually, it's less of a hit, and more of a full-blown punch to the gut. Knocking me backwards for days. It starts as this little voice in my head, reminding me that Joe's gone and he's never coming back, gradually getting louder and louder until I can't think straight, a vice-like grip tightening around my throat until it feels as if I'm choking. It travels down my body to my heart, which is pounding double time as though trying to beat for the both of us. Anything can trigger it. Someone yelling after a Joe on the street. Their Joe. Wearing a jumper I haven't worn since before the accident and finding a familiar short brown hair clinging to the wool, refusing to let go. Today, it was an orchid.

'It's dead.'

'What is? The plant?' Alice asked bewilderedly, her eyes brightening at the extra-large glass of Chardonnay I placed on the beer mat in front of her. I was covering Matt's shift whilst he spent the evening moving Post-it notes adorned with people's names around on Alyssa's seating chart, trying to pretend he understood the intricacies of why Julia couldn't possibly sit next to Bethan. Nothing like a wedding to bring people together.

'Yes, the plant,' I said indignantly, staring forlornly at the once bright pink, now flowerless orchid I'd brought downstairs a few days ago. I'd hoped the sunlight that flooded into the bar for most of the day might perk it up a bit, but its two remaining leaves slumped defeatedly over the rim of the pot, their edges brown and shrivelled. 'Joe gave it to me for our anniversary last year. It's the last living reminder of our relationship and now it's dead, too. Because of me.'

'To be fair, orchids are notoriously hard to keep alive,' Alice offered, before registering my distress, her hand reaching across the bar and finding mine. 'The orchid was just a symbol of Joe's love for you, Jenny, and that lives on. It always will do. This—' she nodded towards the sorry-looking plant, '—means nothing, other than that green-fingered, you are not.'

I squeezed her hand, her pragmatism exactly what I needed in that moment.

'Speaking of Joe,' she continued, her voice taking on a cajoling tone that meant I knew what she was going to ask, 'how have your visions been?'

I sighed, fingers massaging the pressure points on either side of my temple. 'Do we have to do this now?'

'Jenny, if you're not going to see Dr Thomas – yes, I know you didn't show up to the appointment I rescheduled for you – then I have a duty of care as your friend, and a qualified medical professional, to make sure you're okay.' She was sitting bolt upright on her stool as she assessed me over the bar. I felt perspiration beading at the nape of my neck. Eyes like a bloody security scanner, that one.

116

'I'm fine.' I shrugged, faffing about with the napkins for want of something to do.

'Are you getting them more or less frequently?'

'Less. Definitely less.'

Alice's eyes narrowed at the speed of my reply, those green irises fixed on my face.

'I promise,' I added, unblinking.

'Well, that's good.'

I nodded dumbly, my mouth suddenly dry. It was only upon saying the words that I realised them to be true. I hadn't seen Joe yet today, or yesterday for that matter. Was that my doing? Had I been so busy that I wasn't thinking about him as much? The relaxed slump of Alice's shoulders seemed to suggest I'd passed whatever test that was, so then why did it feel like I'd failed?

'How's it going over there? Any SOS signals yet?' Alice inclined her head subtly towards the table in the window, where Jacob and his baseball-cap-wearing date were sharing a bottle of red. Baseball hats, Velcro wallets and a lack of appreciation for Beyoncé were all firmly on Jacob's list of dislikes, so it wasn't off to a great start.

'Nothing yet.' I caught Jacob's eye and gave him an enthusiastic thumbs up. His lips pressed into a thin, unamused line, but the candle on their table still burned. It was his get-out-of-date-free card. If the candle was extinguished, that was my signal to call him with a fake emergency that absolutely required him to leave right that second, only for him to sneak back in through the back door once the coast was clear.

Alice snorted. 'Give it 10 minutes.'

I heard a noise behind me and turned to see Matt emerging from the function room he and Alyssa had commandeered for their evening of wedmin. He looked a little dazed, all wide-eyed and blinking, like a bear emerging from hibernation.

'I need alcohol if I'm to have any chance of making it through this evening,' he groaned, crouching down and plucking a chilled bottle of Picpoul from the wine fridge.

'That bad, huh?'

Matt just threw me a look, downing the inch of wine he'd glugged into a glass with a relieved sigh. 'I had no idea the politics involved in planning a wedding. Personally, I don't see the point in a seating chart. Why can't everyone just sit where they like?'

Alice and I both winced, sucking air audibly between our teeth.

'Alyssa had the same reaction,' Matt said, letting an exasperated hand fall against his left thigh. 'I mean, we're just the bride and groom,' he added, with the speed of someone who'd clearly been biting his tongue for the best part of an hour. 'Don't mind us – let's make sure the whole day revolves around Alyssa's uncle's cousin twice removed who got drunk one Christmas and told everyone how much he hates them, so now can't sit next to anyone. But apparently, he must come because not inviting him would be a *statement*.' He waggled both index fingers in the air, a baffled expression on his face.

'Ah, nothing like planning a wedding to make you want to punch every single person you've ever met in the face,' I mused, nudging my hip against Matt's side with a grin.

'Careful, or I'll sit you next to Alyssa's cousin Rufus,' Matt warned.

'What's wrong with cousin Rufus?' Alice asked.

'Nothing, if an evening of casual racism and not-so-casual misogyny is your thing.'

I grimaced. 'Hard pass.'

Matt's phone chirped in his back pocket. He fished it out, his face softening in a manner that immediately told me it was from Alyssa. I missed that. That warmth deep in the pit of my belly that smouldered whenever I saw a text from Joe, my heart fluttering as though it were about to take flight whenever his name and that ridiculous picture of him with the Snapchat dog filter on flashed up on the screen. I turned away, buffing an already spotless pint glass as I tried to decipher what this feeling was. This chill sweeping over me, like a storm blowing in over the ocean. Sadness? Jealousy? All of the above?

'Sorry to interrupt this fun little pow-wow, but that candle on my table has been unlit for the past three-and-a-half minutes.' I turned to see Jacob leaning unimpressed against the end of the bar, gesturing to said table, where a thin wisp of smoke was twirling from the wick of the snuffed-out tea light. 'Honestly, the service in here is really going downhill.'

'What happened to your date?' Alice asked, eyeing the abandoned wine glass in front of the empty chair where baseball-cap guy had previously been sitting. 'Misplace him already?'

'No, I didn't *misplace him*,' Jacob snarked, doing a poor, high-pitched imitation of his sister. 'His friend called. Something to do with a broken-down car? Which is weird come to think of it, because I swear he said he couldn't drive – I mean, what self-respecting 35-year-old can't drive? Red flag number one – so I'm not sure how much help he's going to be.'

Three pairs of blinking eyes stared back at him, the silence stretching on as we waited for the dots to be joined. Jacob's mouth fell open in horror.

'Oh. My. God. Did he just bail on *me* using a meticulously planned fake phone call? I *invented* the meticulously planned fake phone call!'

'Mate, I've been out of the dating game since the Ice Age and even I know he bailed on you.' Matt grimaced, patting Jacob's arm sympathetically before retreating down the hallway. He turned as he reached the door, pretending to fall to his knees, wine glasses clinking together as he clasped both hands in front of his chest and mouthed *save me!* I smiled at his dramatics, knowing it was purely for my benefit. A show for the sole purpose of making me smile. And it did – especially when Alyssa opened the door at that exact moment and almost fell over my kneeling brother.

'Ah, it's good to hear you laughing again, sweetheart.'

I turned to see Mum descending the stairs from the flat, a giant metal loop of keys jangling against her midriff. I managed a smile. Despite the ache rippling through my chest, its edges jagged and sharp as it tore through me, I managed a smile. I knew how desperately she wanted her Jenny back. The version of me that whistled as she walked and washed her hair twice a week. But there was no going back. And the insinuation, albeit well-intentioned, that I was somehow moving forward, moving on in this world without Joe, made me feel sick.

'You head up if you like, love? I'll do last orders,' Mum offered, registering the shift on my face as I struggled to hold it all together. I nodded, grabbing the orchid and hugging the ceramic pot tightly against my chest as I climbed the stairs to my bedroom. Placing it on my bedside table, I collapsed onto the bed with a sigh, my eyes falling on several of Joe's framed photographs. They were still leaning against the wall, a thin layer of greying dust collecting atop the slim, black frames. Hanging them here felt wrong somehow. They didn't belong in my childhood bedroom, with its too-small single bed and one of everything. One bedside table. One lamp. One toothbrush in the old plastic beaker beside the sink in the corner. And neither did I.

'You know I had a bet going with Alice on how long it would take you to kill that.'

I didn't need to glance over my shoulder to know that Joe was stood in the middle of the room; I could just feel his presence. Sense the atoms in the room shifting. But I did so anyway, his face illuminated by the dim glow of the streetlight in the car park below.

'Your confidence in me is touching, as always.'

'Hey, I'll have you know that Alice bet one week. I – your loving, supportive, loyal fiancé – bet two.' He grinned cheekily. The normally squeaky springs stayed disturbingly silent as he perched on the end of the bed. 'She owes me £20.'

'Well, I'll be sure to remind her.' I yawned, resting my head against the pillow. I wanted to stay up and talk, to stretch out this precious time together as long as possible. But I could feel the inevitability of sleep calling to me, my eyelids heavy. The world took on that strange haziness as I drifted in and out of consciousness, my thoughts and dreams all knotting together, making it impossible to tell where one ended and the other began.

'Alice was right, you know,' I heard Joe whisper. Or maybe I was already dreaming.

'Hmm?'

'The love it represents will never die.'

I smiled sleepily, the silhouette of the orchid the last thing I saw before my eyes closed completely.

I glanced at my watch, the end of my biro tapping noisily against the spiral top of my notebook. I was waiting for Luca. Or rather, he was making me wait. It was 17:35, which meant the Wednesday session at the community centre had officially ended five minutes ago, and yet all I had to show for it was a poorly executed doodle of a saxophone in the bottom right corner of an otherwise blank page.

Luca had been avoiding me all day. All week actually. This in itself was not unusual. We generally did a pretty good job at staying out of each other's way, orbiting around the musty old hall like two opposing planets. But unfortunately, conducting an interview required us to be in the same vicinity as each other for at least fifteen minutes, something that Luca had purposefully gone out of his way to avoid. On Friday, it was a leak in the roof that apparently required his immediate attention. On Monday, he'd left as soon as the class was over, almost tripping over the metal bucket on the floor – that he'd deemed the solution to the leak problem – in the process. A washed-out image of me queueing in the rain outside Hove Job Centre floated around my head when I considered what might happen if I didn't have something to show Derek tomorrow. No. I was not about to let Luca Patel be the reason that another part of my life was ripped away from me.

He looked up from where he was collecting sheet music, hitching an eyebrow in surprise at seeing me still sat on the edge of the stage. He scratched at his jaw, a deep scowl of annoyance darkening his face. I was surprised he didn't have more wrinkles on that smooth forehead of his, considering how often it was scrunched in displeasure. I raised a hand in the air, beckoning him over, but he turned away, changing direction so fast that he lost his balance and collided with an unsuspecting Terry. He tried to style it out, giving Terry a jovial punch to the bicep as he launched into an animated conversation about something. *Oh no you don't.* I strode purposefully across the hall, the heels of my boots click-clacking determinedly against the warped flooring as I went.

'Hey Jenny.' Terry beamed at me over Luca's shoulder, which tensed beneath his shirt as I approached, the worn cotton failing to hide his unease. 'You wouldn't believe the number of people who've sent me your article. Even the 'lecky I work with was reading it on his phone the other day and I didn't know he could read!'

'It was the most popular article on our website last week.' I bobbed proudly on the balls of my feet like a six-year-old who'd just been awarded a gold star at school.

'Really?'

'Really?' Luca parroted, albeit with distinctly more disbelief than Terry.

'Yes, really,' I said indignantly, taking offence at his unspoken implication that I was somehow exaggerating. 'Speaking of articles, can I steal this one away for a few minutes, Terry?' I grabbed Luca's forearm in a vice-like grip as he pretended to spot someone across the other side of the hall.

'Be my guest. Kiki and I need to make a move anyway. It's film night and I promised her we'd watch *The Greatest Showman* . . . again.' Terry groaned theatrically as he swung Kiki's bag over one arm, the strap of the bright pink *Dora the Explorer* backpack too small to fit around his giant shoulder. I watched him stride over to where Kiki was sat on the floor, tongue sticking out in silent concentration as she performed the very technical bunny ears method on her shoelaces. Luca's arm jerked beneath my hand but my grip tightened.

'You just can't keep your hands off me, can you, Thompson?' His voice was heavy. Suggestive. Smug.

I snorted in disgust, but something about the way my engagement ring winked up at me against the bare skin of Luca's forearm made my insides churn and I snatched my hand away, hiding it behind my back. Luca took the opportunity to march over towards the piano where abandoned percussion instruments still littered the floor. I followed him like a disgruntled shadow.

'Come on, Luca, why do you have to make everything so bloody difficult?'

'Me? Difficult?' Luca guffawed but he was stalling, and he knew it.

'I thought you wanted to get the word out about this place? Or do you not care whether you stay open anymore?'

'Of course I care,' he snapped, a lightning bolt of anger flashing across his face. And something about the way his shoulder slumped with defeat told me he *did* care. More than I perhaps realised. 'What do you want to know?'

I quickly pressed record on the Dictaphone app on my phone, placing it on top of the piano. He recoiled, a muscle twitching in his jaw.

'OK, let's just start with an easy one,' I said gently. 'How did you first learn about this place?'

'My Dadaji,' Luca snapped. Zero explanation.

I dipped my head encouragingly, but Luca didn't get the hint. Or perhaps he did, and he chose to ignore it. He sighed wearily, as if *I* was majorly inconveniencing *him*.

'My Dadaji, that's my paternal grandfather,' Luca explained, 'was the one who set this whole thing up, almost 20 years ago.' His face softened immediately when he mentioned his grandfather, his eyes creasing at the corners with obvious affection. 'He was a professional piano player turned music teacher back in Calcutta, but he couldn't afford to requalify when his family moved over here in the 60s, so he got a job as a janitor at the local primary school. The only one he could get as an immigrant.' His voice was jaded, worn around the edges by the trials suffered by many a generation before him. 'Anyway, he started helping out with the after-school clubs, eventually volunteering to run a music group. It was nothing fancy, just a couple of kids sitting round an old piano for an hour after school each day whilst Dadaji belted out Elton John and Stevie Wonder. But he saw how much they loved it. How kids that other teachers had just written off as *difficult* or *disruptive* would blossom, thanks to him.'

'So, is that where your love of music came from?' I kept my tone light, but my eyes were curious.

He nodded. 'Our house was always full of music. I think I learnt to play the guitar before I could even walk.'

'And what about your dad? Is he a musician, too?'

'I wouldn't know. He walked out on us when I was two. Not seen him since. He's got a whole other family now – wife, kids, Cockapoo.' I blinked, his emotionless delivery making me question whether I'd heard him correctly, but seeing his knuckles turn white around a maraca confirmed I had.

'Oh.' There was a very long pause where neither of us quite knew where to look. I watched his face darken, a frown scrunching his features into an ugly, confused mess. I guess it wasn't any easier, being abandoned by choice. 'Well, your Dadaji sounds like an amazing man.'

Luca's face softened a fraction, his fingers unclenching. 'He is.' I breathed a sigh of relief at his use of the present tense. My pen stilled as I reviewed my notes, a big glaring question mark forming on the page.

'So, how did *you* end up here?' I asked, looking around at the musty hall.

'The school ended up selling its sports field to a developer, yet more budget cuts, no doubt,' he muttered with a disapproving shake of his head. 'But it meant they

126

needed the hall for football practice, so Dadaji had to come up with a plan B.'

'Giving up wasn't an option for him?'

Luca shook his head. 'Not even in his vocabulary. He's stubborn like that. Like a dog with a bone. Come to think of it, you remind me of him quite a lot.'

My lips pursed but I ignored the blatant dig.

'So, this was plan B?' I met Luca's gaze head on as he waited for a reaction that I refused to give. He nodded, the briefest hint of disappointment that I'd not taken the bait. As though that was our thing, or something. He'd push and I'd push back. A never-ending tug of war.

'Well, technically it was plan C. Dadaji ran the classes out of our front room for a while, but there were so many kids it wasn't a sustainable solution. Plus, there was an incident involving a permanent marker and Mum's William Morris wallpaper that forced him to find this place. It had been empty for years, ever since the council moved into that concrete monstrosity down by the seafront. Believe it or not, it was in an even worse state back then.'

My eyes followed Luca's around the hall, falling on a pigeon nestled in the gap where the roof met the wall.

'I'll have to take your word for it.'

A drop of leaky-roof water landed with a plop on my forehead at precisely that moment, trickling down my face as though in protest at my cynicism. A smile teased the corner of Luca's mouth. Of course, he enjoyed that.

'I'd love to meet your Dadaji at some point. Maybe interview him for the paper?'

Something resembling sadness swept across Luca's face, his cheeks slipping a centimetre or two. 'He moved back to India last year, always dreamt of spending his final years in Calcutta. But he wouldn't go until he was sure this place was in safe hands.'

'And that's when you took over?' I deduced, the final missing piece of the puzzle slotting into place.

Luca nodded once, stubbing the toe of his boot against a loose bit of skirting board. 'Safe hands, my arse. One year in, and we're already in danger of having to close.' He raked his fingers roughly through his hair, tugging at the ends as though intent on ripping them straight out of his scalp. He was still gripping the maraca with his other hand, holding it so tightly I was afraid it would splinter into a million tiny pieces. The intensity of it prompted something to shift inside me, as though I was having to make room for a new way in which to view Luca Patel – or at least, this softer, caring version of him that I'd not seen before. Luca flinched at the unexpected contact as I reached out to take the maraca from him, our fingers momentarily overlapping.

'Not if I can help it,' I said gently. 'Dog with a bone over here, remember?'

His grip loosened, shifting slightly so that the tip of his forefinger was now over my pinky.

'My Dadaji used to say that music could heal the wounds that medicine could not.' Luca smiled to himself, as though remembering the words after the longest of times. 'And that's all we're trying to do here, for the adults as much as for the children. Music has always been there for me, through the good times and the bad. And I know how important it is to have a place you can go where you feel safe and heard. Where you can get lost in the music, and not feel so alone in whatever battle you're fighting. Because we're all battling something, right?'

I nodded dumbly, my mouth too dry to speak as his words hooked something deep in my chest, pulling it taut. I relinquished my hold on the maraca, my hand suddenly feeling useless and obsolete by my side. I fixed my eyes on my notebook, scared to meet Luca's gaze for fear he'd be able to see right through me to the darkness that lay within.

'And what are you battling, Luca Patel?' I asked playfully, speaking into my pen as though I were a field reporter with a microphone before angling it in his direction. But it must have been one question too many, because he turned away, leaning down to pluck a drumstick from beneath a chair. When he straightened back up, the mask was firmly back in place.

'You mean other than your annoying questions?'

And we were back to deflection. I recognised it better than most, seeing as I was a black belt in the discipline myself. But what did Luca have to hide? I pressed the stop button on my phone to end the recording. The interview was over.

Just then, a commotion by the door made us both look up. A red-faced, slightly flustered Jacob stood in the middle of the double doors, surrounded by a mound of camera bags and lighting equipment.

'Sorry I'm late, Derek had me over at Mile Oak Farm photographing a supposed UFO landing site,' Jacob explained, rolling his eyes in a way that said *don't ask* before turning to face Luca, camera in hand. 'Ready for your close-up, Mr Patel?'

Luca's face dropped, glaring accusingly at me. 'You didn't say anything about a photograph.'

'That's the spirit.' Jacob beamed, carrying on as if he hadn't even heard him. 'Just one step to your left? Perfect, now just act casual. Relax.'

But Luca looked the opposite of relaxed. He flinched as soon as Jacob's flash went off, his whole body stiffening like a plank of wood.

'Just pretend you're back at school and you're having your prom picture taken.'

'I didn't go to prom,' Luca said flatly. Jacob looked horrified. I pretended to play an imaginary violin, my awkward sawing motion through the air the point at which I realised I had zero idea how to play a violin.

'What are you doing?'

'Playing my teeny-tiny violin for poor ickle Luca,' I teased, laughing at my own joke.

'Well, the joke's on you, because I don't know what you're doing, but it's not that. What's your arm even doing?' Luca frowned at my left arm, which was straight out in front of me at a 90° angle. Jacob shooed me out of the way before I could answer, circling Luca in search of an angle that didn't make him look like – well, that.

'Just relax, pretend we're not even here,' Jacob suggested.

'I *am* relaxed,' Luca grumbled, his lips unmoving as they remained frozen in his attempt at a smile. He looked like he was suffering from a severe bout of constipation.

'Maybe let's try a few over by the piano?' Jacob gave me a *this is going to be harder than I thought* eye bulge as he shepherded a reluctant Luca to the opposite side of the hall.

I chuckled quietly to myself as I shoved my notebook back in my bag, Luca's blatant discomfort surprisingly entertaining. A handful of remaining adults – parents of those children still rounding up their belongings and trying to locate missing shoes – had congregated into a semi-circle, little ginger-haired Harry's mum covering her mouth with one hand as she whispered something to the others that made one woman's face turn full-blown tomato. They were all staring intently at something on the other side of the hall, and I followed their collective gaze to see Luca sat at the piano, his long fingers moving gracefully over the black and white keys, his relaxed shoulders no longer bunched awkwardly around his ears. That one lock of hair longer than the rest fell partially across his face as he dipped his head, his t-shirt straining across his back as his whole body rose and fell in time with the music, as if the delicate melody were emanating from his very core. The waning sun streamed in through the opposite window, emphasising his cheek bones, which seemed to have been carved specifically with moments like this in mind.

It was the first time I'd seen Luca smile. I mean, really smile. Not the sarcastic smirk he normally taunted me with. I watched the way his nose wrinkled ever so slightly as he threw his head back at something Jacob said, eyes sparkling with something other than irritation or mockery for once. Provided he wasn't talking/goading/arguing/ being his general self, he was – well, handsome. No, hot. Luca Patel was hot. And now I was hot. Why was *I* hot?

He looked up then, his gaze – softer than normal – catching me watching him. His lips parted, his chest rising and falling with a sudden intake of breath. I turned away quickly, my heartbeat thumping in my ears as I fussed unnecessarily with the contents of my bag, checking three times for my car keys before realising they were already in my hand.

'Jenny, you're missing the show.' Harry's mum winked at me as I turned to leave, fanning her face with one hand as the other women descended into another fit of girlish giggles. I glanced innocently over at the piano, as if noticing it for the first time. Luca was still staring at me. I felt a bead of sweat prickling between my shoulder blades.

'All yours, ladies.' I smiled politely, the weight of Luca's gaze warming the nape of my neck as I hurried towards the exit.

10

'How long do you think I have to stay?'

'Jenny, you've only been there for like, 30 minutes,' Alice laughed, letting out a big, *I'm six hours into a night shift* sigh as I watched her fall backwards onto one of the on-call hospital beds.

'36 minutes, actually,' I said petulantly, batting my necklace – a Temu shot glass made from cheap plastic – over one shoulder. 'And in that time, I've already been scarred for life from pinning the penis on a horrifyingly life-sized cardboard cutout of my brother, and having to put up with Alyssa's annoying friend Kristina with a K who's been married three times and was shocked to hear I was 30 and – *God forbid* – single. She keeps looking at me like I'm a frickin' rainbow-pooping unicorn or something.'

'You're not thinking about doing a runner just so you can go home and see you-know-who, are you?' Alice was suddenly sitting bolt upright on the bed, scrutinising me intently through the phone. I forced my mouth into a smile.

'Of course not,' I lied. But the truth was, I would much rather be home with Joe right now than spending the night playing Mr & Mrs with my brother's fiancée and her mums-gone-wild group of girlfriends. 'And you can say Joe's name, Alice. He's not bloody he-who-must-not-be-named!'

I jumped as a pair of black peep toe stilettoes appeared at the bottom of my bathroom stall, that instant flash of panic as the door rattled against the flimsy catch and I imagined someone barging in on me on the toilet. Not that there was anything to see. I was fully clothed, phone balanced precariously atop the toilet roll dispenser as I perched just as gingerly on the closed toilet lid, trying to touch as little as possible. Then again, the fact that I was a grown-ass woman hiding in the disabled loo was arguably more embarrassing than being caught with my knickers round my ankles.

'Occupied!' I yelled.

Black Stilettoes tottered unsteadily to the next stall, the shared wall between us rattling when she slammed the door shut with the excessive force of someone who was already five tequila shots in. A stray tampon and an XL wide-fit foil Durex packet – *wishful thinking sweetheart* – skidded across the floor into my stall as her handbag fell to the floor. Well, at least she was prepared for every eventuality.

'Excuse me, I did not spend the best part of two hours making you look socially acceptable only for you to hide in the bathroom all night,' Jacob said sternly, wagging his finger at the camera. I tugged at the hem of the black skin-tight dress Jacob had insisted I wear, after declaring everything else in my wardrobe either *too bleurgh* or *so 2012*. It was short. As in, I had to be careful I didn't flash everyone my nude M&S control pants when I sat down, short.

'What the fuck are those?' Jacob had cried earlier that evening while I was getting ready, his face contorting with disgust at the reams of elasticated material.

'These are a necessity. They keep everything in,' I'd explained breathlessly, mid-way through the five-minute body-wiggling battle to get them on. I won. Just.

'Keep everyone out more like,' I'd heard Jacob mutter.

I caught sight of my reflection in the tiny square in the bottom right-hand corner of my phone, blinking twice just to check it was really me. My hair hung in soft, delicate waves around my face, courtesy of Jacob and his GHDs. Smoky eyeshadow and lashes that were not my own made my eyes look wide and awake for once, my cheeks a healthy rosy colour, my lips a bold, seductive red. Alice's left eyeball filled her half of the screen as she moved the phone closer. She let out a low whistle. 'Damn, Jacob, I don't know how you did it, but Jenny, you look hot.'

'Hey!'

'Alice is right, I'm a bloody miracle worker,' Jacob declared, ignoring my half-hearted protest. 'Now get out there and show off the fruits of my labour.'

'Yeah, go have some fun. One of us should.' Alice yawned, closing her eyes.

'Fine,' I grumbled, with the reluctance of someone who'd just been told to walk over hot coals. Which, at this stage, would have been preferable. I jabbed my finger against the screen to end the call, only for my phone to fall to the ground with a loud clatter. I leaned down to retrieve it, trying to remember if I had any wet wipes in my bag.

'They're right, you know.'

My cheeks stretched into a smile. I couldn't help it. It was a natural reaction. Like ice melting in the afternoon sun.

'You *should* be having fun,' Joe reprimanded, looking down at me from where he was leaning against the bathroom door, one Chelsea boot resting casually against the wall.

'I am having fun.'

'Oh sure, life and soul of the party in here.'

I rolled my eyes at him, sticking my bottom lip out like a child.

'Do you remember that night we ended up in that secret bar in the Lanes?'

I smiled. Of course, I remembered. We'd only popped into the tiny, unassuming Italian delicatessen to grab some picky bits for dinner. But when I asked the silver-haired, olive-skinned man behind the counter if he had any Coppa di Parma, he'd smiled knowingly and beckoned us towards the back with a wave of his hand. The next thing we knew, he'd opened what, from the outside, appeared to be your standard, if a little outdated, fridge door – but instead of cured meats and cheeses, we were met with a long corridor, flashing lights and the rich, mellow sound of a live saxophone blasting from the other end.

'How could I forget?'

'Well, considering the number of Negronis we drank that night, you'd be forgiven if you had.'

'That was a good night,' I mused, the memory playing out in real time in my head. The dimly lit room with its miniature, tassel-hemmed lampshades lining the walls. The spindly wooden tables and chairs, the kind you see outside cafes on the cobbled streets of Paris, all empty as people jostled for space on the dance floor. The way Joe had spun me around until I was dizzy, his breath hot and sweet against the nape of my neck. How I'd somehow ended up atop the bar, arm in arm with two women I'd never met before, cancanning to the live band's rendition of 'Tu vuò fa' l'americano'.

'I'll tell you one thing, that girl would not be hiding in the bathroom on a Saturday night.'

I looked down at my feet. 'Well, maybe I'm not that girl anymore.'

'Of course you are,' Joe clapped back, his voice so sure. That made one of us.

'I don't know who I am without you, Joe,' I admitted quietly, almost embarrassed to say the words. But they were the truth. Our lives had been tightly interwoven for so long that neither made sense without the other. But now there was a loose thread, the kind to slowly unravel everything that you'd built, like a piece of yarn dangling from the hem of a jumper. And here I was, unravelling. Joe crouched down, his knee doing that clicky thing it did whenever he took stairs two at a time. I sat on my hands, trying to resist the urge to reach out and trace his jawline with my fingers. Feel the familiar dip of his dimple beneath my thumb. I didn't want him to go just yet. He waited until I lifted my head, his eyes pulling mine to his.

'You are Jenny Thompson,' he said, firmly. 'And you're going to get out there, drink a Sex on the Beach through a penis straw, and bloody well let your hair down.'

I smiled despite myself. 'My hair's already down.'

'Umm, s'cuse me?' slurred a voice to my right. Crap, I'd forgotten Black Stilettoes was still here.

'Sorry, just on the phone.' I winced at my own lie, banking on the fact she was too drunk to realise.

'No problem, babes, it's just you've got something of mine?' A set of bright pink talons appeared under the partition, the kind that were so aggressively long I wondered how she even went to the toilet without causing herself serious injury. Joe snorted with laughter as the hand hovered expectantly between his ankles, the tips of her fingers fluttering impatiently. Our eyes found each other, and it was game over. A giggle bubbled from between my lips in one loud, hysterical burst, and I had to clamp my hand over my mouth to stop it. Using a clean piece of toilet roll, I picked the condom packet off the floor and dropped it into Black Stilettoes' outstretched fingers.

Okay, a couple of hours and then I can make a discreet exit without anyone noticing, I told myself, finally emerging from the safety of the bathroom and pulling on the cardigan I'd managed to stuff in my bag without Jacob noticing. The bar was rammed, the air vibrating with the carefree, louder-than-normal voices of people letting loose on a Saturday night, no 6 a.m. alarm clocks or work presentations to worry about the next day. I navigated my way through the crowd, having no trouble finding our table thanks to the creepy, eyeless masks of my brother that all nine women were now sporting. I mentally adjusted the countdown in my head to ninety minutes. Kristina was the only one not wearing a mask, even though I could see several spares in the middle of the table. No doubt she didn't want the cheap elastic ruining her voluminous blow-dry.

'There you are, Jenny, what took you so long? Did someone get lucky in the bathroom?' Kristina cackled. The multitude of empty shot glasses in front of her and the way one of her eyes took a while to catch up with the other – or maybe that was just the Botox? – told me she was already three sheets to the wind. I smiled tightly at her as I perched at the end of the booth, carefully crossing my ankles in that way I'd seen the Princess of Wales do on TV. Alyssa, who looked stunning in a white feather-cuffed jumpsuit that shimmered from every angle, was sat to my left.

'I'm so glad you came tonight, Jenny.' She beamed, turning her back to the rest of the group. 'I hope you don't think I was being insensitive at all by inviting you? I just thought, well—'

Her kohl-lined eyes desperately scanned my face in that way people do when they hope you'll finish their sentence for them. Navigate them towards safe ground.

'It's fine,' I reassured her, coming to her rescue. I must have said *it's fine* and *I'm fine* a thousand times since the accident. Never have I said something so often that I didn't mean. But when people ask, they don't really want an answer. Not the real one, anyway. 'I'm so happy for you and Matt, honestly – you deserve each other.' Alyssa grasped my hand in hers and gave it a gentle squeeze.

'So, Al, when are you and Matt going to start trying? Is a honeymoon baby on the cards?' trilled a blonde-haired woman whose bright pink sash told me she was one of Alyssa's bridesmaids. All the other women joined in, their excited murmurs like a pack of cooing hens. I bristled slightly at the blatant assumption. And from a woman at that. One who I'd bet all £207 in my bank account had felt the pressure of such assumptions herself, but who, now that she'd ticked the wife and mother boxes – judging by her nuclear family Whats-App picture – had somehow forgotten the pain and stress such throwaway comments could cause. It's like you turn 30 and immediately morph into the bloody crocodile from Peter Pan. Tick, tick, tick. I grabbed a tequila shot from the tray in front of me and knocked it back, shoving a lime wedge in my mouth to stop myself from saying something I might regret.

'We're not in a huge rush. I think we want to enjoy some time just the two of us first, you know?' Alyssa smiled, adjusting her pearl-encrusted BRIDE-TO-BE sash with one hand. Nine blinking Matts and an eyebrow-twitching Kristina all stared back at her in dumb silence, as though she'd just admitted she liked drowning puppies for fun or went round cutting off little girls' braids with a pair of kitchen scissors. Why do we do that? Take every casual comment or passing thought from a woman's lips to be some giant statement for all womankind? Like we're all cookies cut from the same rigid mould?

'But obviously we want kids,' Alyssa backtracked quickly, clearly feeling the need to reassure everyone. 'Hopefully three. Two boys and a little girl.' There was an almost audible sigh of relief around the table, everyone's shoulders lowering an inch or two.

'Ooh, a mini-Alyssa, I bet she'd have your eyes,' the woman opposite me prophesied, sparking an animated conversation about possible baby names. I had to fake a coughing fit when someone suggested Blaze. Kristina, apparently as uninterested in playing the hypothetical baby-name game for Matt and Alyssa's as yet unconceived children as I was, leaned across the table.

'Hannah, when are the strippers getting here?' she stage-whispered, winking at Alyssa's maid of honour.

'I already told you, Kristina, there aren't any strippers.' Hannah sighed with the impatience of someone who'd already had this conversation multiple times. 'It's not that kind of hen do.' Kristina looked like someone who'd just been told Santa Claus wasn't real.

'What?! I thought you were joking! Look, Hannah, I have not had sex for nine months. *Nine longgg months*,' Kristina hissed angrily, her knuckles white as they gripped the edge of the table. Ha, so much for marital bliss! 'There are only so many times a woman can read *Fifty* Fucking *Shades of Grey*, and I've reached my bloody limit. I don't think it's too much to ask for some greased-up, muscular stranger to gyrate in my immediate vicinity for one evening!'

'That singer keeps looking over here, maybe you can satisfy your – needs – there?' Hannah suggested, diverting Kristina's attention to the stage as we all shook with laughter. I glanced over at the raised platform, saying a silent prayer for the poor guitar-wielding musician that Kristina was now attempting to make eye contact with as she sucked suggestively from her penis straw. Wait, was that—?

Fuck. It was Luca. The guitar-wielding musician was Luca. Christ, could this night get any worse?! He was wearing all black – black t-shirt, black jeans with rips at the knees, black beaten-up leather jacket. And he was looking over at our table. At me, specifically. His dark eyebrows knitted together as he sang about broken hearts and first loves, clearly unsure whether it *was* me or not.

'I'm just going to get a drink,' I mumbled to Alyssa, slipping out of the booth.

'Oh, we've got another round coming—' she began, but I was already halfway across the dance floor. I let the crowd swallow me up, breathing a sigh of relief when I reached the bar and could no longer feel the weight of Luca's gaze on me. I held up a hand, trying to get the bartender's attention.

'It *is* you.'

I closed my eyes, taking a long, calming breath before turning to my left. Something told me I was going to need it. Luca's mouth was curled into a victorious smirk, as if we'd been playing hide and seek and he'd just won. I watched his eyes, somehow even darker in the dim light, travel down the length of my body and back up with the speed of a seasoned pro, chasing goosebumps over my skin.

'I'll admit I didn't recognise you there for a second, Thompson. You look—' he paused, registering my I-dare-you-to-finish-that-sentence hand on hip '—different.'

My jaw clenched. So I looked a bit more together than all the other times he'd seen me – I'd brushed my hair for starters and yes, the clean clothes were probably also a first – but he didn't have to be so obvious about it. I ignored him, leaning over the bar as I tried yet again to get the bartender's attention. He was chatting to two women down the opposite end of the bar who kept flashing obvious looks at an oblivious Luca. One of them whispered something to her friend and she giggled, reaching for a cocktail napkin.

Luca turned, both his elbows leaning on top of the bar. 'I would say I'm surprised to see you here, but at this point I'm really not. You just can't stay away from me, can you?'

I rolled my eyes. 'Trust me, this is the last place I want to be right now. Ah, *finally!*' I groaned with relief as the bartender sauntered over to us. But instead of asking me what I wanted, he slid a napkin across the bar. It had a phone number scrawled in the bottom right-hand corner, a lipstick kiss stamped across the top. Something told me it wasn't for me.

'Luca, you've got an admirer, mate.' The bartender grinned, nodding his head in the direction of the two women at the opposite end of the bar, one of whom was wearing the exact shade of coral lipstick that decorated the napkin. Luca offered them a polite smile but I noticed it didn't quite reach his eyes. He pocketed the napkin, confirming he was one of those. The type of guy to accept another woman's number whilst his girlfriend was waiting for him at home.

'Can I get a whiskey please, Andy? Neat. And whatever my friend here's drinking.'

I snorted at Luca calling me his friend, having half a mind to refuse his offer of a drink, but I'd probably die of thirst by the time I got served myself. 'Gin and tonic, please. Double.'

'I guess we should probably swap numbers,' Luca suggested flippantly, producing his phone from his back pocket.

I snorted. 'I have no desire to be another name in your little black book, thank you very much.'

Luca raised an eyebrow. 'I meant for the article. You know, in case you need anything? I AirDropped my contact details to your phone, just tap to accept.'

'Yeah, I don't want to tap that.'

'You sure about that?' His bicep strained against the fabric of his t-shirt as he turned, leaning his head in his palm to better view my discomfort.

Ergh, he was seriously the worst.

'You know, if I didn't know any better, I'd say he was flirting with you.'

I almost choked on my drink. Joe had appeared behind Luca, leaning with his back against the bar. Something about seeing the two of them together like that, shoulder to shoulder, made my insides squirm.

'*What the bloody hell are you doing here?*' I hissed at him, one eye on Luca who'd leaned over to say something to the bartender.

'Nice to see you too,' Joe drawled, feigning offence. When I didn't smile, he held his hands up in surrender. 'Geez, can a guy not go for a drink on a Saturday night without his girl flying off the handle?'

'Joe, this isn't funny,' I hissed with as much menace as a whisper would allow, my eyes flitting anxiously from Joe to Luca and back again.

'Hey, I don't make the rules, honey. If I'm here, it's because you want me here.'

'I *do not!*'

Joe clasped his hands over his heart, one shoulder recoiling back as if he'd been shot.

'You wound me, woman.'

I knew he was joking, just being classic Joe, but guilt swirled cold and sour in the pit of my stomach.

'I mean, obviously I want you here, just not *here*, here,' I clarified gently. 'Anyway, you clearly need your eyes tested because he's not flirting with me. He's got a girlfriend. Several apparently.'

'Who has?' Luca turned back to face me, a cut-glass whiskey tumbler in hand.

My cheeks flushed. 'No one,' I said quickly. 'What are you doing here, anyway? Shouldn't you be up there singing?' I gestured impatiently towards the stage.

'My set's finished. Apparently there comes a point when people would rather listen to drunk strangers butchering cheesy hits than a paid professional.' As if on cue, the bartender tapped his fingers atop a microphone.

'One. Two. One. Two. Ladies and gentlemen, it's Saturday night, which means one thing and one thing only . . . it's karaoke night!' he announced, much to the crowd's delight. Luca's eyes were fixed firmly on my face, his pupils dancing with amusement. 'Don't be shy, we're taking sign-ups at the bar, and to kick us off tonight, we have Jenny Thompson. Jenny, the stage is yours!'

My stomach fell out the bottom of me. I turned slowly towards Luca, my face like thunder.

'What did you do?' I hissed angrily. But the crooked smirk on his face told me he knew *exactly* what he was doing.

'Uh-oh, I'd take cover if I were you, mate,' Joe warned, grabbing a cocktail menu and pretending to hide behind it.

The bartender looked over in my direction. 'I think someone's getting cold feet over here. Can I get some love in the room for Jenny, please, let's see if we can't get her up on the stage. *Jenny. Jenny. Jenny.*' More and more people started chanting my name, over and over. Even Joe joined in. God, this was an actual living nightmare.

Luca doubled over with laughter, gesturing to the chanting crowd. 'The people have spoken.'

I felt a hand on my shoulder and turned to see Kristina standing behind me, shoulders back, surgically enhanced boobs forward. Her lips looked extra glossy. As though she'd just this second applied a fresh coat of lip gloss.

'Jenny, they're calling you,' she said, fluttering her eyelashes at Luca.

'Yes, thank you, Kristina, but there's been some kind of a mix up. Excuse me—' I barked at the bartender.

'What's the matter? Scared?' The way Luca's lips pressed together to keep from laughing made my teeth grind. As though he thought he'd already won. Well, we'd see about that. I grabbed Luca's whiskey tumbler, downing the entire thing and trying not to wince as the neat amber liquid burnt my throat. I took a step towards him, my breathing heavy, my mouth mere inches from his ear. He smelt of old leather and the faint, salty undertone of sweat.

'You should be the one who's scared, you'll be out of a job after this.' I smirked, Luca's whiskey propelling me towards the stage with a false sense of confidence. But when someone thrust a microphone into my hands, the heat of a spotlight landing on my face, my legs turned to jelly. I raised a hand against the glare, squinting through the sea of bodies towards the bar where Kristina was trying to show Luca how she could tie a bow in the stem of a cocktail cherry using only her tongue.

My heart was beating so loudly that I was certain the microphone would pick it up, broadcasting my anxiety for the whole room to hear. But then I spotted him. Leaning against one of the pillars, hair flopping all over the place as he grinned encouragingly from behind his glasses. I stared imploringly at Joe, wishing it was him up here instead of me. He was so much better at karaoke than I was. Joe gave a small shrug of his shoulders, as if he were agreeing with me.

Shania Twain's 'Man! I Feel Like a Woman!' blasted from the speakers behind me, and I mumbled the opening lyrics into the microphone, my voice lost before it even reached the front row of the crowd, none of whom were paying any attention to who was on the stage. None except Luca, that is, who'd somehow escaped Kristina and fought his way through the throngs of people for a front-row seat to my public humiliation. I winced as the microphone let out a jarring, high-pitched noise and I saw Luca's shoulders judder with silent laughter. But there's something about hearing Shania Twain sing that iconic opening line that flips some sort of internal switch in every woman, and I suddenly felt like I could do anything. Climb a mountain. Smash through a brick wall. And most definitely wipe that stupid, smug smile off Luca Patel's face.

As the beat kicked in, I turned so my back was to the audience, purposefully dropping one shoulder so my cardigan slid provocatively down my right arm before landing in a pool at my feet. A wolf whistle echoed throughout the room and by the time I turned back around, the crowd had swarmed closer, a hundred faces now fully invested in the show. I pulled the microphone free from the stand, strutting across the stage with a newfound confidence. I belted out the next verse, raising a game-on eyebrow at Luca as I whipped off my shot glass necklace and twirled it around in the air. The crowd cheered as I found my mark, Luca recoiling backwards before cocking his head with a grin, a silent *touché* of acknowledgement. I dropped to the floor, straddling the microphone stand like a prize thoroughbred as I paused, waiting for Luca's eyes, which were currently somewhere around my thighs, to catch up with my face. He ruffled the back of his head, those dark eyes smouldering with something dangerous and electrifying when they sparked with mine. I grinned, the thrill of victory coursing through my veins at the look of utter disbelief on his face.

The crowd went wild as I jumped off the stage, Alyssa and the other hens fangirling like delirious teenagers at a Taylor Swift concert in the corner as I worked my way along the line, microphone lead trailing along behind me. Luca was the only one still seated; everyone else was on their feet, the floor vibrating with a hundred dancing revellers belting out Shania right along with me. I stopped in front of him, circling his chair slowly like a lioness stalking her prey. All the women around me hollered in solidarity, cheering me on as I planted a shoe on the seat of Luca's chair, forcing his legs apart to avoid being impaled by my stiletto. His gaze lingered briefly on my ankle, lips parting as if he were playing the part of some man in a Jane Austen novel, before dragging his eyes up my bare leg, pausing for a second too long on the scooped neckline of my dress. *Mr Darcy, my arse.* He shifted in his seat as I continued to move my hips against the side of his chair, his visible discomfort like fuel to my already-raging fire. His chest heaved beneath my fingers as I traced a slow, lazy pattern across the cotton of his t-shirt, his jaw jutting to one side in a hard lock.

'I know what you're doing. You might have won all these other people over—' he gestured to the jeering crowd, his grip tightening resolutely on the arms of the chair, '—but it's not going to work on me.'

I shrugged one shoulder in a way that said I knew otherwise, noticing his left heel bouncing to the rhythm of the beat. I whipped the microphone cable hard against the sticky floor with a sharp crack, but still Luca didn't move. As I took half a step back, I watched that dimple appear in his hitched right cheek. The mark of someone who thought they'd won. The corner of my own mouth ticked as I lassoed the excess cable round my head, the roar of the crowd building to a crescendo as I landed the loop over Luca's head, pulling it taut. For a beat, nothing happened. His jaw shifted to the other side, some silent negotiation passing between us as neither one of us backed down. But then he broke into a grin, holding his hands up in surrender and climbing to his feet. The crowd surged around us until there was nowhere else to go, our bodies forced together, the pressure of his hips against mine. It felt strange to feel another man's body against my own, but I found myself leaning into it, a lightning bolt of electricity searing through me wherever we were touching. Right thigh. Hip bone. Left pinky finger as it grazed against the tear in his jeans. My boobs when someone jostled behind Luca and he stumbled even closer, my chest pressed hard against his. His hand found my wrist, twirling me around as I launched into the second verse.

'I've gotta hand it to you, Thompson, you never fail to surprise me,' he yelled in my ear, his breath hot and sticky against the nape of my neck. He threw his head back and laughed, hair in disarray, skin glistening with sweat. My stomach flipped traitorously. I hadn't seen him smile like that before. Warm and genuine, his eyes melting into two pools of sweet chocolate. There was something intoxicating about it. Something so strong it was hard to look away. To ignore the heat that had started swirling between my thighs. With only one way to go, I stepped back onto the safety of the stage as the final chorus kicked in.

My eyes scanned the dimly lit room, searching the shadows for Joe. But he was nowhere to be seen, the pillar he'd previously been leaning against now occupied by a drunk couple who looked like they were attempting to eat each other's faces off. Something cold washed over me and the bubble in which Joe and I existed together popped, disappearing into the stale air of the bar, as though it had never even existed. I turned away sharply, but my heel snagged on a tangle of cable and the next thing I knew, I was hurtling face-first off the front of the stage.

11

I now understand why they call it a hangover. It felt like
the darkest of clouds was hanging over my head, rain
pounding down against my skull with no intention of
stopping any time soon. You know you're in a bad way
when you feel like you might need sunglasses to open the
fridge. *How was it possible to be this thirsty after drinking
so many liquids last night?* My mouth was drier than the
Sahara Desert, but making it to the kitchen required actual
physical movement, and after the wave of nausea that hit
me when I attempted to roll over, it was clear that wasn't
going to happen any time soon.

I was face-down in a sea of pillows, one side of my face
roasting from the sun I could feel streaming in through
the gap in the curtains, the way it always did whenever
Joe didn't shut them properly. Something scratchy was
tickling the backs of my bare legs and I tugged at it, producing a grey woollen blanket that I'd never seen before.
Somehow, I managed to lift my head up long enough
to register the four-inch gap in the curtains through
squinted eyes, before the room started spinning and I
let my head fall fast and heavy into a pillow. I was never
drinking again. Like, ever.

The sheets were worn and bobbled beneath my fingertips as they reached out towards Joe's side of the bed. He always slept on the left. The side closest to the door, so that any hypothetical intruders would have to *go through him first*, as he put it. Just like he always walked on the side of the pavement closest to the traffic and twisted his fingers through mine whenever we crossed a road. A sigh escaped my lips as my palm traced the familiar dip in the mattress, the memory foam still moulded to the contours of Joe's body, refusing to forget. I opened one eye, wincing against the sunlight as I searched for Joe's smiling face in the frame that lived on the bedside table. But there was no frame. No bedside table at all. Just a taped-shut cardboard box with a leather-bound notebook, a pencil in need of a good sharpen, and a full pint glass of water sat on top. It took all my energy to drag myself into a sitting position, my back flush against the bedframe as I waited for the room to stop spinning. I gulped giant mouthfuls of water, even though my brain told me to sip it, frowning suspiciously at the leather jacket hung from the bedpost. It wasn't Joe's, and yet something about it looked familiar. My brain, which currently felt like it was submerged underwater (or one too many shots of tequila), kicked into gear just long enough for me to register that I wasn't in my tiny box room above the pub. I was in mine and Joe's old bedroom. In our old flat. No, in *Luca's* flat. *Shit!*

I scrabbled about on the bed, wrapping the scratchy grey blanket around myself like a protective shield. *What the hell was I doing here?!* Had I gotten confused on the way home, autopilot propelling me down the same streets I'd walked for years? And where was Luca? Oh my god, did we—? No. There's absolutely no way. I mean, we couldn't have. Right? My eyes fell reluctantly on the left-hand side of the bed, mildly mollified to see the duvet – which apparently, I'd slept on top of? – still tucked neatly down that side of the mattress. Two pillows stacked on top of one another, their cases smooth compared to those I'd pummelled into oblivion on my side, one of which had half of last night's make-up smeared across the top. I turned it over, hoping Luca wouldn't notice.

As I did so, I caught sight of my puzzled expression gawping back at me from a large mirror sat atop three other cardboard boxes. I was still wearing the black dress from last night, although it had ridden up, exposing my flesh-coloured control pants, which I was relieved to find still present and correct. Not that anyone could easily remove those bad boys, even if they wanted to. Myself included. My hair looked like I'd walked through a hurricane and been electrocuted all at once, sticking out at gravity-defying angles from all the hairspray Jacob had used. Coupled with the mascara-rimmed panda eyes and red lipstick smear travelling from my mouth to right cheekbone, it's safe to say I'd looked better. A quick glance around the room produced no sign of my shoes, but I did spot my phone placed neatly on top of my bag on the floor by the bed. I reached for it, hopeful it might contain some clues as to how I'd ended up in Luca's bed last night. But no amount of finger jabbing or button clicking would coax the black screen into life. The battery was as dead as I felt right now.

The familiar squeak of the shower turning on had my eyes darting towards the hallway. Steam was swirling underneath the bathroom door, a pile of discarded clothes on the floor outside. I recognised the black t-shirt Luca had been wearing last night. A pair of grey Calvin Kleins on top. The thought of still being here when Luca emerged from the shower was motivation enough to propel me out of bed, hugging my belongings to my chest as I tiptoed into the living room. The tension in my shoulders eased a fraction when I saw the back cushions of the sofa had been removed, a blanket flung back to reveal the dent in the middle where Luca must have slept. My eyes scanned the room, spotting one of my shoes underneath the dining table. I tried not to think too hard about how it got there, dropping to the floor and shimmying commando-style beneath the table to retrieve it.

'Morning, sunshine.'

I jumped, bashing my head on the underside of the table.

Luca was stood in the doorway. Hair slicked back, steam billowing around him like one of those corny aftershave adverts. He was barefoot. Bare chested. Bare everything really, except for the impossibly small towel secured around his waist. God, it was hot in here. Must be the steam. I resisted the urge to fan my face with my hand.

'Good morning,' I said stiffly, rubbing the bump I could already feel forming beneath my bird's-nest hair.

'How are we feeling this fine day?' His voice was doing that annoying singsong thing people do whenever they ask you a question they already know the answer to.

'Fine. Great, actually,' I lied, not wanting to give him the satisfaction of seeing how much I was suffering. Luca chuckled, as though remembering something I was not privy to, the bare skin by his ribs brushing against my forearm as he slipped past. I snapped my arm back as though I'd been burned, biting the inside of my cheek as my elbow collided with the wall. Thankfully Luca didn't notice; he was too busy pulling a bag of coffee down from the cupboard we used to keep the tinned goods in. My eyes roamed the space. Illegible scribblings on the backs of envelopes stuck to the fridge door. An unfamiliar green bottle of Fairy Liquid beside the sink. Apple, rather than the lemon version we used to buy. This was no longer my home.

'So – last night,' I prompted casually, hoping he would fill in the blanks for me.

'Yeah.' Luca breathed heavily, lifting his chin in apparent agreement at something I'd just said. Or not said? 'If you'd have told me yesterday my night was going to end with Jenny Thompson in my bed, I'd have said you were crazy.' He chuckled, pressing a button on his expensive-looking coffee machine so that it whirred into life.

I stared unblinking at his face, not allowing my eyes to slide down his bare chest to where the towel was slung around the v of his hip bones, a neat line of dark hair guiding my gaze from his belly button down to the edge of the towel. Not that I wanted to look. It's just that thing when you know you shouldn't do something, and your brain automatically does it. Kind of like if I said *don't think about red buses* and a hundred red double-deckers would pop into your head. Well, wet, half-naked Luca was my big red bus.

'So, I slept *here* last night?'

His lips twitched, apparently amused by my case of temporary amnesia. A bead of water fell from his hair, running over his collarbone, down to somewhere I didn't dare look.

'Evidently.'

'And – you also slept here last night?'

His smile broadened as he crossed his arms over his chest. His bulging biceps didn't make the whole maintaining eye contact thing any easier.

'Do you not remember what happened last night?'

'Of course I do,' I lied.

'Oh, really?' He took a step towards me, a lion stalking its prey. 'So, you remember giving Shania Twain a run for her money last night?'

I closed my eyes, an awful flashback of me centre stage, riding the microphone stand like I was coming up the home straight at the Grand National, making me cringe with embarrassment.

'Mhmm.'

He took another step forward. 'And then falling off the stage?'

I raised a hand to my temple. So that's why my head was throbbing so badly. 'Yes,' I said tightly.

The floorboards creaked as he advanced some more. 'And turning up at my front door at 1 a.m.?'

I could feel Luca's eyes scanning my face, his teeth tugging at his bottom lip. He was testing me.

157

'Yep.'

He took one final step forward. We were close now. So close that I could smell his shower gel. It smelt of bergamot and sea salt.

'And what happened after? Do you remember that, Thompson?'

My cheeks were burning, my brain desperately trying to filter through memories of tequila slammers and – did I get on top of the bar at one point? – to find any recollection of how the night ended.

I swallowed. 'Did we—?'

Luca just stared at me, his gaze heavy beneath his lashes. His brow had knitted together, slightly upturned in the middle in what anyone else would presume was innocent curiosity, not the calculated torture I knew it to be. The fucker was actually going to make me say it.

'Did we sleep together last night?' I blurted out, screwing my eyes tightly shut as I braced myself for his response. I sensed him lean in, the hairs on my arms standing to attention, his hot breath chasing goosebumps up the side of my neck.

'Trust me, if we'd had sex, that's not something you'd forget any time soon.' His voice was thick and husky, full of unequivocal promise and something darker. Something that made me gasp before I could stop myself, eyes flying open to see Luca's own pupils swirling hot and fiery, his jaw set in a serious line before it dissolved into a winning smile. I resisted the urge to punch him.

'I found you outside the building when I got home last night.' He snorted, finally taking a step back. 'You were pretty wasted, convinced that you still lived here with your boyfriend. Joe, is it?'

My stomach lurched at the sound of Joe's name in Luca's mouth, and I clamped my lips together, afraid I was going to vomit. I nodded; that was about all I could manage.

'Anyway, you kept insisting that I let you in. *Demanded*, actually. Categorically refused to leave until I opened the door.'

I grimaced, a hazy memory of me leaning unsteadily against the red brick wall, my hands clasped in front of my chest.

'Did I beg at one point?'

Luca laughed, confirming my worst fear.

'Seeing as I didn't want to spend the whole night freezing my nuts off on the front doorstep, I let you in.' A flash of me dodging American football-style around Luca in my childish haste to get through the door before him, and then falling ass over tit in the hallway, no doubt flashing him my M&S pants in the process, made me want to hide my face in my hands. 'I thought a cup of coffee would sober you up enough to get you in a taxi, but the next thing I knew you'd passed out on my bed, snoring your head off.'

'I don't snore,' I mumbled petulantly, trying to ignore the proffered cup of coffee that Luca pushed across the kitchen counter towards me. But my need for caffeine was far greater than my principles right now, and I took a sip, ignoring Luca's crooked smile that told me he'd just earned another point on the scoreboard he kept in his head.

As soon as the rich, velvety liquid passed my lips, the pounding in my head dulled slightly. Enough for me to remember the blanket I'd woken beneath, the glass of water placed by the side of the bed, the Luca-shaped imprint on the sofa cushion where he must have slept last night. My face softened slightly as I watched him make himself a coffee in a pint glass. I don't know what shocked me more. The fact he only owned one mug, or that he'd willingly given it to me.

'Honestly, the lengths you went to to get in my bed, when all you had to do was ask,' he teased, banging the used coffee grounds with excessive force into the drawer below.

And he was back again, the thoughtful, caring guy pushed aside as quickly as he'd appeared by the full-of-himself, condescending asshole who was intent on ruining my life. I opened my mouth to let him know I would rather stick pins in my eyes than voluntarily get into bed with him, but the sound of a key jiggling in the lock stopped me. We both froze, two deer caught in headlights, and I watched in horror as Luca's girlfriend let herself into the flat. She was wearing a smart black pantsuit, her cropped cigarette trousers perfectly pressed, the collar of her shirt stiff against her neck. Her phone seemed to be surgically attached to one ear, her head pressed against her right shoulder to keep it in place as she started rifling through various cardboard boxes, oblivious to the two of us stood like statues in the kitchen.

'I'm telling you, he's not a credible witness. If I can just get him on the stand then he'll tear his own alibi to pieces without me even having to say a word.' Her heels clip-clopped against the wooden floorboards as she breezed around the living room, picking things up and putting them back down again with a sigh. One glance at Luca told me all I needed to know. His expression had shifted from smug and self-righteous to one of clear apprehension, the muscle in his jaw tensing as his gaze flitted back and forth between the two of us, while he no doubt tried to come up with a plausible explanation as to why he was wearing nothing but a towel in front of the woman who had slept in his bed last night. Judging by his panicked expression, he was coming up blank.

'Where the bloody hell is that file? No, Tony, I have not lost it. I've just momentarily misplaced it through no fault of my own,' she told whoever was on the other end of the line. 'It's here somewhere, I was looking over it the other night. I was sat right here on the sofa—' she plopped herself down in the divot where Luca had been sleeping, cocking her head quizzically at the discarded cushions littering the floor, '—we'd opened a bottle of Rioja, my case files were on the coffee table, someone was at the door – oh yes, the pizza guy – I put the deposition down, and *aha!*' She did a little victory jump as she bent down and wiggled an A4 cardboard file out from underneath the sofa.

Crash!

Praying for the ground to swallow me whole, I screwed my eyes shut, but not before I saw two sets of eyes land directly on me. No one was looking at the remnants of Luca's only mug, which now lay in shattered pieces at my feet, my attempt to place it silently back on the counter having failed. Miserably.

161

'Tony, I've got to go. Something's just – come up.' Luca's girlfriend spoke quickly into her phone, her eyes never leaving my face as she ended the call. She looked confused. Definitely surprised. Maybe a little mad? God, I hope she wasn't about to go all *Kill Bill* on my arse.

'Jasmine, what the hell are you doing here?' Luca asked, his tone accusatory. Impatient, almost. My mouth fell open at the sheer brazenness of it. A classic male power play. Turning the interrogation around on the woman before she could start asking the questions. If I wasn't technically the 'other woman' in this scenario, I'd have called him out on his chauvinistic behaviour, but something told me it was probably best just to stay shtum.

'I left this here the other night.' Jasmine waved the file in the air, her head ping-ponging back and forth between Luca and me as if she was watching a tennis match.

'This isn't what it looks like,' Luca insisted, holding up one hand whilst keeping a firm grip on his towel with the other.

'No?' Jasmine asked calmly, the weight of her stare landing on me to see if I had a different version of events.

'Yeah, we're just friends. Actually, we're not friends. More like work colleagues. Acquaintances at best. I can't stand him,' I babbled. I was babbling. Luca's eyeballs bulged and I pressed my lips together to keep more word vomit from spewing out. Jasmine raised one eyebrow, shifting her weight onto her left hip, her French-manicured fingers drumming against her trousers. *Shit*.

'You two look . . . *cosy*. Had a little sleepover, did we?' Her cherry-red lips were parted in an expectant O, clearly wanting an answer. *Double shit*.

'Luca slept on the sofa,' I spluttered.

'Thompson was pissed as a fart.'

'I'd maybe had one too many tequilas,' I corrected Luca.

'She basically rugby-tackled her way in here . . .'

'. . . not sure I'd put it quite like that.'

'. . . and then immediately passed out on my bed,' Luca ploughed on, throwing his one free hand up in the air.

I rolled my eyes at his description of events. The silence stretched on, the two of them appearing to have some sort of silent conversation that involved a lot of eyebrow-raising and loaded stares. The creaky floorboards gave away my discomfort as I shifted my weight from foot to foot, Jasmine's gaze darting back to me. Her eyes narrowed.

'Look, the last thing I want is to cause any problems in your relationship,' I promised, my voice coming out a bit squeaky.

'Our *relationship*?' Jasmine frowned, somehow making the word sound dirty. How was it possible that I was making this worse? Were they one of those couples who didn't like labels, or something? I smiled sweetly, my cheeks beginning to ache.

'As much as it physically pains me to give Luca anything remotely resembling a compliment, he was the perfect gentleman last night.'

'No need to sound so surprised,' Luca grumbled, but I ignored him. I'd just spotted my other shoe out the corner of my eye. It was on one side in the hallway, as though someone – clearly me – had kicked it off upon entering the flat.

'Anyway, as lovely as this has been, I should really get going,' I said, grabbing my bag and left shoe from the counter and darting out from the kitchen before anyone could stop me.

'Please don't rush off on my account.' I froze, turning to see Jasmine smiling warmly at me. In any other situation, I'd go so far as to call it friendly. *Did she just wink at me?*

'*Jas!*' Luca snapped. His tone a warning.

'What?' She laughed, flashing her pearly whites. Oh no, we'd progressed to deranged hysteria. I didn't want to stick around to find out what came next. 'Calm down, Luca, I'm not suggesting you should marry – Jenny, is it?' I shrugged meekly when she turned to me for confirmation. 'I'm just saying that the two of you look good together. Besides, you haven't been able to shut up about her these past few weeks.'

Oh my god! My cheeks flushed with embarrassment, my fingers scrabbling to undo the fiddly little buckles on my shoes so I could escape this nightmare. Luca mumbled something incomprehensible, pinching the bridge of his nose. I'd noticed him do it a couple of times now. At work. When he was talking to me. Mostly when he was talking to me. I think it was a stress thing.

'I don't need to be in the office for another hour, why don't we all grab breakfast together?' Jasmine suggested, much to mine and Luca's horror. *Had I accidentally gotten myself involved in some sort of threesome situation? Was that what this was?*

'Jas, I really don't think—'

'I have to go!' I shouted over Luca, the words coming out much louder than I'd intended. I gave up with the buckles, shoving my feet uncomfortably over the straps and wobbling unsteadily towards the door. 'You two seem like a really great couple and all—' *when this asshole isn't getting other women's numbers at bars*, snarked the voice in my head, '—but I'm really not into, you know – *group activities*.'

A giant crevasse had appeared in Luca's forehead and Jasmine's head fell bemusedly to one side as they both blinked at me.

'Hold up, do you think Luca and I are together? Like *together*, together?'

I frowned. 'Well, yeah?'

They both looked at each other for a second before dissolving into peals of laughter, Jasmine doubled over clutching her stomach, Luca leaning against the kitchen counter for support. God, this was going from bad to outright painful.

'Jas is my cousin,' Luca wheezed when he could finally draw breath.

Cousin? My mind rewound to when we'd first met, her opening the door in nothing but Luca's t-shirt.

'I crash here sometimes if I work late,' she explained, answering my unspoken question. 'My office is just around the corner and it's a lot easier than shlepping back to Lewes after missing the final train.'

'Which seems to be a twice-weekly occurrence these days,' Luca chastised. 'And that key I gave you was for emergency purposes only, not so you could let yourself in willy-nilly.'

Jasmine batted his reprimand away with the back of her hand. 'Anyway, Luca's single, Jenny. Like, *very* single,' she added. I blushed. I didn't think this situation could get any more awkward, but somehow the knowledge that Luca wasn't dating Jasmine, that he wasn't dating anyone, made the fact that I was standing mere metres from him and his tiny towel a whole other level of uncomfortable. Luca made a noise somewhere between a sigh and a *fucks-sake* as he turned and semi-jogged towards the safety of the bedroom, muttering something about clothes.

The buckles of my shoes dug painfully into the fleshy soles of my feet, demanding to be removed, so I took a seat on the bench in the hallway, easing my feet free with a sigh of relief.

'Sorry about all the confusion,' I muttered for want of something to say, smiling shyly up at Jasmine who was brushing crumbs from the top of her folder. 'For thinking you and Luca were, you know—'

Her face contorted in horror before winking at me. 'No harm done. I don't know who was more horrified by that prospect – me or Luca!'

I laughed, remembering the way her eyes had almost popped out of her head. 'Most definitely you.'

'Seriously though, Luca's a good guy.' Jasmine chuckled, her eyes crinkling softly at the edges with unmistakeable fondness. 'Still a little scarred from the past – I mean who isn't, am I right? – but he's one of the good ones.'

'Why, what happened?'

'Oh, he was seeing someone for a long time. They were engaged and everything. Rachel *if-I-don't-post-about-it-on-Instagram-it-didn't-happen* Gallagher,' Jasmine jeered with a shudder. Clearly, she was not a fan. 'Anyway, a few months before the wedding he found out that Rachel had been seeing someone else on the side for basically the entirety of their relationship.'

'That's awful,' I gasped, my mouth falling open in shock.

Jasmine pursed her lips. 'That's one word for it. Anyway, it's been over a year and he's still carrying it around like a dead weight. That feeling that he'll never be good enough for someone, you know?'

'From what I've seen, Luca has no problems attracting the opposite sex.' I found myself wondering what he'd done with the phone number from that woman at the bar. Had he just taken it to be polite? Tossed it in a bin on the way home? Or was it still folded neatly in the pocket of his jeans? Saved and waiting for later? Jasmine tilted her head, not disagreeing with me.

'Sure, but that's nothing serious. That's why I got my hopes up when he wouldn't stop going on about you. Honestly, the past few weeks it's been Jenny this, Jenny that.'

'Well, don't believe anything he's told you.' I smiled shyly, brushing a wayward strand of hair away from my face.

'Oh my gosh, here I am trying to set you up with my cousin and you're already spoken for. She's a beauty, can I see?' Jasmine squealed excitedly.

My brow furrowed with confusion. But then I followed her gaze to my engagement ring, the oval-shaped diamond showing off in the morning sunlight, casting iridescent rainbows all over the walls as though demanding to be seen. Guilt flooded through my veins, cold and sharp, at the realisation that for a second, just one second, I'd forgotten I was wearing it.

'Oh, umm—'

But Jasmine had already skipped towards me, her olive-toned fingers taking my left hand gently in hers as she made the customary coos that all women make when presented with a sparkly ring. Pigeons every last one of us.

'So, who's the lucky guy?'

'He's, umm . . .' I thought about telling her. Coming clean. But the words lodged themselves in the back of my throat, unwilling to be spoken out loud. I coughed but they stayed there, solid and unmoving, making it difficult to breathe. 'Joe,' I croaked eventually. 'His name's Joe.'

'Well, you tell Joe that he's a very lucky man,' Jasmine said, brushing off the front of her trousers as she straightened up.

I picked up my shoes, suddenly eager to leave. 'I will.'

12

'I'll be two minutes. Five, tops,' I promised Jacob, who was making himself comfortable in the passenger seat of my car. In the time it had taken me to exit said car, he'd already pushed his seat back as far as it would go, reclined to an almost 180° angle, and had his shoeless feet up on the dashboard. 'I just need to pick up some of Luca's grandfather's old photographs.'

'I'll be here,' Jacob called back, eyes closed as he waved one hand lazily in the air.

The late spring sun beat down on the cracked tarmac of the community centre car park, giving off a faint smell of hot tar. I saw Ivan sat on the stone steps out front, a strawberry-scented cloud of smoke surrounding him as he puffed on a vape, the sides of his cable knit cardigan cocooned tightly around his body despite the warm, early May sunshine.

'All right, Jenny?' He nodded. 'We've not seen you in a while.'

Something heavy and uncomfortable pressed deep in the pit of my stomach. I hadn't been to the community centre all week. I'd wanted to. I'd even sat in this very car park for over an hour on Monday evening, the backs of my trousers sticking to the car seat as it grew increasingly dim outside, my fingers gripping the door handle. But something stopped me from exiting the car. The very same something that had me replying to Luca's texts in a strangely formal way ever since the whole 'waking up in his bed' fiasco. Last night when I'd texted him to say I'd swing by today to grab the photos, I'd actually signed off with *kind regards*. Kind fucking regards! Every time I thought about him, that same scene played out lazily in my head – the intensity of Luca's gaze as he stared at me from beneath lashes still glistening with shower droplets, the flimsy-looking knot in his towel that looked as though any second it would just—

'Oh, you know, work, schmerk.' I shrugged noncommittally, the back of my neck suddenly very warm.

Ivan exhaled a sickly-sweet plume of white smoke, but the way he bobbed his head, like one of those dog figurines that sat in people's cars, told me he suspected another reason.

'Well, I'd better—' I gestured wordlessly to the door, doing some sort of weird double-pistol gesture I'd never done before in my life, and Ivan shuffled to the side, laughter rumbling at the back of his throat as he let me pass.

It took a second for my eyes to adjust from the bright sunshine to the dim light of the hall, as I squinted about the room in search of a box or envelope somewhere with JENNY written across it in giant, no-need-to-actually-talk-to-Luca letters. No such luck. I sighed, my gaze landing on Luca as if pulled towards him by an invisible string. Taut with tension, ready to snap at any moment.

He was at the far end of the hall, a jumble of mismatched chairs surrounding him from which ten pairs of feet swung several inches above the ground. They were trading a beat back and forth, Luca tapping a simple rhythm out on the drum wedged between his knees, and each child then taking it in turns to pass around a small hand drum and repeat it back to him. He was wearing a plain white t-shirt with an unbuttoned plaid shirt over the top, the sleeves of which were rolled up to reveal the perfect amount of forearm. How was it that he could wear a flannel shirt and look like . . . well, *that* – but if I did, I looked like I'd misplaced my axe? My cheeks flushed at the sudden, vivid memory of Luca in the kitchen last week, one arm flexed against the doorway as droplets of shower water ran slowly down his bare—

OK, they are just arms, Jenny. Cool it. Honestly, one glimpse of a half-naked, wet male and my uterus was ready to disregard hundreds of years of progress when it came to gender stereotypes and single-handedly volunteer to continue the human race. I mean, if someone had to do it . . . *No, pull it together, woman.* Luca looked up, his dark eyes catching mine and for one panicked second, I thought he might have heard my thoughts. He muttered something to Ivan who'd just returned from outside, passing him the drum before strolling over to where I was lingering awkwardly in the doorway, like an uninvited guest in someone's house. An unwelcome heaviness pressed against the sides of my stomach as I watched him approach, every muscle in my body tensing in anticipation.

'Hi.'

'Hi.'

I watched Luca's lips part and then close again, his brow furrowing as though he was suddenly unsure of what to say, his normal sarcastic aside never coming.

'I'm here for the photos?' I prompted, filling the silence.

'Yes, right. Photos.' Luca spun on his heel, striding through the dust motes dancing in the sunlight. 'I thought you'd said Monday.'

'Right, yeah, sorry about that. Work's been crazy,' I said as I followed him to the piano.

'Weird, I thought I saw your car driving away as I was leaving.'

I made some sort of noncommittal noise at the back of my throat, a cross between a snort and a questioning *huh*, but otherwise didn't trust myself to say anything more.

'I'm sorry about the whole Jasmine thing last week,' Luca said suddenly, his hand running roughly through his curls, giving the ends a sharp tug. 'She can be a bit much sometimes. Well, all the time, actually.'

'So, it's hereditary then?' A smile hooked at the corner of his lips, his eyes glistening as we resumed the game of chess we'd been playing since the first day we met.

'Here we are, one shoebox of memories as promised.' Luca handed me a battered old box, the cardboard so worn that the logo on the side was now nothing but a faded black smudge. Our fingers brushed, the pad of his thumb skimming across the inside of my wrist where my pulse was thrumming. He cleared his throat, taking a step back. 'I haven't had a chance to look through it yet, but my Dadaji seemed to think there might be

something of interest in there for your article. Something that might help.'

'No, this is great,' I said, riffling through the various
photographs and newspaper clippings to distract myself
from the weight of Luca's gaze. 'How's the fundraising
going?'

Luca didn't say anything, but the way his jaw locked
in a hard, tense line told me exactly how it was going. Or
not going. There'd been a flurry of donations after the
first article ran, but since then it had died down and it
was clear they were still a long way off their target.

'You still have a few weeks left until the concert,' I
said encouragingly, hugging the box tightly to my chest.
Luca nodded but his eyes were fixed on the back of the
room, a faraway look on his face as though he were
picturing an alternate reality. One where the hall was
no longer filled with music and laughter, where the front
doors were padlocked shut, papered over with posters
of club nights and circus shows.

'I just can't bring myself to imagine a time when this
place is no longer here. What sort of world do we live
in if that's allowed to happen? It's a lifeline for so many,
a safe haven where anyone can come and feel like they
belong, no matter how lost they might be.' Luca's voice
trailed off, eyes blinking fast and furious like a lightning
storm flashing across his face. He shook his head, his fingernail ticking over the edge of the piano. 'You wouldn't
understand.'

'Understand what?'

'What it's like to lose something you think you'll have
forever.'

I forced myself to blink. To breathe. *He doesn't know*, I reminded myself. But it felt like he'd taken an ice-cream scoop to my chest, a giant, melting chasm where my heart used to be.

'Well, we'd better make damn sure that doesn't happen, then.' I forced a smile, swallowing the razor-sharp lump in my throat, but still my voice had to scrape by to get out. I turned my attention to the photographs in my hands, not trusting that the tears wouldn't come if I stared for one second longer into Luca's hooded eyes.

'Wait, is that you?!'

I squinted at a sepia photograph of a middle-aged man sat cross-legged on a patch of lawn, the image drained of almost every drop of colour in the decades that had passed since it had been taken. An impressive-looking beard covered most of the man's face and neck, and yet his beaming smile was still the first thing I noticed. The second was the toddler running around in the background. He was holding a tambourine triumphantly in the air, a familiar cheeky grin on his face as if he'd just done something he shouldn't have. He was also butt naked.

'Give me that.' Luca lunged towards me with a horrified look on his face, but I was ready for him, darting to the side and holding the photograph up for closer inspection.

'Why am I not surprised that you were an exhibitionist even back then?' I teased, skipping around the opposite side of the piano as Luca made another failed attempt to claim the photograph for himself.

'I knew I should have checked the contents before giving it to you. That is *not* going in the paper.' Luca's eyes narrowed wolfishly as he slowly circled the piano. My heart raced as the two of us continued this slow, agonising dance, him going right, me going left, until I found myself on the side closest to the door. He held my gaze, unblinking as he followed my eyes to the double doors, a challenging cock of his eyebrow that said I dare you. I faked right and then made a run for it, but didn't get far before Luca's arm hooked itself around my waist, hoisting me off the ground as easily as a leaf on the breeze. He pulled me tightly against him, one of my legs between both of his, all my softest parts against all his hardest. His hand skimmed the underside of my shirt as he grabbed me, his touch rippling like fire across the bare skin of my stomach. I gasped, every single muscle seeming to melt at the sudden contact.

'Aha!' Luca shouted, snatching the photograph from my fingers and holding it aloft triumphantly.

'Are you two fighting?'

We turned to see a little girl, her rainbow-tights-clad feet glued to the floor as she twisted her little body from side to side. It bothered me that I couldn't remember her name, just that she'd lost her brother six months ago. Leukaemia. As though that were her identity now.

'Of course not.' I smiled, shimmying free from Luca's grasp and squatting down to her level. 'We were just playing a game.'

'And Miss Thompson lost,' Luca added smugly, tapping the back pocket of his jeans into which he'd slipped the incriminating photograph. I rolled my eyes at him, quickly attempting to straighten my shirt.

'Miss Thompson, are you a fan of *The Jungle Book*?' Luca asked loudly as I made to leave, spinning to look at me with the utmost seriousness as he swung his guitar across his chest. From across the room, ten pairs of excited eyes blinked expectantly up at me as Luca began strumming the tune of 'The Bare Necessities'.

'Oh, well, I should really be going—'

'You don't like *The Jungle Book*?' little ginger-haired Harry frowned, his mouth falling open in disbelief as though I'd just told him that Santa wasn't real. Nine more gasps echoed around the hall like a sudden gust of wind, an uncomfortable silence descending as Luca's fingers stilled on the strings.

'No, I love it! *Huge* fan. The biggest!' I corrected myself quickly, glaring at Luca until he started playing again. 'You're doing that annoying lip-twitching thing. Don't think I don't know what you're doing,' I hissed at him, taking the wooden stick with bells on it that Kiki ran to give me with a shy smile.

Luca walked back over to the children, dropping to his knees, and tapping out a beat on the pair of bongos for Harry to take over before waltzing back over to me.

'It's called a smile. You should try it sometime,' he said dryly, his scent – warm and surprisingly familiar – wafting over me as he came up behind me, close but not quite touching. My breath caught in my throat as his fingers wrapped around my wrist, and I tried to resist the urge to step back into him. 'Like this.' His voice vibrated right through me as his fingers interlaced with mine until I wasn't sure where I ended and he began, shaking whatever instrument I was holding in time with the beat. His grip loosened, leaving my skin peppered with goosebumps as he began a conga-style procession around the hall, a chaotic trail of percussion-wielding infants behind him. They were each playing their own tune and yet somehow, it all seemed to belong, weaving together to create something beautiful. Perfect, not so much. Following the script, definitely not. But beautiful none the less.

'There you are. I was about to send out a search party.'

I glanced at my watch. *Had I really been here over an hour?!*

'Sorry, I didn't realise the time.' I grinned sheepishly at an approaching Jacob, noting a scattering of crumbs stuck to the front of his crochet knitted t-shirt. 'I see you helped yourself to the emergency bag of crisps in the glove compartment. You do know those have been in there for over five years?'

Jacob turned a delicate shade of green, brushing most of the incriminating evidence over the floor.

'I'll just go grab my stuff,' I added, leaving him chatting to Luca as I went to retrieve the shoebox. With my back to them, the hairs on my arms stood to attention, bristling at something despite the sun beating down through the windows.

'Sorry we kept her so long, mate,' I heard Luca mutter faintly.

'Ah, no bother. It's nice to see her this passionate about something again. I've not seen her like that since before the accident,' came Jacob's voice.

'Accident?'

'Yeah, Joe's accident.'

'Joe, as in Jenny's fiancé, Joe?'

The box slipped through my fingers, landing on the floor with a thud as my head snapped up just in time to see the confusion on Luca's face. I waved my hands frantically in the air, trying to get Jacob's attention, to signal to him to stop, but he wasn't looking my way. *Shit*.

A mix of adrenaline and something else flooded through me, propelling me across the room before I could even register what was happening. But by the time I reached them, everything about Luca's face told me I was already too late. His eyes, heavy with a cocktail of sadness and pity that I knew all too well, found mine, full of questions I couldn't answer. Like why I'd never corrected him whenever he'd mentioned Joe. How I'd let him believe we were happily engaged. Gone along with it, in fact.

'Wait a second, you didn't know?' Jacob frowned, looking first at Luca and then at me. I stared at the shoelace of my left trainer, unsure of what to say.

'No, I didn't know.' Luca breathed out. 'I thought—' But his voice trailed off. I watched his eyes land on the third finger of my left hand where my engagement ring hung heavier than normal. Confusion, realisation, sorrow all swirled across his features as I watched him rearrange the pieces in his head. I blinked, looking away, having no desire to see the final picture.

'*Shit*. I've fucked up, haven't I? Jenny, I'm sorry.' Jacob blushed, swivelling to face me. 'I thought he knew, I thought you – God, me and my big mouth.' He smacked his palm against his forehead, silently berating himself.

'It's fine,' I said, forcing a tight smile. But it wasn't fine. Luca knowing meant that I couldn't pretend any more. At least not around him. It felt as if the walls were steadily closing in, the space in which Joe still existed getting increasingly smaller, the prospect of it disappearing completely looming ever closer. I kept swallowing even though my mouth was bone dry, as if that would help keep my feelings inside. The silence stretched on, awkward and uncomfortable, broken only by the occasional squeak of Jacob's Vejas against the varnished floor as he bounced anxiously on the balls of his feet. Luca's mouth parted and then closed again like a goldfish.

Jacob cleared his throat.

'I'll just—' He gestured vaguely over one shoulder, one hand gripping his upper thigh as though physically having to restrain himself from legging it straight for the exit. 'Meet you at the car?'

I nodded, keeping my chin glued to my chest to avoid catching Luca's eye as I hurried towards where my bag was slumped by the piano stool. I needed my bag to go home. And I needed to go home to see Joe. Home. The word jarred in my head, echoing round and round like a broken record caught on repeat. When had I started calling the pub home? Mine and Joe's flat was home. *He* was home. My Joe. A daydreamer, an eternal optimist, the last person who still used full-blown punctuation in text messages. And forever, the love of my life.

My left hand fished my bag out from under the stool, my right hoisting the cardboard box clumsily under one armpit. But my hands were clammy, the lid slick against my palm and the bottom gave way, falling with a loud thump to the floor, black-and-white photographs scattering in all directions. One lodged itself under the battered toe of a black leather boot that appeared in my line of vision. I knew even without looking up that it was Luca's. He must have followed me across the hall. We both dropped to our knees at the same time, taking it in turns to return the photographs to the box in silence. His fingers hovered over mine for a second, as though contemplating taking my hand in his. But he didn't.

'Jenny.'

My breath caught at the back of my throat and I looked up to see Luca kneeling before me, dark straight lashes framing his wide eyes. It was the first time he'd called me by my name. Normally, I was just Thompson to him. But hearing my name in his mouth made my heart leap into a full gallop.

'I'm sorry about what I said before – about you not knowing what it's like to lose someone.' His voice was soft, a deliberate slowness to his words indicating that he was choosing each one very carefully, his face twisting with something resembling embarrassment. 'I never would have said that if—'

'If you knew my fiancé died?'

He recoiled as though I'd just slapped him. But I didn't have the energy to choose my words with the same care that he was. I just wanted, no *needed*, to see Joe. Snatching the final photograph from Luca's hand I shoved it into the box and ran for the door, my shoulder ricocheting painfully against the doorframe as I went. I heard Luca calling after me but I didn't turn back.

13

I have this theory about love. It's all-consuming, somewhere along the way creeping into every nook and cranny, colouring every memory with its distinctive rosy hue. It's bold and unapologetic, not afraid to make mistakes or colour outside the lines, until one day you realise you can't see someone walking down the street swinging an orange Sainsbury's Bag for Life without remembering the argument you and your other half had one time in aisle six. When they couldn't make a decision on what to have for dinner and you stormed off, but they eventually tracked you down in the ice-cream section, holding a bouquet of flowers and the ingredients for pasta pesto. And that's cute when they're around, a funny anecdote to entertain friends with over dinner, or a shared glance exchanged outside a Sainsbury's Local reminding you of it all over again.

But what happens when they're gone? Where does that leave you? Broken? Incomplete? Immobilised, like I was right now? Forgetting why I'd even come into the pub storeroom to begin with as the naked lightbulb swung back and forth above me, illuminating the dingy three-metre by three-metre concrete floor where one

New Year's Eve Joe and I had made love. I shivered as I remembered how the cool stone had felt beneath my bare legs, the pleasant weight of Joe's body on top of me, all his parts slotting neatly between mine as though we'd been moulded specifically with each other in mind. My hand reached up, finding the spot on the back of my head that had bashed repeatedly against the side of a beer keg, the rhythmic clanging of metal drowned out by a distant, muffled cheer of *Happy New Year* and the cry of Joe's name escaping between my lips.

'Penny for your thoughts?'

I glanced over at Joe who was perched atop a stack of cardboard boxes, the memory fading to nothing in the musty air between us. Warmth bloomed across my cheeks. We both knew that he knew exactly what I'd been thinking. But we continued the charade all the same, neither of us wanting to pop the bubble by acknowledging Joe's unnatural ability to read my mind.

I pouted. 'They're worth more than that, don't you think?'

A smile flickered across Joe's lips as he got to his feet, stalking slowly across the room towards me. He moved one step closer and then another, something hot and fiery crackling behind his lashes as his continued advances forced me to retreat, a breath escaping my lips as the heel of my shoe hit the hard wooden edge of the wine rack that ran the entire length of the wall. He'd backed me into a corner. Quite literally. And there was nowhere on earth that I would rather be.

'They're fucking priceless,' he whispered in my ear, ducking his head to the space where my neck met my shoulder. He inhaled, a low moan rumbling through him as though my scent alone would be his undoing. I closed my eyes, chest heaving with longing as I sensed his hands brace against the wooden beam above my head, physically restraining himself from getting any closer. When I opened them again his nose was hovering a millimetre from mine, so close that my fingers itched to grab great fistfuls of his jumper and yank him towards me. Joe's lips parted, his smile widening in recollection. 'Especially the ones where you're naked and I'm doing that thing you like with my—'

'Jenny!'

Our eyes swivelled towards the door just as the old metal handle started to turn. My breath caught in my throat, echoing around the musty, cobweb-filled storeroom as my heart hammered against my ribcage, the way it always did when I knew Joe was about to leave me. Again. I stared up at him, his chin dipping slightly to the wool of his jumper as he smiled. A smile that said *I'll see you soon, then.*

'There you are,' Matt sighed, opening the door just enough to crane his ruddy-cheeked face around. He frowned at me. 'You OK? Look a little flushed . . .'

I puffed a stray strand of hair out of my face, my eyes fixed on the patch of concrete floor where Joe had been standing, as though if I stared hard enough, he might reappear. 'Fine,' I eventually croaked, a chill setting deep in my bones.

Matt just nodded, apparently satisfied with my monosyllabic response. 'We need more of the Chardonnay too, whilst you're at it. Oh, and don't forget the tonic waters,' he added, nodding his head at the pile of neatly stacked boxes that not two minutes ago Joe had been sat on. Tonic water. *That's* why I'd come in here.

'On it,' I said with a tight smile, bending down and running my palm over the top of the cold cardboard before hoisting two boxes onto my hip. You'd think I'd be used to it by now. Joe being there one second and the next, just not. Gone in the blink of an eye, in a single heartbeat. But it never got any easier. Having someone you love taken from you prematurely. I carried the boxes back to the bar, repeating the journey four times over, something heavy turning over in my chest every time I entered the empty room.

I don't really know how I spotted him. It was mid-Saturday afternoon, and some football match Matt informed me was a *big deal* was showing, so the pub was packed, people spilling out into the beer garden for the first time this year. Maybe it was the raucous cheer as someone scored that made me look up at precisely the right moment. Or maybe it was something else. The same something that caused a familiar tingle to shoot down the length of my spine as I saw Luca stood in the flagstone entrance, hands buried in his pockets, gaze roaming about the room. I'd not seen him since the whole Joe revelation. He'd tried calling. Twice. But I didn't want to have to explain myself. To admit that I'd let him believe my fiancé was still very much alive because the simple truth was just too painful to voice out loud. But also because I liked the idea that Joe and I, together, still existed in someone's reality. Even if it wasn't mine.

My heart began to race. I had about three seconds before he spotted me. And so, I did what any self-respecting thirty-year-old woman would do in my situation and dropped to the floor so fast that I fell smack on my arse. My head whipped one way and then the other, desperately searching for an escape route, but the pile of yet-to-be-unpacked boxes was still blocking the doorway, meaning there was no way around without standing up in Luca's direct line of vision. And *that* was not an option.

'Err, you OK down there?' Matt asked, frowning down at me as though I were an unwelcome bit of toilet paper stuck to the bottom of his shoe. A snicker from where Jacob was perched on a stool told me he'd already clocked Luca.

'Stop looking at me!' I hissed, slapping the backs of Matt's legs until he turned to face forwards, staring bewilderedly at Jacob in the hope he might provide some answers. 'Talk to me, Jacob,' I barked.

I heard Jacob's stool creak, picturing him doing his classic fake upper-body stretch, arms splayed out wide, body twisting from side to side as he snuck a glance over each shoulder whilst causing everyone within a 20-foot radius to turn and stare in his direction. Subtle it was not.

'Target six o'clock. Approximate distance 25 feet. He's reaching for something in his jacket . . . God, it should be illegal for anyone that hot to wear leather. It's really not fair on the rest of us.'

'*Jacob!*' I growled, wrinkling my nose at something foul-smelling in the bin beside me.

185

'Right, sorry. He's coming this way, 20 feet and closing in . . .'

I crouched lower to avoid detection. 'Remember, I'm *not* here. Got it?'

'Yes, got it,' Matt huffed, moving out of reach of my hands.

'15 feet,' Jacob confirmed. I hugged my knees tighter to my chest. '10 feet. 5. 4. 3. 2. 1—'

'All right, Jacob.'

I wedged myself further into the cut-out space underneath the sink as Luca's voice echoed directly above me. Matt's eyes flicked between me and Luca, with the furrowed brow of someone trying to solve a complicated maths equation at the sight of his grown-ass sister contorting herself into a painful-looking position that she'd most likely need assistance getting out of.

'Luca? Fancy seeing you here!' I winced at Jacob's over-the-top, not at all casual greeting. The man couldn't do subtle if his life depended on it.

'Don't think we've met. I'm Matt, Jenny's brother,' Matt said, extending a hand across the bar.

'Luca.'

'What can I get for you, Luca?' Matt asked.

'I was hoping to catch Jenny. Is she working today?'

'I've not seen her,' Jacob blurted out quickly. A little too quickly. I rolled my eyes, grateful for Matt's more measured response.

'She's not working today,' he confirmed, sneaking a quick wink down at me. I jabbed two fingers towards my eyes and pointed sharply upwards. 'She helps out every now and then but she's better at drinking the drinks than pouring them, if you know what I mean!'

Matt winced, his right leg buckling slightly as I uncurled one of my feet from where it was wedged beneath my bum and rewarded him with a sharp jab to the shin.

'Yep, I sure do,' Luca chuckled knowingly. I frowned. *What the hell did that mean?*

'Now there's a story I want to hear,' Jacob said eagerly, stool legs jarring gratingly against the floor as he scooted closer. My heart leapt up into my throat. I still hadn't told Jacob and Alice about the whole sleepover at Luca's and I planned on keeping it that way.

'I just came to return this,' Luca said, by some small miracle sidestepping the opportunity to regale my brother and best friend with embarrassing details of how I'd rugby-tackled my way into his flat at 1 a.m. stinking like a brewery and then passed out in his bed. I heard him place something on the bar, sliding it across the countertop, just as my right leg went into spasm. I clamped one hand over my mouth to stop the scream of pain vibrating at the back of my throat, the other desperately massaging the twitching muscles in my right calf. But my leg seemed to take on a life of its own, kicking out in protest at being stuck underneath my full weight for so long, and striking Matt in the back of the knee in the process.

'*Oww!*' His legs buckled, his elbows leaning atop the bar the only thing stopping him crumpling to the floor as they caught his fall. '*What the hell, Jenny?*'

I closed my eyes, willing the ground to swallow me whole. Peering up, I saw an angry-looking Matt, an amused-looking Jacob and a frowning Luca all staring down at me.

'Yes. I was just, err – yes.' I jumped to my feet, gesturing vaguely to the floor as though that were sufficient explanation for my hiding. Luca's teeth teased at his bottom lip.

'Have you been down there this whole time?' he asked, eyes twinkling with amusement.

'Of course not,' I scoffed, with a level of conviction I hoped would ward off any requirement for further explanation. Luca cocked one eyebrow dubiously, his lips pressed tightly together in a way that told me he was not convinced. 'Besides, who's stalking who now?' I went on. 'Let me guess, you just happened to be passing?'

'He came to return your wallet,' Matt explained, still rubbing the back of his leg as he waved my battered leather card holder in front of me. Huh, I must have dropped it leaving the community centre the other day. The fact that several days had passed and I hadn't even noticed it was missing said a lot about the current contents of my bank account. Or lack thereof. Warmth flooded my cheeks as I shoved it in the back pocket of my jeans.

'Thanks,' I muttered. 'But you really didn't have to come all this way just to return it.'

Luca shrugged. 'I did try and call . . .'

My cheeks burned some more. So, that's why he'd phoned. Another cheer rumbled from one side of the bar to the other like a Mexican wave, all the red-football-shirt-wearing men leaping to their feet while everyone dressed in blue sat with their head in their hands. Luca took a step forward, one forearm propped against the bar as he leaned in closer.

'Plus, I didn't know when you'd next come by the community centre after the other day . . .' Something uncomfortable knotted in my stomach.

'We really don't have to talk about it.'

Luca shook his head, but it was more at himself than at me. 'I made an assumption about your life when I had no place to. I mean, we hardly know each other. So – I apologise.' Across the bar, his eyes held mine. Wide and imploring and laden with something I'd not seen before. Sincerity, perhaps?

'It's fine. Consider it forgotten,' I said with an awkward smile, keen to steer us back to safer ground. This whole him-being-sincere business was creeping me out. 'Besides, if we're being honest, I made a few assumptions about you when we first met.'

Luca's mouth twitched with interest. 'Oh really? Like what?'

'Like . . .' I made a show of mentally running my finger down a very long list, 'you being a conceited asshole, for one. Obviously, I don't think that anymore.' I blinked innocently. 'Now I just think you're an asshole.'

Luca's laugh made his eyes flash a colour I'd never seen before, a shot of warm amber rippling through his ink-dark irises that was so beautiful I wanted to hear him laugh again just so I could see it a second time.

'You know what, I think I will get that drink,' Luca announced, slapping one hand on the counter as he claimed the stool next to Jacob. 'Something tells me I'm going to need it if you keep doling out compliments like that.'

'You asked.' I shrugged, pouring him a pint of whatever was on draught without even asking what he wanted and sloshing most of the contents over the sides of the glass as I placed it on the beer mat in front of him.

'How did you guess that I prefer to lick my beer straight off the bar?' But he raised the glass to his lips all the same, closing his eyes as he took a long sip. 'Speaking of *excellent* customer service—' he paused, staring pointedly at me, but I ignored his dig of a segue '—I'm playing at Brighton Music Hall next Saturday night. You should come.' The way Luca was staring at me made it seem as though the invitation was for me and me alone. My mouth fell open before I could stop it. *Wait, was this . . . was he . . . was he asking me on a date?* 'You should all come,' Luca added, and my shoulders relaxed a fraction when his eyes swung to Jacob and Matt, my bottom jaw finally remembering how to close.

Jacob's hand came down flat on the bar. 'Count me in!'

I glared at him, my eyeballs screaming *traitor* across the counter. *What?* his eyebrow said back.

'I'm on the late shift next Saturday but Jenny's free,' Matt volunteered for me.

'Um, excuse me? Since when did you become my social secretary?' I huffed, taking offence at the automatic assumption that I didn't have any plans. Which I didn't. But still, *he* didn't know that.

'Oh, I'm sorry. When was the last time you weren't in your pyjamas by 5 p.m. on a Saturday?' Matt asked, folding his arms across his chest. My cheeks flushed.

'2002,' Jacob teased, all three of them cackling with laughter.

'Just say yes, Thompson.' The way Luca's smirk stretched from ear to ear made my teeth grind with annoyance. Like he knew what was best for me.

'Why? Because every woman must accept any invitation that a man deigns to offer us?'

'No,' he said slowly, a lost look in his eyes, as though unsure how he'd navigated himself into a conversation around gender stereotypes. 'Because it'll be fun. That is, if you even know how to have fun.' He shrugged, feigning disinterest.

'I'm fun,' I said pointedly, lifting my chin at Jacob for backup, but he just dropped his head lamely from side to side before taking a giant gulp of wine. Matt was no better. He looked away when I turned to him, suddenly very interested in the game on the big screen. 'I *am* fun,' I insisted, resisting the urge to stamp my foot.

Luca grinned. 'Sounds more believable the more you say it! Come on, you know you want to really.'

'She does.' Matt nodded, answering for me.

My hand found my hip. 'I really don't.'

'You do,' Luca said simply, bumping one shoulder conspiratorially against Jacob's. 'She does.'

'She really does,' Jacob agreed.

'I do not!' I insisted. 'What is it with men and thinking they know better than all women?'

Luca held one hand to his chest in mock offence. 'I would never dare to suggest I know better than all women, Jenny.' His eyes flicked to mine. 'Just you.'

I threw the tea towel I was wiping the bar with in his direction but sadly he caught it before it could make contact with his face. Shame.

14

The number 2 bus on a Saturday night was one of those rare, magical places where two worlds collided. For the weary-looking travellers resting their heads on the juddering window, name tags bobbing against their work uniforms, the day was finally coming to an end. But for the dolled-up faces aglow with excitement at the prospect of what the evening ahead might bring, it was only just beginning. If my mum were here, she'd say there was some sort of life lesson there. Something about all endings being new beginnings. I tipped my chin in the direction of a man and woman on the opposite side of the bus, two rows in front.

'Mum and Dad having their first solo date night since baby,' I guessed. The dark circles beneath their eyes spoke of sleepless nights and 3 a.m. feeds, but the way their faces melted as the man flicked through photo after photo of a dark-haired, chubby-cheeked baby on his phone told of a love only a parent can truly comprehend.

'And right now, she's seriously doubting her mother-in-law's ability to keep their tiny human alive,' Joe added as we watched the man answer an incoming call, mouthing something silently to the woman before she grabbed the phone from him, her free hand performing some sort of frantic rocking motion in the air as she spoke to who-ever was on the other end of the line.

We were sat in our usual spot on the back row of the top deck, me next to the window on the left-hand side, Joe to my right. It was the perfect vantage point from which to play our favourite game. The one we always played whenever we were on the bus, or sat outside a cafe, taking it in turns to pick a stranger and write their life story.

'OK, my go.' Joe's eyes narrowed behind his glasses as they scanned the top deck of the bus, his lips pressing together in that way they did whenever he was concen-trating on something. He inclined his head in the direction of a young girl who'd just emerged from the stairwell. 'What about her?'

My eyes swivelled to the front of the bus, watch-ing the girl lurch unsteadily towards a vacant seat as the bus pulled away, grabbing onto a pole to stop her-self from falling. She glanced shyly around as though to check no one had seen this embarrassing series of events, her cheeks flushed with teenage humiliation. She couldn't have been older than sixteen, her rainbow-beaded phone strap swaying back and forth with the rhythm of the bus as she opened the camera app, her face filling the screen as she carefully applied a fresh coat of lip gloss.

'First date. Boy she's had a crush on forever at school finally asked her out. Sits behind him in maths class – no, English,' Joe auto-corrected, nodding his head approv-ingly as though that were the better fit.

'She lied to her parents about where she was going tonight, told them she was heading to a friend's house to study,' I pitched in, watching her remove an unseasonably thick turtleneck jumper and stuff it in her bag, revealing a black, lacy top with delicate spaghetti straps underneath.

'Do you remember that time we said we were having a sleepover at Jacob and Alice's but instead we camped out on the beach?'

I grinned, turning to look up at him. 'You mean the night I almost died of hypothermia?'

'Gah, it was romantic,' Joe maintained.

'It was February and you pressured me into going skinny-dipping.'

Joe raised an eyebrow. 'Hey, I don't remember you complaining when I suggested that particular activity. Besides, I warmed you up nicely afterwards, didn't I?'

My cheeks reddened as I remembered that night. Our first time. All fumbling fingers and shy glances and *is this OKs?* as our goose-pimpled bodies explored one another under the light of the moon, the waves lapping hungrily around our waists, before we zipped ourselves into a single sleeping bag, Joe's breath warm against my ear.

My phone buzzed in my jeans and I wiggled it out, a text from Jacob waiting for me.

You almost here???

'Ah, the classic triple question mark. Someone's in trouble,' Joe teased, reading the message over my shoulder.

'It's your fault I'm late,' I huffed, pursing my lips as I tapped out a reply to Jacob. I'd been ready half an hour before Google Maps told me I needed to leave, but I'd paced up and down the hallway for over 45 minutes waiting for Joe to show. Except he didn't. It was the first time I'd been home alone that Joe hadn't appeared at all. A fact I was trying really, *really* hard not to think about.

'Where were you, anyway?' I whispered accusingly, hitting send and sliding the phone back into my pocket.

'Oh, you know, places to go, people to see,' Joe said light-heartedly, stretching his legs out in front, one ankle crossed over the other.

'You're a figment of *my* imagination, the only person you should be seeing is me,' I muttered through clenched teeth, irritated he'd not been showing up as frequently the past week.

'Says the woman on her way to a date.' I knew Joe was just teasing, trying to make light of the situation as he always did. But it struck a nerve.

'It is *not* a date,' I said coolly. 'There's a whole group of us going. What else would you have me do on a Saturday night? Sit at home waiting for you to show up?'

The regret was instant, cold and sour-tasting in my mouth. I pressed my lips tightly together, but it was too late. The words were already out there.

'Ouch,' Joe breathed, his glasses slipping down his nose as his eyebrows shot the other way. I sighed, pressing my fingers to my temples.

'I'm sorry, I didn't mean that. It's just—' I paused, my fingernail scratching at the fabric of the seat, '—I just miss you, that's all.'

Joe closed his eyes briefly, his jaw clenching as though my admission had caused him actual physical pain – even though I knew that to be impossible.

'I miss you too,' he whispered eventually, his head hovering a centimetre above my shoulder.

I glanced out of the window. We were outside the big M&S on Western Road; just three more stops. I watched as an elderly couple crossed the street, arms linked, hands clutched tightly together. They were wearing one layer too many in that way people of a certain age often do, the map of wrinkles on their faces telling the most incredible story. One of laughter and happiness and past worries, all of which they'd shared together. The woman produced a packet of Werther's Original from her handbag, the man automatically reaching for one in a silent exchange so seamless it looked as though it had been performed a hundred times. It made me hopeful that the world had been kind to them, had allowed two young people who had fallen in love many decades ago a lifetime in each other's company. I wondered how couples got to that age unscathed? Happy. Together. Their arms still intertwined. They were the lucky ones, I guess.

'Excuse me, is anyone sitting there?'

I turned to see a middle-aged woman laden down with shopping bags on either arm, her fringe stuck to her dewy-looking forehead. She was staring hopefully at the empty seat next to me. The one that just five seconds ago, Joe had occupied. The hole in my chest widened some more.

'No,' I smiled tightly, shuffling closer to the window. 'No one's sitting there.'

Jacob was hard to miss as he stood waiting for me at the top of the stairs leading down to the lower promenade. He was wearing an oversized asymmetrical jumper made entirely of mohair or the pelt of some other poor innocent creature, the left side falling further down his ripped white jeans than the right, a line of tiny metal studs trailing down either arm. He tapped the screen of his phone to check the time, the toe of his neon-pink Converse drumming impatiently against the gum-strewn pavement.

'Hey! Sorry I'm late.' I grinned apologetically, pulling Jacob in for a hug before he could chastise me for my tardiness. As we pulled apart, he did a double take, his mouth opening as though about to say something, but nothing came out; instead, he silently gawped at me.

'What?' I asked, my hand automatically flying to my hair. 'Is my hair doing that weird static thing?'

Jacob shook his head, mouth still opening and closing as though his brain were trying to remember how to form words. 'Nope, your hair looks good. Your outfit looks good. Jenny Thompson, you look *hot!*'

'*Shhhh!*' I shushed him, my cheeks burning as several heads turned in our direction, eyes travelling down my bare legs. I tugged at the distressed hem of my denim skirt, cursing the bold woman who'd strutted up and down in front of the hallway mirror an hour ago, a certain confidence to her that had abandoned me suddenly.

'Say cheese.' The flash of Jacob's phone took me by surprise as he snapped a picture, a whooshing sound two seconds later confirming he'd already sent it to someone.

'What are you doing?' I asked, my cheeks flooding with heat. At this rate I needn't have bothered with blusher.

'Just keeping Alice up to speed.' Jacob shrugged innocently, his phone buzzing in his hand.

'*Is she wearing lipstick??!! Aubergine emoji, tongue emoji, winky face emoji,*' I read over Jacob's shoulder, rolling my eyes. 'It's tinted lip balm actually,' I said pointedly, rubbing my lips together. Determined to change the subject, I nudged Jacob. 'Anyway, what about you? I'm loving the outfit. It's giving me chic but aggressive camel vibes.'

Jacob made a face. 'I don't like camels. Anything that can go a week without a drink can't be trusted. Speaking of drinks, I might die of thirst shortly if we don't find a beverage.' Jacob bugged his eyes out and I rolled mine, linking my arm through his as we descended the stairs towards Brighton Music Hall.

In the alfresco venue, people were spilling off the ends of the wooden picnic benches that dotted the sea-facing terrace, all littered with empty beer glasses and perspiring wine coolers that sparkled beneath the festoon lights strung high above. It was still mild, the heat from earlier in the day warming the evening air as jackets lay abandoned on benches, sunburnt shoulders and candy-cane-striped tan lines on full display. Three hollowed-out beach huts on a raised wooden platform formed the stage, a neat row of fully functioning beach huts in cute pastel shades flanking it on either side. The sun shimmered behind the stage, ribbons of golden light streaming across an endless horizon of blue.

'*Jenny! Jenny, over here!*'

'Looks like someone's trying to get your attention.' Jacob nodded his head in the direction of one of the tables near the front where Jasmine was holding a wine glass aloft, beckoning us over.

'Oh, that's Jasmine, Luca's cousin,' I said, grabbing Jacob's hand and navigating a safe path through the crowd.

'Figures, with those cheekbones. Honestly, what is with the genes in that family?' Jacob muttered, sounding half-impressed, half-irritated.

'You made it! Luca said he'd invited you, but he wasn't sure if you were going to come,' Jasmine cried as we eventually emerged through a scrum of lads wielding Coronas, jumping to her feet and pulling me in for a hug. 'And wow, you look a-mazing!'

'Mhmm, doesn't she?' Jacob mumbled under his breath, raising an I-told-you-so eyebrow at me.

'Well, you've only ever seen me in last night's clothes with crazy bedhead, so I feel like the only way was up.' I laughed nervously, letting my hair fall in front of my face.

'Wait, what's this about last night's clothes?' Jacob's head appeared at my shoulder and I bit my tongue, forgetting I hadn't told him or Alice about my accidental sleepover at Luca's.

'How rude of me. Jasmine, this is Jacob. Jacob, Jasmine,' I said quickly, thrusting Jacob forwards in the hope that he wouldn't ask any more questions.

'I'm the best friend,' Jacob announced, his hand hovering in the space between them. Jasmine ignored it, placing her tiny hands on his shoulders and planting a kiss on either cheek.

'I'm the cousin,' she declared, before producing two glasses of wine as if from nowhere. 'And the fun one,' she whispered with a wink, pressing them into mine and Jacob's hands.

'A girl after my own heart,' Jacob whooped with delight, raising the glass to his lips and taking a long sip. 'I like this one, Jenny, we can keep her.'

Jasmine hooted with laughter, several men in the immediate vicinity shamelessly ogling her, not that she noticed. She flicked her long, black hair over one shoulder and gestured for us to sit.

'I read your article about the community centre the other day,' Jasmine said, her kohl-lined eyes closing briefly before flashing open with that same intensity that I recognised in Luca. 'You clearly have a talent for writing, Jenny, just like my cousin.' She turned and nodded in the direction of the stage. I followed her gaze, my stomach doing a little somersault when I realised that the music I'd been tapping my foot along to was Luca's. He was stood in the middle of the stage, guitar slung over one shoulder on a worn leather strap, the smile of someone doing what they were born to do stretched wide across his face.

'You seem to make a great team, you and Luca,' Jasmine commented, her eyes creasing in a way that made me wonder whether Luca had told her about Joe.

'Don't they just,' Jacob agreed, batting his eyelashes innocently at me across the table. I crossed my ankles, taking a sip of my wine to resist the urge to kick him under the table. If his jeans weren't dry clean only, he might not have been so lucky.

The evening passed in a rosé-filled blur, the sun dipping further and further behind the horizon before it disappeared altogether. I slowly found myself relaxing, laughter bubbling freely out of me as though it had been contained for too long and was finally spilling over. It was so natural that I couldn't help but think how different I felt, sat on that uneven wooden bench with a folded-up coaster wedged under one leg. I felt light and almost whole, not weighed down or ripped apart like I had for most of this year.

'This final song's for anyone out there who's ever had their heart broken,' Luca breathed into the microphone, his fingers picking lightly across the strings of his guitar as he spotted me in the crowd. He blinked, a look of surprise flashing across his face for the briefest of seconds before softening into a smile that made my insides fizz. He held my gaze as he started to sing and I found I couldn't look away, everything and everyone around me seeming to fade.

> *You promised we'd stick it out through thick and thin,*
> *But then the walls came down, my world's tumbling in,*
> *And I'm left picking up the pieces of this mess you made,*
> *You left my heart all broken and frayed.*

The hum of the crowd had quietened, heads turning towards the stage, shoulders swaying as they listened to the words that hit so deep inside me it was as though Luca had seen inside my very soul.

When I smell your perfume on a stranger in the street,
My heart breaks in two, it forgets to beat,
I thought all love ever did was break and end,
But on the Monday when I met you . . .

Luca's breath echoed down the microphone as he paused, just long enough for his eyes – heavy with too many emotions to name – found mine once more.

. . . I watched it begin again.

Luca's fingers strummed with finality across the strings, everyone around me jumping to their feet as the crowd broke out into rapturous applause. But I couldn't move. My heart was thumping in my chest as if I'd just run a marathon, my fingers gripping the edge of the table as my brain whirred into rewind, a rush of speeded-up colours and memories as I flicked back to that day. The day I'd first met Luca. I was on my way to work so it had to be a weekday. But was it a *Monday*? Even if it was, it didn't mean it was *that* Monday. The one Luca was talking about. Statistically, in fact, it was highly unlikely.

'You OK?' Jacob mouthed at me when he saw I was the only one still seated.

I nodded with a smile, jumping to my feet before he could put two and two together. I reached for my wine glass, downing its contents in one, but I'd misjudged quite how much was left and a trickle of wine escaped out the corner of my mouth, running down my chin.

'Hi,' came a familiar voice behind me.

I swallowed audibly, quickly wiping my chin on the neckline of my t-shirt before spinning around. Only I forgot I was still stood in the gap between the table and the connecting bench, the wood slamming into my shins as my top half buckled over. My cheek landed hard against Luca's chest, his hands gripping the bare skin of my arms to cushion my fall.

'Woah, easy there. People might think you're falling for me, Thompson,' Luca teased, the left side of his mouth curling upwards. I straightened up, but not before I felt his heart thumping against my ear, beating double time in tandem with my own. I suddenly didn't know where to look, faffing about with tucking my hair behind my ear even though it was already there. Luca dipped his mouth closer to me so I could hear him better over the crowd.

'I'm glad you came.' His voice was low. Husky.

'Me too.'

'What did you think of the set?'

I nodded enthusiastically, giving a dorky thumbs up which instantly made my cheeks warm with regret. But I didn't know how to articulate it. That feeling of having witnessed someone perfectly express how I'd been feeling for so long. Luca opened his mouth as if to say something else, but another band had already taken to the stage, the sound of an electric guitar playing the opening bars of

Kings of Leon's 'Sex on Fire' sending everyone flocking onto the dance floor.

'Ohmygod, I *love* this song!' Jacob squealed with delight, grabbing my hand and dragging me along after him. I looked back helplessly and saw that Jasmine had done the same to Luca, whose protests she either couldn't hear or was choosing to ignore as she pushed him after us. We found a small circle of space among the throng of bodies, Jacob jumping on the spot in time with the beat. As the chorus kicked in, he grabbed both my wrists, raising them skywards as he sang up at the stars like they were paid spectators at his own concert. He dropped to one knee, performing some sort of air guitar solo, much to the delight of the surrounding crowd. I giggled, feeling any remaining tension melt away, my hips loosening as they started to sway in time with the music. At first Luca and I were on opposite sides of the tiny circle that our group had formed, but the space between us got smaller and smaller with each new song and it wasn't long before my hips were bumping against his, skin sparking against skin as our arms touched. I stumbled slightly as someone tried to push their way past, but Luca steadied me, his hand against my hipbone. And suddenly, we were no longer just dancing. We were dancing *together*, his hand still on my hip, mine finding its way to his shoulder. It felt right, natural even, our bodies moving as one as if we didn't even have to think about it.

It was becoming harder to concentrate on what song was playing, where Jacob was, anything that wasn't the feeling of Luca's hand against the dimples at the base of my spine. A gentle yet firm pressure that made me want to press my body even closer against his, to take his little finger – which was brushing against the bare skin above the waistband of my skirt – between my teeth and see if he tasted like he smelt. Warm and spicy, like aged leather.

People started to drift apart around us, limbs stilling by their sides, and I realised with a surge of disappointment that the song was over. Luca took a small step back, his hand falling from my hip as he swept his curls out of his face. But then his mouth was against the sensitive bit of skin behind my ear, his breath sending shivers down my spine.

'Do you want to get some air?'

I nodded, suddenly dizzy, and let him take my hand, leading me away from the dance floor, round a barrier, past a security guard who Luca greeted with a lift of his chin, and out onto the promenade. A couple sat with their feet dangling over the edge of the esplanade, shoes mere inches from the pebbles on the beach below, a grease-stained bag of chips ripped open between them. Smokers congregated against the wall, cigarette tips illuminating their faces as a cloud of grey smoke hovered above them. But the further we walked, the fewer people there were until, eventually, it was just us. Like we were the last two people left in this world.

'I like to walk along here after a gig, come back down to earth a little bit. Just me and the ocean.' Luca exhaled, running his fingers along the metal railings as we walked.

'Oh, sorry; should I leave you to it?'

'No, no,' he said quickly, his fingers weaving themselves through mine as I hesitated, unsure whether to turn back or keep going. He pulled me along after him, making the decision for me. 'It's nice to have the company for once.'

And so we walked, listening to the sound of the music growing fainter with each step, but it wasn't until we'd passed three beaches that I realised our fingers were still interlinked. I looked down at my hand in his, surprised to see how natural it looked, like two pieces of a puzzle slotted together. Luca seemed to realise at the same time, his own eyes dropping to the space between us with a frown, and we both let go with a shy, blinking-too-fast smile.

'I liked that last song you played,' I said, clearing my throat a little too loudly.

'Oh yeah?'

'Mmm, I think it was my favourite.'

There was a pause before Luca replied. 'Really?'

'What?' I asked, half-laughing up at his dubious expression. 'What's wrong with that?'

Luca shook his head, some unspoken thought burying itself into the v that had appeared on his forehead. 'Nothing, it's just – out of all of my songs that's probably the most depressing.'

I frowned. 'I don't think it was depressing. It was honest. Raw. It was kind of beautiful, actually.'

'Beautiful,' Luca mused quietly to himself, both elbows leaning on the mint-green railings as we came to a stop.

'Did you write it about Rachel?'

I heard his breath catch sharp and fast at the back of his throat and his head snapped to look at me, a flash of surprise across his face at the sound of her name. And something else. Something darker. Gone was the loose-hipped, carefree guy I'd been dancing with not ten minutes earlier. He'd been replaced by this tense version of Luca who couldn't quite meet my gaze, the muscles in his forearms rippling beneath his t-shirt.

'Jasmine might have mentioned her,' I admitted guiltily, wishing I'd kept my mouth shut.

Luca's jaw clenched, his knuckles turning white around the railings.

We stood in silence for a long time, nothing but the sound of the waves lapping at the pebbles on the beach below, the air thick with salt and words unspoken. That stomach-twisting feeling of having said the wrong thing squirmed inside of me, causing my feet to scuff noisily against the pavement.

'Yes,' Luca said eventually. He was still staring determinedly at the horizon, the sky now so dark that it was almost impossible to tell where it ended and the ocean began. 'Yes, I wrote it about Rachel,' he repeated, faltering ever so slightly when he said her name. 'And someone else.'

My heart sped up in my chest but I asked a different question to the one I really wanted to ask. 'Did it help?'

I hated the hope in my voice, lingering pathetically in the still, warm air between us. Luca didn't answer for a while and I wondered if he'd heard it too. And realised that I wasn't asking just for him, but also for me. My eagerness to find some secret solution, some miracle cure that would stop this constant ache in my heart, made my eyes drop to the floor. Eventually Luca let out a long breath, as if he was letting go of something, blood rushing back to his fingers as he loosened his grip on the railings.

'Did it help me forget that the woman I thought I was going to spend the rest of my life with was having an affair with her boss for the better part of our entire relationship? No,' he answered simply, a small apologetic shrug of his shoulders like he knew I was hoping for a different answer. 'But there's something powerful about being able to confine all that crap into a three-minute song and then walk away. That's why I play it last. It gives me somewhere to channel all those emotions – to acknowledge them, to grieve them, but then leave them all on the stage. They would have totally consumed me by now otherwise.'

'People haven't always been there for you, but music has.'

Luca nodded. 'Something like that.'

His hand fell to his side, his fingers brushing against mine once more. But this time neither of us moved away. We stood there, shoulder to shoulder, staring out at the ink-black sea, our index fingers slowly intertwining as my breath escaped in giant white puffs. The air heavy with expectation, silent except for the sound of the waves lapping at the shore below.

'You're not wearing your ring.' It was more of a statement than a question, Luca's voice drifting on the still night air. But when we turned to each other, I saw his eyes scanning my face, searching for an answer. I looked down at my hand in his, our fingers interlinked, his thumb over mine. The intimacy of it surprised me, seeing our woven hands cast their shadow on the pavement behind us. It was only then that I saw my ring finger was bare. Nothing but the faint indentation to prove I'd ever previously worn it. I felt the world shift for a second, as though the earth was rotating faster than normal, trying to snatch something away from me that I was desperately clinging on to. Panic bubbled up inside me, the weight of it crushing my airway like a hand tightening around my throat. I snatched my hand free, what had previously felt so right suddenly feeling very, very wrong.

'Sorry, should I not have—?' Luca frowned, his voice trailing off as he shoved his hand deep into the pocket of his jeans. I felt an unexpected pang of guilt for making his shoulders sag that way, but the guilt I felt for forgetting my ring, tonight of all nights, overshadowed it completely.

'I – I must have left it at home,' I stammered, but my brain was working overtime, retracing my steps. I was definitely wearing it yesterday. One of the tiny claw feet had snagged on the hem of my jumper as I was leaving work, pulling a thread loose. Did I take it off before showering this morning? Was it lying forgotten in the little china dish on my bedside table? Or had it fallen off somewhere, lost forever? A sharp pain shot through my chest at the thought, and I gasped, some nonsensical part of my brain telling me to clamp my hand over my heart or it might very well break in two.

This was what always happened. Every single time I tried to pretend for one second that I was moving forwards. It was like quicksand pooling around my ankles; the more I tried to take a step forward, the deeper it pulled me down. I wanted nothing more than to run back home right that second, in the tatty old ankle boots that Joe had bought me for my 25th birthday. The ones that had had a tiny stone stuck in between the grooves of the right sole for as long as I could remember.

'Jenny,' Luca said softly. So softly that it made me feel worse. I didn't deserve his kindness, or his sympathy, or whatever enormous thing he was trying to convey with just that breath of a word. He took a step towards me, but I ducked away before his outstretched hand could reach me.

'I have to go,' I said quickly, biting the inside of my cheek so hard I could taste the metallic tang of blood.

'Oh. Right. Well, at least let me walk you—'

'No need, I can walk myself.' I was already striding away from him, towards a taxi that had just pulled into a lay-by next to the pier.

'Jenny!' Luca called after me, his voice travelling over my shoulder in the wind. I was running now, my lungs burning for oxygen as I sprinted as fast as my legs would carry me towards the waiting car. I yanked the back door open, trying not to look at my ringless finger under the dim glow of the streetlight, and hurled myself into the back seat. I clamped my eyes tightly shut, the blood pounding in my ears not enough to silence the petrifying thought that my forgotten ring, on tonight of all nights, was somehow symbolic. That it meant something.

'It *doesn't* mean anything,' I whispered furiously to myself. 'I just forgot to put it on, that's all.'

'What's that, love?' came the cabbie's voice through the flimsy plastic screen. My eyes blinked open to see the taxi driver's gaze fixed on me in the rear-view mirror, probably trying to gauge if I was a puke risk or just plain old crazy.

'Nothing,' I said quietly, my fingertips tracing the soft circle of skin where my ring used to sit. 'Please just take me home.'

15

'You should call him.'

I gawped at Alice, mouth open. As if she'd just suggested I jump off Beachy Head stark naked.

'Call who?'

Alice rolled her eyes, her pursed lips confirmation that she wasn't willing to play this game. She took a sip of her wine, suddenly very interested in her nail beds. She was waiting me out and I knew it, but it didn't make it any less annoying.

'Why would I call him?' I huffed eventually, dropping the *I don't know who you're talking about* act. I wiggled the third and fourth fingers of my left hand, a habit I'd developed ever since I'd found my ring lying forgotten on my bedside table when I got home from Luca's gig. The metal band felt cool and reassuring against my skin.

'Because you haven't stopped thinking about him since Saturday night.'

'Because you just gave me vodka instead of gin,' Jacob spluttered, grimacing as he returned his glass to the beermat in front of him.

'Because you've been polishing that same pint glass for fifteen minutes.'

I put the glass pointedly down on the bar, watching it sparkle under the lights as I tucked the tea towel under the tie of my apron.

'Because your face is the colour of a tomato right now.' Jacob grinned. He was enjoying this game way too much.

'Because—'

'OK!' I held up both hands in surrender, cutting Alice off before she could add yet more fuel to the already-blazing inferno. Alice swapped her half-full glass of Chardonnay for Jacob's vodka tonic much to his delight, a snail trail of condensation marking their silent exchange.

'What's the big deal anyway? You see each other practically every week already.' I'd always envied Alice's ability to view everything in black and white. Occupational hazard for a doctor, I guess. But this *thing* with Luca was so far from black and white. It was an ever-changing kaleidoscope of colours, some of which I'd never even seen before. The heat I'd felt on Friday night when his fingers had touched mine was a blistering hot red. The sense of happiness I'd started to feel at the prospect of seeing Luca at the community centre, a bright sunshine yellow. The ripples of green when I clocked Harry's mum purposefully drop her car keys in front of Luca, her Pilates-toned derriere angled in his direction as she bent down in slow motion to retrieve them. A washed-out grey-blue surrounding the whole picture, a swirling mix of confusion and sadness.

'He's a *friend*, right?' The probing lilt of Alice's voice confirmed she thought otherwise, but she knew me too well to dive right in and say what we both knew to be true. Luca wasn't a friend. I wasn't sure what he *was*, of anything really, but after Saturday night, I was certain he *wasn't* a friend.

I blinked, processing.

'I guess.'

'So, *friends* phone each other and thank them for a fun night.'

I rolled my eyes at her, grateful for the sight of Old Sam, one of our regulars who'd had a full head of brilliant white hair for as long as I could remember, approaching the bar. Some things at least never changed. I busied myself with pouring him a pint of Guinness, not needing to wait to hear his order which had been the same for the past fifteen years. As the dark, stormy liquid swirled in the glass, I glanced back over at Alice who was hunched over her phone, her face illuminated with a soft blue glow as she scrolled purposefully through something on the screen. Jacob was leaning over, whispering something intently in his sister's ear – although she simply shook her head, batting him away when he tried to snatch the phone from her.

'Keep the change.' Old Sam smiled, pressing a crisp £5 note into my hand. He was probably the only patron left who still paid in cash. As I slotted his £5 note neatly into the designated section of the till, I frowned. The spot at the side of the register where my phone always sat while I was on shift was empty. I patted the back pockets of my jeans, rooted around in the front pocket of my apron. Empty. A lump lodged itself at the back of my throat as my eyes darted back to a suspiciously pleased-looking Alice. She had my phone in her right

hand, the name *Luca* appearing on the screen as a ringing tone buzzed aggressively through the speaker.

'Give me that!' My feet left the floor as I performed
a full-body lunge across the bar, swiping the still-ringing
phone from Alice's hands.

'Hello?'

His voice took me by surprise, the phone slipping
through my fingers onto the floor with a clatter. For one
panicked second I froze, all three of us looking down as
though it were a grenade about to explode, before Luca's
voice buzzed through the speaker once more.

'*Hello?*'

I dropped to the floor, all fingers and thumbs as I hot-
potatoed the phone from one hand to the other, before
eventually managing to take it off speaker. My thumb hovered over the End Call button, all red and enticing. But I
knew he'd only call back, so I raised the phone to my ear.

'*Yo!*'

Jacob spluttered most of his drink over the bar top,
Alice almost falling off her stool. I'd never said *yo* in my
entire life, so God knows why that was the first word
that popped into my panicked brain.

Luca sighed impatiently, clearly not recognising my
voice, which wasn't surprising considering the whole *yo*
debacle. 'Sorry, who is this?'

I winced.

'It's Jenny. Jenny Thompson.'

There was a pause.

'Hello Jenny. Jenny Thompson.'

My grip tightened around the phone, every second of
silence that ticked by more painful than the last. Why

was this so awkward? It's not like anything happened the other night. We'd walked. We'd talked. Nothing more. Maybe the fact nothing had happened *was* the issue?

'Did you just phone to say hello, or—?'

'Yes. I mean, no. I was . . . I was just phoning to . . . Apologise. For. The. Other. Night.' My voice was almost robotic as I followed along with the words Alice was mouthing at me across the bar.

'No apology necessary,' Luca said simply, and my heart slowed a fraction in my chest.

'Well, sorry for being all weird and disappearing on you like that.'

'Hey, I would have done the same. If you see a taxi on a Saturday night at peak time, you've just got to take it. Those things are about as rare as unicorns.' I heard my breath echo down the phone, a sigh of appreciation at all the things Luca had chosen not to say. All the things he knew I wasn't ready to talk about.

'Was that it?' His voice was warm with humour as it crackled down the phone.

'Um . . .'

Alice mouthed something at me that I couldn't make out.

'I, err . . .'

Jacob performed some sort of weird hand-to-mouth action, miming cutting something in front of him and chewing it. What was this, fucking charades? I'd always been terrible at charades. No one wanted me on their team at Christmas.

'Food!' I blurted out before I could stop myself. The silence on the other end of the line was so deafening I had to remove the phone from my ear and check Luca hadn't ended the call. I wouldn't have blamed him if he had.

'Sorry?'

'I said, do you eat food?' I shook my head at the words coming out of my mouth. How was that any better? Judging by the way Jacob covered his face with his hands, he shared my pain.

'Yes, Thompson, I eat food.' Luca's tone was light, tinged with humour, and I could just picture that teasing hint of a smile playing with the corner of his mouth.

I pushed my bottom lip forward with my tongue.

'Of course you do. You are human,' I groaned, spinning in a circle and yanking at the end of my ponytail with more force than a woman who already lost a considerable ball of hair in the shower every day should. Alice had produced a medical pad from her bag, pen lid clamped between her teeth as she hastily scribbled something down before turning the page to face me.

Ask him if he wants to grab dinner!!

I shook my head at her, trying to ignore her aggressive stabbing of the page with her pen to get my attention. Oh, fuck it.

'How about you come to the pub for dinner on Friday? My treat, for disappearing on you the other night.' I only realised I was holding my breath when Luca's answer came, short and blunt.

'I can't.'

'Oh. Sure. No problem. Forget I even asked,' I said, forcing a casual indifference despite the sting of rejection.

I was about to hang up when Luca added, 'I'd like to, it's just . . .'

'It's fine,' I said abruptly, cutting him off before I could hear whatever lame excuse he'd come up with in those five seconds of awkward silence.

'If you'd let me get a word in, I was going to say I've already got plans on Friday night.'

Of course he did. This was the guy who had women throwing phone numbers at him left, right and centre. He probably had a date lined up every night this week.

'Wild Friday night plans, you know how it is!' Luca added, his voice light and playful as though he could sense my discomfort down the phone.

'Oh, sure, I've actually got plans on Friday myself,' I found myself saying. Jacob and Alice both frowned at me, clearly struggling to keep up with the conversation.

'Really?'

'Yep.'

'Because you were the one who suggested Friday in the first place . . .' Luca reminded me. There was no hiding the amusement in his voice now. He was backing me into a corner, and he knew it.

'Yeah, well, I only just remembered. My diary at the minute is just *wooo*—'

Alice tapped her pen against her glass, giving me a sobering shake of her head, whilst Jacob just gawped at me open-mouthed, like I was some exotic animal in a zoo.

'Ah, that's a shame.' Luca's voice vibrated in my ear. 'Why's that?'

'Well, I was going to ask if you fancied joining me? I need to make a start on getting the community centre vaguely presentable for the concert, so I've got a hot date with a mop and some bunting, but there's always room for one more.'

My cheeks flushed, realising I'd jumped to the wrong conclusion when it came to Luca. Again. I stared across the bar at Alice and Jacob, both of them blinking expectantly at me, Alice quite literally on the edge of her seat. I squeezed my eyes shut and tried my best not to overthink it.

'Sure.'

'Shall we say 7:30?'

A flock of tiny butterflies took flight inside my belly, leaving me breathless.

'7:30. Yes, perfect. That's my favourite time to meet.' I cringed, shoving my whole fist into my mouth to stop yet more word vomit spewing out. Jacob and Alice gave each other the *did she really just say that* side-eye, lips pressed into tight lines to keep from laughing.

Luca just chuckled on the other end of the phone.

'I'll see you then.'

'See ya,' I said awkwardly, before stabbing at the End Call button and throwing my phone on the counter with a sigh of relief.

'I genuinely have no words for what I just witnessed,' Alice said soberly.

Jacob looked perplexed. 'How the hell did you manage to get a date after that absolute car crash, and I can't get one after messaging a guy for two months?'

'It's *not* a date,' I said firmly, twisting my engagement ring round and round my finger. Calling it that did something weird and twisty to my stomach, like I was approaching the top of a roller-coaster and knew the drop that awaited me on the other side. 'I'm just going to help him set up the community centre, that's all.'

'That's all,' Jacob mimicked to his sister, the two of them dissolving into fits of giggles. When they eventually came up for air, Jacob turned to me with a judgemental eye. 'OK, in all seriousness though, what are you going to wear?'

'You don't still have those knickers with the hole in, do you?' Alice said sternly. 'I've told you before, Jenny, so-old-they're-falling-apart is not the same as crotchless panties.'

My cheeks flushed, my pulse beating hot and fast beneath my skin. Just the thought of Luca seeing me in my underwear was enough to make me hot with embarrassment, my thighs sticking uncomfortably to the insides of my jeans. Not that there was even a remote possibility of Luca seeing me in my underwear. Right?

Oh God.

As someone who has an unhealthy love for anything with an elasticated waistband, there have been very few occasions in my life when I've felt overdressed. In fact, only one comes to mind. I was five years old and adamant that feeding the ducks at our local park was the perfect occasion to wear my sparkly replica of Belle's dress from *Beauty and the Beast*. With my yellow organza ballgown and matching butter-coloured wellies, the ducks had given me some very judgemental looks. But stood in the doorway of the community centre, I realised I was, without a doubt, 100% overdressed.

Luca had made out like we'd just be moving a few chairs, maybe hanging a bit of bunting. Then again, he'd also made it sound like it was just going to be the two of us. So, I was somewhat surprised when I arrived at 7:30 p.m. on the dot to find a small army of men, all dressed in overalls, pushing paint rollers up walls and skimming plaster over holes. It was like something out of *60 Minute Makeover*. I stared regretfully down at my heeled sandals, only just realising that an open toe was a very bold choice for someone whose non-pedicured feet had been in hibernation all winter. The fingers of my right hand tugged at the hem of my dress, which skimmed just above the knee, as though willing it to magically grow a few inches. The plastic handle of the takeaway bag I was carrying cut sharply into my fingers, the grease-stained cardboard boxes heavy with battered fish, chips with lashings of salt and vinegar, and a sausage for me.

'*You're the only person I know who doesn't order fish at the fish and chip shop. You just can't say no to a cheeky sausage, can you?*' Joe's voice rang in my ears and, as I closed my eyes, I could picture his eyebrows jiggling mischievously at the double entendre. I turned, glancing over my shoulder. Nothing. The flagstones behind me were empty and cold. He wasn't there. Of course he wasn't, but my heart sunk an inch deeper in my chest all the same.

Loitering in the shadow of the doorway with Joe's voice still ringing in my ears, I was seriously fighting the urge to just go. No one had seen me. I could message Luca from the car, pretend something had come up. I could be home watching a movie with Joe in less than fifteen minutes. Twenty if I stopped by the Tesco Extra en route and picked up a tub of Ben & Jerry's. But as I reached for the door handle, Luca looked up, his eyes somehow finding mine through the chaos, like two magnets drawn together. He balanced his paintbrush atop the open tin of paint beside him, straightening up with the pained squint of someone who'd spent far too long in a crouched position. He walked towards me, his scruffy trainers and paint-splattered forearms making my floaty, floral dress feel even more ridiculous.

'You made it.' The surprise in his voice was undeniable, a flame blazing in those dark mahogany eyes as they travelled quickly down my body and back up again, Adam's apple bobbing in his throat.

I lifted my chin a fraction, ready for battle. 'Of course,' I said defensively, feigning offence at the suggestion that I might not have shown up, even though just thirty seconds earlier I'd been mentally planning my escape. He held my gaze for a second longer than necessary, those autumn-coloured eyes making my heart race.

'Sorry about all this.' Luca gestured apologetically to the group of men beavering away behind him. I spotted Terry up a step ladder in the far corner, another man I didn't recognise holding it steady on the ground below. Ivan was on the stage, turning one way and then the other as he attempted to untangle the giant mass of fairy lights that were currently climbing their way up his legs. 'I might have mentioned it to a few of the guys, and the next thing I knew they'd all turned up wanting to help.' He raked his fingers through his hair, leaving a thin streak of white paint at the ends.

'It's fine, really. Put me to work!'

Luca's eyes fell to my shoes with a dubious look, clearly concluding that I was not suitably dressed for an evening of DIY.

'Ivan's already mopped the floors, so you could make a start at setting out the chairs if you like?'

I gave him a look, kicking my shoes off to one side as I coaxed my hair up into a messy bun, the floor cool beneath my bare feet.

'You really don't know me at all, do you? I'll have you know that I'm a dab hand with a paintbrush,' I remarked, bending down and swiping a roller from an abandoned paint tray. 'Besides, this place is in dire need of a woman's touch.'

'I can't argue with you there.' Luca laughed, strolling over to a cardboard box and returning with a once-orange, now entirely paint-splattered, pair of overalls that looked about three sizes too big for me. 'Can I interest you in this sexy little number, madam? I'm told they're all the rage in Paris.'

'Why thank you, kind sir,' I giggled, playing along with his false grandeur by dropping into a rather wobbly courtesy.

His eyes twinkled with delight, his breath hot against my collarbone as he leaned in to whisper, 'Don't say I never give you anything.'

I shivered involuntarily, each consonant landing like a raindrop against my skin, his lips mere centimetres from my neck. As Luca placed a hand fleetingly on the small of my back, I felt something quieten inside of me, that constantly taut string that was always pulling me to and fro between the past and the present, wound so tight I feared it might snap, loosening a fraction under his touch. I tried not to overthink it as I watched him stroll across to his half-painted skirting boards, stealing a glance over one shoulder when he thought I wasn't looking. As our eyes met, something passed between us. The shared understanding that something was different. I was used to Luca looking at me with a sort of loaded, condescending eyeroll, as though my very presence on this earth was of great inconvenience to him. But the way he was looking at me now, the muscle in his jaw clenching repeatedly, his lips parted, made every inch of my skin feel like it was on fire. It felt exciting. And scary. And intoxicating all at the same time.

And hot. Very, very hot.

I started on the back wall, tipping a generous amount of the palest yellow paint into a plastic tray and working my roller up and down until the soft white sponge was completely coated. It was oddly satisfying watching the chipped, tired-looking magnolia disappear beneath a cheerful coat of Fuzzy Duckling, and I focused on the steady rhythm of my roller moving up and down, up and down. Luca was on the opposite side of the room with a dust sheet beneath him, working a paintbrush along the fiddly edges, the pink of his tongue just visible between his lips. The tension in my body rose as we slowly edged towards each other, sparking and crackling like kindling catching fire, as I orbited the room clockwise and Luca circled counter-clockwise until we eventually met along the far-right-hand wall.

'Fancy seeing you here,' I joked lamely. Luca's fore-arms were covered in a light dusting of paint, tiny flecks of pale yellow like a constellation of golden freckles against his olive skin.

'I have to hand it to you, Thompson, it's not easy to pull off stained, twenty-year-old overalls, but as always, you continue to surprise me.' My cheeks flushed at the compliment. I was back to being Thompson again. But it didn't have the same mocking undertone as before. It felt playful. Mischievous almost. Like the twinkle in Luca's eye.

'This thing is twenty years old?!' I cried in outrage, glancing down at the faded jumpsuit that, despite my rolling the legs up five times, was still trailing on the floor.

'Hey, boss, you didn't compliment me on my outfit,' came Terry's voice over the creak of the ladder as his heavy boots descended one by one. I giggled as he struck a pose at the bottom, both thumbs hooked over the strap of his tool belt, the dozen or so pockets already adorning his cargo trousers apparently insufficient storage. He flung one ankle over the other as he looked moodily up at the ceiling.

'Nor me,' Ivan joined in, pointing one finger, John Travolta-style, up in the air before jumping a good foot off the ground to reach Terry's high five.

Luca chuckled, unfazed by their ribbing. 'What can I say, boys? You've either got it or you haven't.'

'You saying Jenny's got it then, boss?' Terry grinned, sharing a *nudge nudge wink wink* with Ivan. He was clearly enjoying himself way too much to notice the two pink spots that had appeared on Luca's cheekbones. Or mine, for that matter.

'I'm saying *you* don't,' Luca said smartly, expertly sidestepping any hole Terry was trying to dig for him. Terry closed his eyes, one hand flying to his chest as if he'd been shot, the other clutching the side of the ladder as all six foot five of him fell dramatically to the floor. After a few seconds, he opened one eye, surveying his silent audience. He chuckled throatily, throwing me a wink before climbing back up to a standing position.

'After watching that, I can see where Kiki gets her performance skills from,' I whispered down to Luca, whose shoulders shook with laughter as he angled his paintbrush neatly along the edge of the skirting board. We worked in silence for a few minutes. Not the awkward kind. The kind that two people comfortable in each other's presence are happy to pass the time in, no pressure to fill the void with pointless small talk.

'So, when's the big day?' Luca asked eventually, straightening up and bending his neck this way and that.

I froze. My eyes automatically swivelled to land on my engagement ring, which had twisted itself around, only the silver band visible. I shimmied it back around with my third finger, brushing the diamond face with the pad of my thumb.

'Your brother's wedding?' Luca's delicate emphasis made my cheeks flush.

'19th July.'

Luca raised a questioning eyebrow at my less than enthusiastic response.

'I'm happy for him, for both of them. Truly. It's just—' I stopped myself, bending down to pour some more paint into the plastic tray.

'You thought it would be you,' Luca finished for me, an unapologetic shrug of the shoulders that told me he understood exactly how I felt.

'I'm jealous of my own brother's happiness. God, I'm a terrible human being,' I groaned, hiding my face shamefully in the crook of my elbow. The fabric smelt musty, the faint tang of white spirit cutting through the stale odour.

'You're not jealous of his happiness, you're just wanting a little slice of your own. That doesn't make you a terrible human being, it just makes you human.' A memory passed briefly over his face and I bit my cheek as I remembered Luca's own happily never after.

'Sorry, I didn't mean to dredge up the past.'

'Don't be.' Luca shrugged, the steady rhythm of his paintbrush unwavering. 'The past is what makes us who we are. But to quote my Dadaji . . .' He cleared his throat, putting on a deep, authoritative voice with an accent stronger than his own. 'If you let the past define your present, you quickly lose any hope of a future.'

My roller stopped. His words, despite their theatrical delivery, caused something to shift inside of me, my throat suddenly thick like cotton wool.

'He sounds like a wise man. Clearly the apple fell *very* far from the tree.' I bumped my hip bone lightly against his shoulder, feeling some inexplicable need to navigate us safely back to our normal, light-hearted dynamic.

'If I can even be half the man he is, I'll be happy.'

'Who's to say you're not already there?'

Luca lowered his paintbrush, his eyes big and round as they searched my face. He blinked fast once, twice, three times, before his mouth stretched into a crooked smile.

'And who's to say the wedding won't be fun?'

I look at him flatly. 'Being a single guy in your thirties at a wedding is fun. Being a single woman in your thirties at a wedding is like being one of those abandoned puppies in a cardboard box by the side of the road, everyone throwing you pitying looks as they walk past, keeping a wide berth in case finding yourself unexpectedly single and alone in your thirties is somehow catching.'

Luca chuckled. 'Well, there's your answer, then. Don't go alone.'

'Right,' I scoffed, as if he'd just suggested I turn up stark naked. His eyes widened as if to say *why not?* 'Alice is working and even though Jacob said we could go together, I already know he's going to bring a date and then I'll be the awkward third wheel.'

There was a short pause, nothing but the squelch of my roller filling the silence.

'I could always go with you, if you like.'

I dropped my roller. It landed with a dull splat on the dust sheet below, showering Luca's hair with a fresh sprinkling of yellow.

'*Shit!*' I dropped to the ground, dabbing at the mess with a wet cloth. 'Sorry, I didn't mean – it just slipped out of my hand.'

'I'll pretend I believe you.' Luca grinned, wiping at his face with the cuff of his sleeve and leaving a pale-yellow smear just below his temple. 'So?' I could feel him seeking my gaze, dipping his head to try and catch my eye. I feigned ignorance, buying myself a few precious seconds.

'So, what?'

Luca's head tilted to one side, his broad chest rising with a deep breath. 'So, what do you say we go together? You know, as friends,' he added quickly.

'Oh, you don't have to do that.'

'I know,' he said simply. 'But I want to. If that's what you want, that is?'

I reached for my roller, suddenly wanting something to do with my hands.

'OK.' I blinked, surprised by the speed and ease in which the word tumbled out of my mouth, ready and waiting on the tip of my tongue.

'OK.' Luca nodded, turning back to his skirting board. I watched his right cheek hitch slightly, both eyes closing for a split second as he performed a mini fist pump, and wondered what it all meant. If he could feel it too. This fizzing sense of anticipation brewing in the pit of my stomach.

'That's me, folks. I need to get back and relieve the sitter.' Terry's voice made me jump, his heavy-soled boots unpausing as they clomped towards the exit. I looked around the empty hall and realised everyone else must have already left, my watch confirming it was well past 9 p.m.

'Thanks again, Terry, I owe you one,' Luca called, raising a hand in the air. Terry gave a two-fingered salute before disappearing into the night air. The echo of the door swinging closed suddenly made me very conscious that Luca and I were alone. I caught him looking at me, those big, gold-rimmed eyes trained unashamedly on my face, warm and curious in a way that triggered that flip-flop sensation in my belly.

'What?'

'You've got a little something—'

'Oh.' I wiped blindly at where he was pointing, my fingers coming away clean every time. 'Did I get it?'

Luca smiled. 'Not quite.' He took a step forward, closing the distance between us entirely. I breathed out unevenly, watching his chest rising and falling faster than normal. 'It's just – there.'

'*Hey!*' The paintbrush Luca had just produced from behind his back dabbed clumsily across my face, leaving a cold streak of paint down my right cheek. My eyes narrowed. 'Oh, it's *so* on.'

I got him on the forearm, a thick swipe of yellow running from his wrist to the inside of his elbow. His grin widened. Brandishing his brush like a fencing sword, he lunged forward, landing another blow to the sleeve of my left arm. Bouncing on the balls of my feet, I aimed for the face, but Luca dodged quickly to the side, grabbing my paintbrush-wielding hand in his. He spun me around, so quickly that I heard myself gasp, my own arm pinning me against his chest. I could feel the contours of his body through the worn coveralls, his belt buckle pressing against the soft, fleshy part at the base of my spine.

'Care to admit defeat?' Luca teased, his breath warm against my ear.

'Never,' I vowed, twisting free from his grip and reaching down to swap my paintbrush for the roller. Luca hesitated at my choice of upgrade. 'What's wrong, Patel? Start something you can't finish?' My roller struck gold, gliding up the right side of his face and forming a perfect half-beard from jaw to ear. I smiled triumphantly.

'Oh, I always finish. Don't you worry about that.' Something flashed hot and molten behind his eyes, confirmation that his dual meaning was no accident. My breath hitched audibly in my throat, an unexpected rush of desire scorching through my veins, throwing me off-guard. And off balance. My foot caught in the trailing end of my trouser leg, sending me lurching forwards and straight towards an unsuspecting Luca. The floor rushed up to meet us and I screwed my eyes tightly shut, every muscle in my body bracing for impact. But then I felt Luca's arms wrap themselves around me, strong and sure as they pulled me tightly against his chest, cushioning my fall.

When I opened them again, we were about as close as two people could possibly be. Noses practically touching. A tangled mess of limbs as our hearts beat furiously against each other through our overalls. Luca's mouth formed a perfect O beneath me, his gaze flitting from my eyes to my mouth. Eyes. Mouth. Eyes. Mouth. And for one wild, terrifying moment, I thought about kissing him – how easy it would be to snake my arms around his neck, twist the ends of his hair between my fingertips as I pulled his lips closer to where I wanted them—

'*Ahem.*'

Someone cleared their throat behind us and we sprang apart, scrambling to detach ourselves from one another. Terry was stood in the doorway, rubbing at his stubble with one hand, an amused look on his face.

'Sorry, didn't mean to . . . interrupt.' It looked like he was trying very hard not to laugh. Warmth flooded my cheeks. Why did it feel like I'd just been caught with my hand in the cookie jar? 'Just forgot my keys,' he explained, his boots echoing in the silence as he sauntered over and swiped a handful of metal off one of the chairs.

'As you were,' he called over his shoulder, jangling his prize noisily in the air as he disappeared through the doorway, dipping his head as he went. The door slammed shut once more, the moment gone, vanishing into the night along with a chuckling Terry. A swirl of cool air hurried in from outside, biting against the bare skin of my arms. I shivered.

'It's getting late. I guess we should probably call it a night too,' Luca said reluctantly, his eyes fixed on mine as though willing me to disagree. And just like that, my whole body was ablaze once more, one look from Luca enough to restart the burning flame in the pit of my belly.

I nodded. 'Probably.'

16

'What do you think it means?'

Jacob craned his neck closer to my phone, re-reading the text message we'd been poring over for the past five minutes. The same text message that had prompted me to send an emergency SOS message to the group chat at 7 a.m., resulting in Jacob showing up at the pub twenty-seven minutes later, out of breath and slightly red-faced, eye mask still atop his head.

'OK, hear me out,' he said, nursing his cup of coffee with the tenderness a mother would her baby. 'Call me crazy, but what if—' he paused for dramatic effect '—he wants you to meet him for dinner tonight at 7 p.m.?'

I rolled my eyes at Jacob's fake sincerity, flicking him between the eyes before swiping my phone off the kitchen table. I read the text one final time before slipping it into my pocket.

Dinner. Tonight. 7pm.

That was it. No details. No explanation. Not even a bloody question mark. As if my attendance were mandatory. The sheer presumption of it all irked me a little, but another part of me fizzed with excited anticipation, something fluttering nervously behind my breastbone at the thought of going on a date with Luca.

'Yes, thank you, Einstein. Thank God you came over, otherwise I'd never have worked that one out,' I drawled, taking another sip of coffee. 'I mean, do you think it's a date?'

'Of course it's a bloody date!' This time, it was Jacob's turn to roll his eyes. My teeth halted their worrying of my bottom lip, panic causing every tiny muscle in my body to freeze. Jacob must have seen it on my face because the next minute, he was backtracking. 'Or,' he added quickly, one finger in the air, 'it could just be two people having dinner together? I mean you've got to eat, he's got to eat, why not eat together?'

'Mmm,' I murmured quietly, running my index finger round and round the rim of Joe's *Star Wars* mug, the edge of my nail catching on the hairline crack down one side. It had been eight months. Eight long months without Joe and it still felt like a betrayal even thinking about going on a date with someone else.

'Look, it doesn't have to be a date if you don't want it to be. It can just be dinner. A chance to escape your mum's for the night, get a change of scene, have some fun. You do remember fun, right?'

I took a loud slurp of coffee, ignoring his question.

'Hey Siri, what does it mean to have fun?' Jacob asked, his eyes trained on my face even though he was talking to his phone. After Alice and me, Siri was probably the most important woman in Jacob's life. The display lit up, a robotic female voice echoing around the kitchen.

'Fun is defined by the Oxford English Dictionary as light-hearted pleasure, enjoyment, or amusement; boisterous joviality or general merrymaking.'

'You hear that?' Jacob angled his head towards the phone. 'General merrymaking. Doesn't that sound delightful?'

'Know-it-all,' I mumbled into my mug, glaring accusingly at Jacob's iPhone as the screen returned to black.

'Look, if you're still worried, I'll be your get-out-of-date-free card and phone you half an hour in so you can bail if need be. What do we think, the classic *I've been knocking on your door for ten minutes, don't tell me you forgot you said I could crash at yours tonight*?' Jacob wailed, flapping his hand dramatically in front of his face. 'Or I could pretend I've been arrested? No wait, I've got it – kidnap!' He mic-dropped his half-eaten croissant, crumbs flying everywhere.

'Wait, have you been kidnapped or are you the kidnapper?'

'Hmm, both equally likely options,' Jacob mused with the utmost seriousness. 'Let's go with the former.'

I forced a smile, but my heart was still hammering in my chest. I wished Joe was here so that we could talk about it, but the truth was I'd stayed awake until 3 a.m. last night waiting for him and he'd never showed. I didn't know what filled me with more fear, the fact it had been eight days since I'd last seen him, or that, if I was honest with myself, I already knew what he would say.

'Hey,' Jacob said softly, 'it's just dinner.' Those three words somehow answering every question that he knew I needed an answer to, as only a best friend could. *No, it doesn't make you an awful person. No, it doesn't mean you love Joe any less. Yes, I will 100% take one for the team and go in your place if required.* I smiled, reaching out and squeezing his hand across the table.

'It's just dinner,' I repeated to myself, typing out my reply and clicking send before I could change my mind.

I could see him.

He was stood on the corner of the intersection, dressed in black jeans and a crisp white shirt that looked fresh out the packet, the collar stiff and tall against his neck, the sleeves rolled up his forearms. I loitered just out of sight, watching Luca for a minute as he checked his watch, then his phone, then his watch again, running his fingers through his tousled hair. He paced three steps one way and then three steps back, turning sharply on his heel as he went. Wait, was *he* nervous? I watched as he looked down at his shirt, chin on his chest as his fingers undid another button, teasing the neckline open a fraction before shaking his head and quickly doing it back up. I stifled a giggle, the bundle of nervous energy in the pit of my stomach calming a fraction with the realisation that perhaps he was just as anxious as me.

I took a deep breath, running my palms down the silk fabric of the dress Jacob had helped me pick out. I'd wanted something new. Something I'd not worn before and, specifically, not worn with Joe. Something that had no memories attached to it until the ones I chose to make tonight. A blank canvas. Luca's head snapped up the second my heels click-clacked across the cobbles, the crisp seams along his shoulders lowering a fraction as he watched me approach. I stared fixedly at the floor, focusing on putting one foot in front of the other without falling over.

'Jenny.'

I loved the sound of my name in his mouth. The way he caressed the J. Like he was tasting it. My cheeks flushed as Luca's eyes travelled up my bare legs, over the curve of my waist, to the low V of my neckline.

'You look beautiful,' he breathed, his palm like fire against my waist as he drew me towards him, pressing his lips lightly against my cheek. Lingering. I could smell his aftershave, a smoky, earthy musk that made my insides twist with a mix of desire and anticipation. God, he smelt good.

'You don't look too bad yourself.' I smiled shyly, tucking a wayward strand of hair behind one ear as it danced in the evening breeze. We stood in silence for a moment, the streetlight above us flickering on even though it was still light out.

Luca cleared his throat, one arm stretched out wide. 'Shall we?'

I nodded, falling into step beside him. We passed a row of small independent shops, all shrouded in darkness bar the final building on the end, which bathed the last few squares of pavement in a warm, welcoming glow. The faint sound of music buzzed from behind net-curtain-covered windows, which were so fogged up with condensation that you could barely see in. Luca held the door open for me and I tried not to think too hard about how my bum brushed the front of his trousers when I squeezed past. The rich smell of ragu greeted me as soon as I stepped inside, wholesome and comforting in that way only proper home-cooked food can be.

'Ah, Signore Luca!' A greying man with bushy eyebrows that sprouted off in every direction other than the one they should hurried towards us. He was dressed in chef's whites, with a black apron straining valiantly across his middle and a great beaming smile plastered across his face. Something about his smile seemed familiar, the way it pulled my own mouth up at the corners prompting an uncanny sense of déjà vu. He clasped Luca's hand in both of his and pumped it fiercely up and down, a light dusting of flour floating in the air between them.

'Matteo.' Luca greeted him warmly, clapping him on the shoulder once he regained possession of his hand. 'Thanks so much for squeezing us in.'

Matteo threw his hands in the air before resting them on his belly. 'Ah, it is nothing. Anything for Signore Luca and his lady friend.' He peered round Luca towards me, his eyebrows performing an excited dance across his brow.

'Jenny, lovely to meet you.' The air rushed out of me as Matteo ignored my outstretched hand, pulling me in for what I could only presume was a hug, his soft, rotund stomach stopping us from fully embracing. He smelt of red wine and freshly cracked black pepper.

'Signorina, the pleasure is mine. Ah, Luca, you didn't tell us she was so beautiful, eh?' Matteo scolded, gesticulating wildly with one hand and flipping Luca with a dishtowel with the other. I realised that Matteo was fluent in three languages – Italian, English, and the one he spoke with his hands. I felt my cheeks flush.

'*Luca!*'

I watched over Matteo's shoulder as a mop of sandy-brown hair sped through the restaurant, weaving in and out of the tables with ease before launching itself at Luca's legs, tiny arms wrapping themselves around his knees.

'Woah, slow down, mister.' Luca smiled, ruffling the boy's hair affectionately. I recognised Andrea immediately, with those too-big-for-his-face brown eyes and the distinctive red and black football jersey that he'd never not been wearing whenever I'd seen him at the community centre. So that's where I recognised Matteo from.

'Hello, Miss Jenny.' Andrea smiled his big toothy grin up at me, his hand rubbing shyly at his face, not quite meeting my gaze. Matteo looked down at his grandson with nothing but love and adoration before turning back to us.

'Come, I have *special table* prepared, just like you asked,' Matteo stage-whispered to Luca loudly enough that the whole restaurant probably heard, prompting two pink spots to bloom on Luca's cheeks. Matteo gestured for us to follow him through the restaurant, Andrea placing his tiny hand in mine and leading me through a maze of red checked tablecloths and mismatched wooden chairs. We went through a swing door at the back of the restaurant that led to the kitchen, past a wood-fired oven and a rosy-cheeked, white-haired woman stirring a pot of delicious-smelling tomato sauce. Matteo introduced her as his wife, Magda, who planted a kiss on both my cheeks and then another on Luca's, holding his face tenderly in both her hands and speaking very fast Italian. She beckoned for us to follow her to the back door.

'Oh.'

I stopped dead, poor Andrea jolting backwards from the sudden change of pace. It was as if stepping through their creaky stable door had transported me all the way across Europe, to a little slice of Italy hidden away down the backstreets of Hove. The garden was wild, all cracked terracotta pots and mismatched paving slabs, with vines crawling up the brick walls that flanked it on all sides, but there was a beauty to the untamed landscape. The olive trees, uneven and natural, swayed in the warm breeze, which smelt of lemon balm and oregano, herbs spilling over the tops of their pots in carefree abundance. A small wrought-iron table and two matching chairs had been set up in the middle of the garden, the single red rose and about a hundred tealights flickering in old jam jars on the paving slabs speaking of a woman's touch.

'It is OK?'

I turned to see all four of them staring at me, their eyes wide and unblinking in anticipation. A warmth bloomed deep in my chest at the thought of Luca arranging all of this. Of Matteo and Andrea carefully selecting the perfect rose. Of Magda lighting each candle in turn, positioning them just so. The sentiment. The care. The thought.

'It's perfect.' I smiled, weaving the silk tie of my dress back and forth through my fingers, until I realised that one wrong tug could result in my dress unravelling and quickly stopped. I pressed my lips tightly together, fighting back a giggle when Andrea grabbed onto the other side of the chair with Luca, the two of them pulling it out for me. Andrea snatched the menu from Magda's hands and passed it to me with a shy smile before Matteo shooed him back up the flagstone path.

'Think I've got some competition,' Luca remarked with a raise of his eyebrow. I laughed, feeling my shoulders relax.

'Pfft, we don't need menu,' Matteo announced dismissively, swiping the faux-leather folder out of my hands before I could even open it. 'I can make anything you like, your wish is Matteo's command.'

'Oh, umm – I'll have a ham and pineapple pizza then, please.' I smiled, remembering the giant pizza oven we'd passed in the kitchen.

Matteo's mouth fell open in horror.

'Pineapple? On the pizza?!' he cried, looking horrified and a tiny bit nauseated by the suggestion. He looked at Luca. I looked at Luca. But Luca just leaned back in his chair, teeth glinting in a way that told me he was enjoying every single second of my torture. 'And I'll have my usual, please, Matteo!' he said with a grin. Before I could rectify my mistake and order literally anything else, Matteo was already retreating up the garden path, the fingers of his right hand pursed together as his wrist waved back and forth in disbelief.

'I think that's *the* most offensive thing anyone's ever said to any Italian. Like, ever.' Luca chuckled, his eyes sparking playfully in the candlelight as he poured red wine into two glasses.

I groaned, burying my face in my hands.

'Seriously though, pineapple on pizza?'

'What? It's delicious.'

'It's criminal,' Luca countered, his face deadly serious.

I giggled, a tiny snort escaping before I could stop it.

'Joe used to say the exact same thing!' My laughter died a quick death, hanging awkwardly over us like an unwelcome rain cloud on a summer's day. 'Sorry,' I muttered, fidgeting with the edge of the tablecloth. 'I don't know why I said that.'

But when I looked up Luca's smile was still in place, his head cocked to one side as though trying to work something out. 'It's fine. I'd actually like to know more about him.'

'Who, Joe?' I frowned, unable to keep the surprise from my voice.

'Yes.' Luca smiled encouragingly, before adding, 'That is, only if you want to talk about him. I totally understand if you don't—'

'No, it's fine,' I assured him, surprising myself by actually meaning it. 'What do you want to know?'

'How did you two meet?'

'At school. He saved me from a public humiliation that, as a 13-year-old girl, would have been the end of my life as I knew it.'

'And you were together for all that time?'

'Sixteen years, four months and nine days.' For some reason I felt my cheeks reddening at this admission, or perhaps the speed at which I'd volunteered the information.

Luca's eyes widened as he tipped his chair backwards, quite literally blown away by that revelation. 'That's pretty special. To find your person and have them stick it out with you for that long. Someone that chooses you each and every day.'

'Pretty special,' I repeated with a small smile.

Luca reached for his wine, swirling the liquid up the sides of the glass. The muscle in his jaw tightened as his eyes met mine across the table, a sad sort of smile tugging at his lips. I watched his hard exterior, the one I'd mistaken for standoffishness when we first met, crack to reveal a soft, gooey centre.

Suddenly, it all made sense. The deflection, the abruptness, the couldn't-be-further-from-the-truth Casanova image that he let people believe because it was an easy way to avoid getting too close. Because whenever he had gotten close to someone, they'd left. His dad. His ex. Even his Dadaji. They'd all chosen someone else, or something else, over him. And somewhere along the way, he'd determined that he was the common denominator. Some sort of problem that couldn't be fixed. It made my heart ache. Luca leaned forward, the single tealight fluttering between us bringing out the flecks of gold in his eyes.

'Do you still believe in love? Even after everything?' he asked.

The candle flickered with a passing gust of wind, threatening to be snuffed out completely before it stilled, burning even brighter than before. I considered Luca's question for a long time, his unblinking gaze causing a pleasant warmth to wash over me from head to toe.

'I think not believing in something doesn't stop you from wanting it,' I said carefully, my teeth catching my bottom lip. 'You?'

Luca's lips parted a fraction, shifting in his seat so that his leg fell against my knee. Casual. Heavy. He didn't move it away. 'I'm a songwriter, Thompson, believing in love is kind of a requirement.'

'Really? Was that part of the job description when you applied?'

The corner of his mouth twitched, an intensity in his eyes that made my insides melt. Thankfully, my phone chirped before I completely liquified into a puddle on the floor.

'Sorry,' I mouthed apologetically, digging in my bag until I found it. Jacob's name flashed up on the screen. My get-out-of-date-free card was calling bang on time.

'You need to get that?' Luca asked.

'No.' I turned my phone off, slipping it back into my bag just as Matteo came bustling down the garden path, a black tray held aloft on one shoulder. It contained a single blue and white plate which he placed in the middle of the table, a spoon balanced on either side.

'Buon appetito!' He smiled, clasping both hands together in delight before scurrying back towards the restaurant. Magda's head appeared around the door, craning at what looked like a very uncomfortable angle, before Matteo shooed her back inside, saying something that required a lot of hand gestures. I stifled a giggle as Luca poured us both some more wine.

'What's this?' I asked, frowning at the generous square of tiramisu sat in the centre of the hand-painted plate, cream oozing out from all sides.

'Dessert,' Luca said with deliberate slowness, as if I were an alien from another planet.

I laughed. 'No. I mean, I thought we were having pizza?'

'Dessert first. Pizza after.'

'You can't have dessert first!' I scoffed, throwing my head back.

His eyes danced as they watched me. He dipped a finger into the cocoa-dusted whipped cream and raised it to his lips.

'Says who?' His tongue swirled around the tip of his finger as he licked the cream off. It was slow. Intentional. But his tongue might as well have been in between my thighs the effect it was having on me.

'Says the world,' I maintained, my voice hoarse.

'No, seriously, what idiot came up with that rule? Some miserable sod who thought it was a good idea to make people wait for the very thing they're looking forward to the most? Life's too short for waiting, Thompson; sometimes you've got to write your own rules.' His eyes didn't leave mine as the spoon disappeared inside his mouth, the low moan of satisfaction rumbling at the back of his throat making me wonder what else might draw that noise out of him.

'Screw it.'

I grabbed the other spoon, filling it with a mound of coffee-soaked sponge and cream. My eyes closed with pleasure as I savoured the sweet, creamy flavours, a sigh of desire escaping audibly from somewhere deep inside me. But when I opened my eyes and saw Luca watching me across the table, my pulse beat hot and fast beneath my skin, and I realised I was far from satisfied.

'You've got a little something—' Luca leaned towards me as if in slow motion. I had to fight the urge to grab his face in my hands and taste the bitter tang of coffee on his lips as the tip of his thumb glided briefly across my own. When it retreated, a smear of white cream was just visible. Luca inspected it for a moment, twisting it this way and that before slowly raising it to his mouth, lips parted, and sucking it clean. Fuck. Who knew tiramisu could be such a turn-on?

I reached for my wine glass, the deep, velvety Barolo doing very little to cool the raging fire burning in the pit of my stomach. A slow smile grew on Luca's mouth, as if he knew the effect he was having on me. Never one to give up without a fight, I crossed my legs, letting my right shoe fall to the floor, the bare skin of my foot gliding brazenly up Luca's trouser leg beneath the table, higher, higher—

His spoon clattered noisily against the side of the plate, one hand clenching a fistful of tablecloth whilst the other shot into the air, palm splayed as he tried to get Matteo's attention.

'Can we get the bill?'

My back hit Luca's front door, which used to be my front door, at the very same moment our lips touched. You could hardly call it a kiss. His lips brushed mine so gently it was barely more than a whisper even though every inch of my body was practically screaming with desire, my heart beating so loudly I swear the whole building must have heard it. His hands found my hips, certain in what they wanted as he pulled me tightly against him, his mouth trailing a path of impossibly soft kisses down the length of my neck.

'Did I tell you how beautiful you look tonight?' he murmured against my skin, catching my earlobe between his teeth.

'Not that I can recall,' I gasped breathlessly, tipping my head back with a moan as his mouth moved down my neck, grazing my shoulder, along my collarbone. My hips bucked impatiently beneath him and I felt Luca smile against my skin, but he took his time making his way further down, pulling the neckline of my dress down to expose my breast, teasing my nipple with his tongue, sucking, biting.

'Well, you do. And this dress,' he mused throatily, his fingers finding the bow that secured it at my hipbone.

'Yes?' I panted, wanting him, willing him to undo me. He took half a step back, his eyes pure fire as he kept hold of the tie, the bow slowly unravelling until the two halves of my dress hung open like a robe. I dropped my shoulders, the smallest of movements enough to send the silky material pooling around my feet.

'Somehow it looks even better on the floor,' Luca breathed, eyes roaming over my nearly naked body as though committing it to memory. I reached for him then, my hands frantic as they scrabbled at the bottom of his shirt, yanking it out of his jeans and over his head in my haste, my *need*, to feel his skin against mine. And then my mouth was on his again, but this kiss was different. It was urgent, decisive, our teeth clashing against each other as we backed into the flat, my dress and his shirt forgotten about on the front door mat. We didn't make it to the bedroom. Luca's hips pinned me against the living room wall and my entire body responded, melting into him as his arms snaked tightly around me, pulling me ever closer until my left leg was somehow hitched around his waist. His pinky finger teased the elastic of my underwear, pinging it once against the flesh of my hip as a low whimper escaped from my mouth.

'So, I take it you're now a fan of having your dessert first?' came Luca's voice in the dark, his hands everywhere all at once. I felt like my body was going to burst into flames at any moment.

'Consider me converted.' I smiled, pulling him towards me once more.

17

I was supposed to be getting coffee. One black drip coffee for me. One flat white for Luca. Luca, who I'd left in a delicious tangle of warm bed sheets with the promise that I'd be right back, the prospect of coffee and freshly baked pastries the only reason he had eventually let me wiggle out from beneath him, reluctantly unhooking my leg from around his hip bone, allowing his wandering fingers to slip from the curve of my waist. But my phone told me that was almost three hours ago. And that I had five missed calls and two voicemails from Luca.

I'd walked the two streets over to Drew's Brews as intended, my hands swallowed up by the sleeves of Luca's sweatshirt, which brushed gently against my bare legs, the skirt of last night's dress dancing in the breeze. I'd closed my eyes, angling my face up towards the late morning sun as I stood patiently in the late Sunday morning queue, flashbacks of last night playing on repeat.

Last night.

It had been – well, no single word existed that came close to describing how I'd felt in that moment. How Luca had made me feel. And I'd felt everything, everywhere, all at once. My toes curled in recollection as

I remembered waking up when it was still dark out to the feeling of Luca's hand tracing the length of my thigh, past the tiny birthmark by my belly button, the tip of his finger brushing the underside of my breast which appeared to have been moulded to fit perfectly in the palm of his hand. The way he'd breathed my name against my lips, his tongue doing magical things as I felt the weight of him hovering over me.

A man collided with me on his way out, a wayward elbow catching my arm and sending us both flying. I saw his shoes first. Brown suede Chelsea boots righting themselves against the uneven cobblestones, a splash of spilt liquid darkening the left toe. My eyes travelled up his jeans, which were slightly faded in that way that told you they were his favourite pair, overworn and under-washed. But it was the jumper, navy blue and hoicked up at the sleeves, that had my heart in my mouth.

'Joe?' His name tumbled so readily out of my mouth that I realised on some level I must have been expecting, hoping even, to see him today. A pair of unfamiliar green eyes frowned back at me from a glasses-less face.

'Sorry, love,' the stranger mumbled in a thick northern accent before hurrying off down the street. I shuffled forwards in the queue, my mind now racing with a single thought. *When was the last time I'd seen Joe? I'd not seen him yesterday, or the day before, or the day before that. Had it been . . . ? No. What about . . . ? No, not then either.* I started to panic, sifting back through the events of the past few weeks, my heart beating faster the further back I went. *Aha, on the bus on the way to Luca's gig. I'd seen him on the bus on the way to Luca's gig!* But that was three weeks ago. Surely it hadn't been that long? I glanced over my shoulder, searching for Joe's face in the line of caffeine-hungry millennials that snaked behind me, pressing my face to the window of the shop to see if he was inside.

'It's Drew's,' I reminded myself quietly, taking a deep, calming breath in through my nose as I scrunched the sleeves of Luca's sweatshirt into a tight fist. 'He always shows at Drew's.'

But he didn't show by the time I reached the entrance, my foot taking over from the person's in front to wedge the door open. Nor did he appear when I'd inched to the front of the queue.

'One black coffee and an oat milk hazelnut mocha with extra whipped cream, right?'

I blinked at the barista, a sharp pain piercing my chest at the sound of mine and Joe's regular order rolling off her tongue, her hand already reaching for the hazelnut syrup. Like we were a package deal. Neither making sense without the other. But I was here buying coffee for another man. A man who was waiting for me, naked and warm in the bed that not so long ago I used to share with Joe. The thought made my stomach tighten. Someone sighed impatiently behind me, the barista's smile fading as I stood frozen to the spot.

'Umm, no,' I managed eventually, my voice cracking with the effort. 'Just a black coffee and a flat white today.'

I had a sudden urge to sit at our normal table in the back, me facing Joe, Joe facing me, like always. But another couple were already there, mugs to one side, heads bent over *The Sunday Times* crossword puzzle in a way that screamed routine. I paid for the coffees and left, but instead of heading back to the flat, my feet took me in the opposite direction, striding purposefully towards the farmer's market along the seafront. It was another place that I could always count on Joe appearing, falling into step beside me as we walked up and down the promenade, perusing stalls selling buckets of fresh olives and signs made from old pieces of driftwood that said things like *sandy toes & salty kisses*. My skin buzzed with that anxious need to keep moving, panic coursing through my veins like hot, molten lava.

It was busy along the seafront. The sun was out, shining down on the neat rows of stalls that magically appeared along the upper promenade every Sunday, and it had brought half the population of Hove out with it. I pushed through the crowds, my head snapping this way and that, desperately searching for that familiar mop of sandy-brown hair amidst the kids with butterflies painted on their faces and the couples walking arm in arm at that leisurely Sunday pace, string bags filled with sourdough and olive oil the price of a house deposit swinging from their shoulders.

He's not here.

I ran my hand through my hair, triggering a flashback of Luca's fingers twisting their way around the strands at the nape of my neck, coaxing my head back as his lips murmured hot, delicious things against the bare skin between my breasts. I shook my head, screwing my eyes tightly shut as I tried to push the memory from my mind, to make room for Joe.

What if I never see him again?

I ground my teeth together, my jaw throbbing from the effort of keeping this heart-wrenching pain inside. Hot coffee sloshed down my front as my grip tightened around the takeaway cups, both lids flying off as a brown patch bloomed like a dead rose across the fabric of Luca's jumper.

And now, somehow, I was here. Sat on the pebbles of Brighton Beach, my dress growing cold and wet beneath me whilst I stared out at the West Pier, as I had a thousand times before. Only this time I was alone. There was no Joe, camera pressed against his face as he skittered across the stones, the *click click click* of his shutter as he took photograph after photograph of the burnt-out metal skeleton of a pier. I never could understand how something so broken, a shell of its former self, could still be standing. How it could look so beautiful, with its now-useless metal beams standing tall and proud as the mist swirled around them.

'Come on, Joe,' I muttered, hugging my knees tightly to my chest as I looked around the empty beach. I swallowed, my throat suddenly thick with panic. My eyes stung with tears as I tried to block out the voice inside my head, the one that kept saying *it's your fault he's not here, you let him fade away.* The voice was so loud that it took up all the space in my head, no room left for anything else. It was only then that I noticed my tears had turned to sobs, tearing raggedly through me. The seagulls joined in with my cries, bringing their high notes to the gentle melody of the waves against the shore, and I watched as a bird landed on a stretch of beach. It pottered around for a moment, its tiny feet performing a rain dance on the wet sand, trying to entice any signs of life to the surface before flying off again, an incoming wave wiping the beach clean. As if the seagull and its pattering feet never existed.

'Where are you, Joe?' I whispered, a single tear rolling down my cheek as I closed my eyes, wishing, willing him to appear. My phone buzzed against the stones beside me, Luca's name flashing across the top. That thing in the pit of my stomach constantly pulling me between the past and the present stretched taut, like the moment of stalemate in a tug of war. I knew I couldn't stay on this beach forever, but equally, I didn't want to leave.

Leaving felt so final, like giving up, and I just wasn't ready to admit that I might never see Joe again. And so I waited, watching the sun rise with a casual elegance to its highest point, teetering at its apex in the sky before it ultimately succumbed to its inevitable descent. My phone buzzed again and I sighed, heaving myself to my feet. My joints were cold and stiff from sitting for so long, but something else was weighing them down as I trudged slowly back up the beach, something heavy and absolute. I paused at the bottom of the steps, unable to resist the temptation to glance once more over my shoulder, a fresh wave of disappointment my only reward.

'Leaving so soon? Personally, I thought I was worth at least five more minutes.'

I misjudged the next step, stumbling forwards and only narrowly avoiding dropping my phone over the side. Joe was stood at the top of the stairs, one brown boot slung casually over the other as though *he'd* been the one waiting for *me*. The initial relief at seeing him was short-lived, swept away by an unexpected wave of anger. The sight of him stood there so calmly, after I'd just run around half of Hove searching for him, made my blood run hot. It took everything I had to resist punching him, imprisoning my hands in my oversized sleeves so as not to alarm the elderly couple on the bench opposite.

'I waited for over an hour,' I hissed, not pausing to see if he was following as I stormed off down the board-walk. Joe had to break into a semi-jog just to keep up.

'Huh. So, kind of like that time you were an hour late for the new James Bond film, then?' he answered cheekily.

My jaw clenched. 'Don't do that.'

'Do what?'

'Try and make light of the situation. There's no light left, OK, Joe?'

We walked in silence for a while, weaving our way through the throngs of people.

'You don't have to wait for me, you know,' Joe said softly, rubbing his palm against the back of his neck.

I closed my eyes, the pain almost too much to bear.

'I don't know how to do that,' I said slowly, fighting to keep my voice steady.

'You don't know how to do what?'

'Not wait for you!' I yelled, tears streaming from the corners of my eyes as I whirled around to face him, hair flying in front of my face. A woman turned to stare at me, placing a protective arm around her little boy and giving me a wide berth as they hurried past. 'I don't know how to do life without you, Joe. I've tried. Believe me, all I've done this year is *try*. Try to move on, but not forget. Try to be strong, but also gentle with myself. Try to live in the present, but not let the past die. But I'll always wait for you, for a thousand lifetimes, Joe, if it means we get to spend just five more minutes together.'

'But it's not real, Jenny,' Joe insisted, an urgency to his voice that hadn't been there before. 'This—' he waved his palm back and forth between us '—this isn't real. What we had *is* real and nothing can ever take that away from us. But the world won't wait for you, Jenny. Life's short – and, trust me, I should know.' For once I didn't find his attempt to lighten the mood endearing, or even remotely funny, my mouth setting in a grim, firm line. 'Don't waste your future by longing for the past.'

He made it sound so simple. Like letting him go was as easy as allowing the string of a balloon to slip through your fingers, watching it float away on the wind, growing smaller and smaller until it disappeared completely from view. Bile rose in my throat and I turned away, my pace quickening as I pounded the pavement, unsure whether I was running from or towards something. Joe ran ahead of me, walking backwards so I was forced to look at him.

'Would you change it?' he demanded.

'What?'

'Would you go back and make it so we never met? Erase every night we spent together, every kiss, every whispered conversation under the duvet, just so you didn't have to endure the pain when it ended?'

I scowled at him, furious that he'd even suggest such a thing. 'Of course not.'

Joe smacked his hand against his thigh as if I'd just proved his point. 'Exactly! So then why are you denying yourself a chance at happiness again? Wouldn't you want the same thing for me if it were the other way around?'

For a second, I wished it *were* the other way around. That it had been me the drunk driver had hit, just so I wouldn't be the one left with a giant hole punched through their heart, an excruciating, constant reminder that something was missing. My feet stilled on the lip of the pavement, the lump in my throat unmoving as I registered where I was. I was stood at one of the traffic-light controlled crossings on the main road that ran along the promenade. The exact spot where Joe had his accident. My hand reached out, holding on to the traffic light pole for support as my mind travelled back to that day, the day my whole world ended.

It had started just like any ordinary Tuesday. But then again, aren't all days ordinary until they're not? The usual slept-through alarms (me), dashing frantically about the flat whilst simultaneously trying to put on socks and brush teeth (again, me), freshly made coffee brewing in the kitchen (Joe), a stolen kiss bouncing off someone's jawbone as we sailed past each other. I hurtled towards the front door like a whirlwind with a hurried *remember to grab some milk on your way home today, yeah?* over my shoulder before the door slammed shut behind me. I'd obsessed about that final conversation for weeks. Months. Chastising myself for not saying *I love you* like I normally did every morning. For not taking a second to stop and look into those ocean-blue eyes of his, to taste his lips on mine. Because you never think that will be the last time. You assume there'll be a tomorrow. You think you have forever. But Joe didn't bring any milk home that day. A drunk driver had seen to that, running a red light and crashing straight into the side of Joe's bike. And just like that, he was gone.

My phone vibrated again, and I dug it out of my pocket. Luca. Again.

'Jenny—'

I turned back to the sound of Joe's voice, his face the last thing I saw as I stepped off the kerb. I didn't see that the little man wasn't green, or that people were still waiting patiently on the cobbled pavement opposite. I certainly didn't see the cyclist approaching from my right, weaving in and out of the waiting queue of cars. All I saw was Joe's pupils widen with horror behind his glasses as I felt the crushing impact, my body crumpling as the ground rushed up to meet me. And then everything went black.

I knew even before I opened my eyes that I was in the hospital. I could feel the stiff, scratchy sheets beneath my bare legs, the open-backed polyester gown bunched uncomfortably somewhere around my hips. The hot, stale air had the bitter taste of disinfectant, burning the back of my throat as I listened to the repetitive beeping coming from somewhere to my left. I tried to ignore the machine, but each beep was louder than the last, mocking me with the reminder that even after everything, my broken heart was somehow still beating. I turned my head away, not wanting to watch the little red line leaping joyously upwards on the monitor. And there was Luca. All six foot something of him crammed awkwardly into the hardbacked chair beside the bed, one hand resting on his thigh, the other stretched outwards, his fingertips resting on the edge of the bed less than a centimetre from my own. His eyes were closed, dark, bruise-like shadows beneath them, as his chest rose and fell in a steady rhythm. I tried to sit up, pushing my hand flat against the hard, plastic-lined mattress, but a sudden sharp pain shot through my ribs like a red-hot poker.

'*Ow!*'

Luca's eyes blinked open as I sucked my breath in sharply between my teeth, my hand flying to my right-hand side, which felt tender and swollen beneath my grazed fingers.

'You're awake.' His voice was thick like cotton wool, speaking of missed sleep and endless worry. 'Are you in pain? Do you want me to get the nurse?'

I shook my head, my hand reaching out to catch his as he jumped to his feet.

'Don't go.'

His brow softened, his eyes warm like melted chocolate as he slowly sat back down, the plastic covering letting out a small sigh as he resumed his position by my side. 'I'm not going anywhere, Jenny. I'm right here.'

'What happened?' I frowned, my brain sluggish and slow as I tried to fill in the blanks. My head was pounding, and I winced as my fingers ran over a neat, raised line of sutures along my hairline.

'You were getting coffee, remember?' Luca said gently.

I nodded slowly, an image of Drew's flashing into my mind.

'Well, you were gone a while. I was starting to get worried, but you weren't picking up your phone, so . . .' Luca's voice drifted off, unspoken questions lingering in the air between us as his eyes scanned my face, searching for answers.

'I was crossing the road,' I said slowly, my brow furrowing with the effort of trying to clear the fog.

'That's right. The cyclist came out of nowhere apparently, the woman waiting to cross on the other side of the road saw the whole thing.'

'*Jenny?*'

All the breath rushed out of me, the sound of my name coming from somewhere down the hall setting off a violent sequence of flashbacks, the fog clearing just enough to reveal the details. A lonely figure in a coffee-stained sweatshirt and floaty red dress sat amongst the pebbles, hugging her knees to her chest. The concerned looks on people's faces as I stormed past them, one lady muttering *bit early, isn't it?* as her friend mimed glugging from an imaginary bottle. The way Joe's glasses kept slipping down his nose as he hurried to keep up with me. Joe.

My head snapped up, towards the sound of fast-approaching footsteps echoing down the corridor. Alice skidded to a halt in the doorway, both hands bracing themselves against the doorframe, her chest heaving beneath her scrubs. She was still wearing a blue surgical cap, a disposable face mask hanging loosely around her neck as if she hadn't bothered to take the three seconds required to remove it.

'Jenny,' she sighed breathlessly, her grip on the door loosening a fraction as she analysed me quickly from head to toe, her breathing slowing with each limb accounted for. 'I came as soon as I heard. I was in surgery and I didn't see my page until—'

'It's fine. I'm fine,' I reassured her, my vision blurring at the edges as she darted forwards, her arms flinging themselves around me. Her eyes were shining when she finally loosened her grip, lifting her torso from mine but keeping a firm hold of my hand, as though she was afraid to let me go.

'You're a total cow for doing this to me, you know that?' She sniffed. 'I was scared shitless when they paged me saying you'd been in an accident.'

I managed a weak smile. 'I know, so selfish of me.'

'*Very* selfish,' Alice maintained fiercely, before her face softened slightly. 'Honestly, I don't even know why we're friends.'

I laughed and then instantly regretted it, my hand flying to my ribs once more. Alice frowned, grabbing the chart hanging from the end of my bed and flicking aggressively through it, eyes skimming over multiple scans and notes. She held an X-ray up to the light.

'Fractured ribs. Mild head laceration. Grade three concussion. You're lucky it wasn't worse,' she concluded, her eyes flicking up to read the monitor beside me and giving a brisk nod of satisfaction. 'What the hell happened? It says here you were in some sort of a collision?'

My eyes dropped to the cheap, scratchy bedsheets, suddenly taking an unnecessary interest in the arrangement of the pillows behind me. Luca got to his feet, fluffing and plumping them for me, which just made the stone in the pit of my stomach feel ten times heavier.

'Jenny had gone out to get us some coffee, and on her way back some asshole cyclist crashed into her when she was crossing the Kingsway,' Luca explained, pummelling one of the pillows. 'The paramedic must have seen I was the last person to call Jenny so they phoned me, told me what happened.'

'Hang on, you were at your old flat? Together?' Alice's eyes flitted from me to Luca to the plastic bag containing my clothes on the table by the window, the red silk tie of the dress I'd worn the night before peeking out one side. Luca turned to me, unsure if he'd said the wrong thing. But I couldn't look at him. I couldn't look at either of them, my fingers twisting a loose thread in my hospital gown back and forth.

'But why were you on that side of the road? Drew's is the other way,' Alice probed, her eyes narrowing suspiciously. My heart began to race, blood pumping in my ears in time to the increasingly rapid beeping of the heart rate monitor. My eyeballs bulged in their sockets, silently screaming at Alice to drop it. Her bottle-green eyes did not miss a trick as they darted to Luca and then back to me, her mouth forming a silent O of understanding.

'Speaking of caffeine, you couldn't be a doll and grab me a coffee, could you, Luca?' Alice smiled sweetly, batting her eyelashes as she plopped herself dramatically on the end of the bed with a sigh, rubbing at a muscle between her shoulder blades. 'Twelve-hour shifts are a killer,' she groaned.

'Oh, sure. Do you want anything, Jenny?' Luca's hand came to rest gently on my arm and I could hardly bear the tenderness of it. I flinched, guilt flooding through me at the look of concern that flashed across his face as he withdrew his hand. 'Sorry, did that hurt?'

I pressed my lips together, forcing a smile. 'It's fine.' The lie felt tacky and reluctant in my mouth. We both watched Luca exit the room, disappearing down the corridor in search of the cafe. Alice waited until he was out of view before she turned back to me, arms folded neatly across her chest. The silence seemed to stretch on forever, the ticking of the clock on the wall opposite marking each uncomfortable second. Tick. Tick. Tick. I could feel Alice's eyes on me, big and wide and expectant. Tick. Tick. I wound the loose thread tighter around my finger, the tip turning bright red.

'What's going on, Jenny? Where were you before the accident?'

Something about her voice told me she already knew the answer, but I couldn't bring myself to say it out loud. Admit that I'd been lying these past few months whenever she'd asked me about Joe.

'I was getting coffee.'

Alice sighed impatiently, jumping to her feet as she paced back and forth in front of the hospital bed. 'That's bullshit and we both know it. I mean, let's just skip over your whole little sleepover situation for one second . . .' She paused, clearly hoping I might fill in some missing details, but when I didn't, she continued her interrogation without even drawing breath. 'Drew's is in completely the opposite direction, Jenny, you had no reason to be along the seafront. You were with him, weren't you? You were with Joe.'

Oof. Alice was still one of the only people that could throw Joe's name into conversation without an awkward pause or painful wince. She was also the only person who

263

could guess what had been going on. Hot angry tears raced each other down my cheeks, the thread breaking off in my fingers. One look at my face was all the confirmation that Alice needed.

'Jenny, you told me that you had a handle on it. That the hallucinations had stopped.'

'They did stop. For a while,' I added, my voice small. 'That's the problem.'

I felt the bed dip slightly as Alice resumed her position by my feet, her trainers dangling several inches above the floor below. She reached out, stilling my fidgeting fingers in hers.

'Jenny, look at me.' Alice's voice was gentle, but she squeezed my hand with an urgency that made me look up. 'These visions of Joe, I know you think they're helping but they're not. If anything, they're doing more damage. I mean, just look where they landed you.' I followed her gaze about the room, over the sad magnolia walls with their copious plug sockets, the standard-issue blue privacy curtain that hung from the rail above the bed, the dull strip lights emitting a low buzz.

'I'm so confused, Alice.' I sniffed, wincing as I took a long, shaky breath in, a sharp pain twisting in my ribs. 'This thing with Luca, it's – well, I don't know what it is.'

'Honey, you've basically been crushing on him since you met, that's what it is.'

'I have not! I hated him when I first met him. For most of the time I've known him, actually.'

Alice rolled her eyes. 'Potato, pot-arto. Put it this way, you've been spending a lot of time with him recently, correct?'

'Well, I've had to for work.'

'And you had a sleepover the other night after your date?'

'Ergh, can we stop calling it a sleepover! What are we, eight years old?'

'Fine. You had sex,' Alice huffed, sounding slightly peeved at my constant interruptions. She held a palm up when I opened my mouth. 'Don't even try and pretend you didn't, you don't wear a dress like that—' she cocked an eyebrow in the direction of the plastic bag '—and not finish the night with it either torn to shreds or on the floor. What I mean is, being with Luca seems to make you happy. The happiest I've seen you in a long time, in fact. But you're scared to go all in because that means you've got something to lose again.'

Even I couldn't argue with that logic.

'I do like spending time with Luca,' I admitted after a while, testing the thought out. 'But the more I'm in his life, the less Joe's in mine, and when I realised that being with him came at the expense of Joe disappearing, I felt . . .' Alice waited, bobbing her head encouragingly. 'I was scared.'

'Right, now we're getting somewhere!' Alice declared, slapping the bed triumphantly. 'Scared of what?'

'Of losing him all over again.'

'And?'

My voice had shrunk to barely more than a whisper, the tight ache of approaching tears at the back of my throat. 'Of opening my heart again only for it to be shattered.'

Alice sat back, letting my words linger between us for a moment. Something inside me had come loose, the truth that I'd been holding on to tightly for so long unravelling around me like a ball of wool.

'Jenny, there comes a point when we all have to let go. No one can hold on forever, and that doesn't mean you love Joe any less or want to forget him, but the thing about looking back all the time is that you can't see where you're going. You'll stumble and fall and hurt yourself over and over again, until the day you find you can't get up anymore. And I can't lose another friend, Jenny. I *won't*.' Alice's bottom lip wobbled as she shook her head, her eyes rolling up towards the ceiling and blinking fast several times to curb the tears glistening behind her lashes. My heart ached for my friend, but there was guilt there too, tight and heavy as it dawned on me what it must have been like for her to get that page. Just like the one she'd gotten the night Joe was admitted.

'Jenny! Sweetheart.'

I turned to see Mum barging her way through the door, her jet-black hair sticking out at all angles, her bar apron still double-knotted around her waist. 'Oh, she's sitting up. You're sitting up.' She sighed, her hand flying to her chest in relief as though the ability to sit at a ninety-degree-angle was a sure sign of a clean bill of health. 'She's sitting up, Jacob. She's all right,' she bellowed down the corridor as a wheezing Jacob appeared behind her, clutching the side of his chest with a pained expression on his face. His shoulders sagged with relief when he saw me, his small smile the only evidence of the silent conversation we shared without either of us saying a word.

'Thank God, because I might need that hospital bed at this rate,' he gasped, collapsing red-faced into the vacant chair beside the bed. Alice rolled her eyes at her brother's dramatic entrance.

'What happened, darling? Are you hurt?' Mum asked, her forehead puckered with worry as she stroked my hair back from my face, the way she always did when I was young and came home with a grazed knee and a tear-stained face.

'I'm fine, Mum, really.'

'Well, I wouldn't call three fractured ribs and five stitches fine,' Alice muttered pointedly. Mum's hand flew to her mouth in horror and I threw Alice a look that told her she wasn't helping.

'What's all this Jacob was telling me on the drive over about you having – *visions of Joe*?' Mum whispered, her eyes wide with worry as she pushed the already tightly tucked bedding further down the side of the bed. Both Alice and I turned to look at Jacob, whose cheeks turned an even deeper shade of beetroot.

'I'm sorry, she practically forced it out of me,' Jacob babbled apologetically. 'Plied me with that Tupperware of biscuits she keeps in the glove compartment of her car.'

'Ah yes, that well-known torture technique. I'm surprised you lived to tell the tale,' Alice snorted, reaching over and flicking crumbs from the front of his shirt. Jacob swatted his sister's hand away with an irritated scowl.

'Is it true, Jenny? Have you been having these, these—'

'Grief hallucinations,' Alice finished as Mum floundered for the correct terminology.

Mum nodded, pointing at Alice. 'Yes, those.'

I wriggled uncomfortably beneath the sheets, suddenly wanting very much to pull them up and over my head. 'Yes,' I admitted, my cheeks warming with embarrassment.

'And how long has this been going on, exactly?' She looked first at me, then at Alice, then at Jacob, who started whistling the tune of Radiohead's 'Creep'.

'Since Joe's funeral,' Alice eventually answered.

'That long?!' Mum exclaimed, her teeth worrying at her bottom lip.

'I thought you said they'd stopped?' Jacob frowned.

'She lied,' Alice replied for me.

'Oh, Jenny,' Mum sighed, her hand coming to rest on my arm. 'Why didn't you tell me? I could have helped.'

'Sorry Jenny, I should never have said anything,' Jacob prattled to my right. 'It's just that your mum can be *very* persuasive when she wants to be—'

'I thought I heard you talking to yourself in your room a few times, but I just assumed you were on the phone or something,' Mum muttered, more to herself than me, her eyes shining with some newfound understanding as she connected the dots. I raked my fingers through my hair, wincing as my nail snagged against one of my stitches. It was too much, the questions coming at me from all sides, the heavy looks of concern like a weight pressing hard against my chest, making it difficult to breathe.

'—and then she got the shortbread out,' Jacob continued.

'Jacob, no one cares about the sodding shortbread,' Alice tutted.

'Well, it's relevant, Alice. You know shortbread's my weakness. I didn't just cave for a bloody rich tea.'

'I'm your mother, I should have known something was wrong. I just never dreamt you were talking to your dead—'

'*Yes!*' It came out louder than intended, the thing winding tighter and tighter inside of me finally snapping. 'Yes, I've been seeing my dead fiancé. Yes, I've been talking to him and going to our favourite places with him and blowing you guys off to spend time with him. And yes, I know that's not healthy, but I don't know how else to do this. To do life without him.'

I'm not sure what made me look up in that moment. Why I tore my eyes from the polyester bed sheets polka-dotted with my tears. Maybe it was the sound of laughter drifting up the corridor from the nearby nurses' station. Or the sudden intake of breath echoing in the silence that followed my words. Or perhaps I just felt him. Standing there in the doorway, three cups balanced in a cardboard coffee holder in one hand, a bunch of cellophane-wrapped flowers in the other. They were aggressively bright, sunshine-yellow daffodils and clashing orange gerbera daisies, like they were trying too hard to be cheerful. But I wasn't looking at the flowers. My eyes were fixed on Luca's face. It was blank, unreadable, but there was something wrong with his eyes – a pain that he was trying very hard to hide. I felt a spasm of unease twist in my gut. *How long had he been standing there?*

'You've been seeing Joe this whole time?' His voice cracked, split open by the sharp sting of betrayal as all my worst fears were confirmed. The beeping next to me was going crazy, my heart threatening to leap out my chest at the pain etched into Luca's brow as I watched the shadow of the past darken his features.

'It's not what you think—' I began, tripping over the words in my haste to get them all out at once, to stop the wall I could see going up, brick by brick, behind Luca's eyes. He cleared his throat, not looking at me.

'The nurse said you're only allowed three visitors at a time, so I'm going to head out.' His voice was emotionless as he set the coffees down on the table, looking around as if unsure of what to do with the flowers before thrusting them into Jacob's lap.

'Luca, please don't go!' I called after him. But it was too late.

He was already gone.

18

No one will ever convince me that time moves to a constant, steady rhythm. Not with the way it drags throughout the week, Monday dripping reluctantly into Tuesday, Wednesday seeming to last an eternity, each day longer than the last, until 5 p.m. on Friday rolls around and then you blink and the weekend's over. The past two weeks since I'd been discharged from hospital had felt like one never-ending Wednesday, the minute hand moving with a slow sort of reluctance around the grease-spattered clock face in Mum's kitchen, the hour hand even slower. I'd not seen Luca since the hospital. Not spoken one word to him. Well, technically I'd spoken a lot of words, via texts, emails, and so many left voicemails that a very well-spoken lady now informed me that *the mailbox you are trying to reach is full* whenever I dialled his number. And . . .

. . . nothing.

I'd watched as the double ticks next to my latest overly long apology turned blue, confirming he'd read it, only for him to go offline again a second later without even the briefest appearance of three dots to show that he'd considered responding. He just didn't want to talk to me. Period. And, it would seem, neither did Joe, who I'd also not seen since that day, the expression on his face before I hit the tarmac still branded on my mind. A constant reminder of that ever-present ache deep in my chest, the hole where something used to be.

'Any messages?' I asked Beryl, pausing at her desk on the way to mine after returning from a particularly harrowing trip to Autumn Lodge, the local care home that had been hit with a chlamydia outbreak. *You're never too old to get a cheeky leg over* was the exact quote I'd scribbled down from one resident, who looked about ninety and was wheeling his oxygen tank behind him en route to collect his course of antibiotics. Beryl swivelled slowly in her chair to face me, her lips pinched into a tight pout of annoyance.

'No, Jennifer. Once again, *no one* called for you,' she said coolly, no doubt still pissed off from the last time I asked her a few hours ago. Or because she didn't take kindly to being a glorified PA, even though it was literally her job to field incoming calls.

'So how are the Viagra-popping residents of Autumn Lodge?' Jacob asked with a grin as I eased myself gently into my chair. After two weeks off work, my ribs were healing nicely and the bruising was all but gone, but they were still tender and I was under strict instructions from Alice to take it easy.

'Apparently the gentlemen operate a colour-coded tie system to state their sexual preferences. Not sure why it's just the men that are allowed to be picky, but I didn't have the energy today to get into a debate about gender inequality with a bunch of Churchill-loving octogenarians. Blue means can't go on top – presumably for medical reasons but I wasn't about to ask for details – while green is code for no foreplay and red means up for anything,' I read, squinting at my scribbled notes.

'Let me guess. A man in a red tie told you that?'

I rolled my eyes at Jacob, hitting refresh on my emails. My heart sank deeper in my chest when Luca's name failed to appear in the list of three unread emails that materialised on my screen. My phone buzzed atop my notebook and my heart leapt upwards again, a constant boomerang of hopeful highs and crushing lows. I lunged for it, all fingers and thumbs as I knocked it to the floor in my haste to see who the message was from.

'Woah there.' Jacob held out a hand to stop me from bending down, reaching for my phone himself and placing it slowly back on the desk. 'Doctor's orders,' he said with a warning tone to his voice. I tapped the screen, everything inside of me plummeting at the sight of my mum's name.

Just checking in love. How's your day going? xx

I sighed, turning the phone over. The subtext to that message was *just checking to see if you've had any visions of your dead ex-fiancé today?* She'd been 'checking in' multiple times a day since I'd been discharged from hospital, fussing around me like a mother bird. Thankfully she'd drawn the line so far at regurgitating food for me, but the way she was going, I didn't think it was far off.

'You still not heard from Luca then?' Jacob guessed, not looking up from his screen. He was reading the latest

'Forbes 30 Under 30' list which just added to my rage. I was tired of fucking '30 under 30' lists. You know who I wanted to see? The 55-year-old who'd just graduated university. Or the 70-year-old who'd set up their first business selling hand-knitted scarves on Etsy. Show me that person. Not the bleary-eyed twenty-somethings killing themselves to exceed some unrealistic benchmark set by a society that declares if you haven't '*made it*' (whatever the fuck that means) by thirty, you've essentially failed.

'Nope,' I said, stabbing my mouse with excessive force on the delete button of one of Beryl's twice-weekly company-wide emails. (This one was requesting that employees refrain from drinking milk directly from the cartons in the fridge. I noticed Rahul shrinking down in his chair to my right, doing a very bad job of not looking guilty.)

'Well, you can talk to him tomorrow night at the concert,' Jacob declared simply, as though that were the answer to all my problems, not the very thing I'd been dreading these past two weeks.

'Call me crazy, but I think two weeks of radio silence means he probably won't be jumping for joy at seeing me in person. Besides, whatever this' – I waved my hand through the air, racking my brains for a way to describe what Luca and I had – '*thing* was between us, it was a mistake.'

Jacob paused his scrolling, spinning in his chair to face me.

'Oh no, you don't get to do that,' he said, wagging his ballpoint pen at me.

'Do what?'

'Give up on the chance of anyone getting close to you after being scalded one time.'

'I think my fiancé dying did a lot more than just scald me, Jacob,' I snapped. 'It fucking destroyed me, burnt everything to the ground until there was nothing left.' The deluge of emotions I'd been holding in these past few weeks were teetering on my lashes, threatening to overflow at any moment.

'I know it did,' he said softly, wheeling closer until our knees were touching. A shadow passed across his face that made me instantly regret my outburst. Sometimes I forgot that I wasn't the only one who'd lost Joe, that I didn't have a monopoly on grief. 'But Luca healed you in a way that none of us could this past year,' Jacob continued, dropping his head until he caught my eye. 'He brought you back to life, sparked something in you that had been snuffed out, and that's been a beautiful thing to watch. Nothing has the power to hurt as much as loving someone, Jenny, but nothing heals quite like it either. I mean, Christ, I would have given up this whole dating game years ago otherwise.'

'I've tried, Jacob. I've phoned, I've texted, I've emailed. I even arranged for the restaurant we had our date at to send him a pizza with I'M SORRY written on it in tiny pieces of pepperoni. He returned it. Uneaten.'

'Well, that's just wasteful,' Jacob tutted, horrified that anyone would turn down pizza. 'It's a good thing that the Jenny Thompson I know doesn't give up easily, then,' he said, holding my gaze challengingly.

My eyes narrowed. 'Seriously? You're really appealing to my competitive side right now?'

'Is it working?'

'Not even a little,' I lied, pushing his chair back towards his desk.

A familiar wheezing *ahem ahem* behind me made me close my eyes; this was *so* not what I needed right now. I took a long, calming breath in for five seconds before spinning around in my chair, forcing my face into something vaguely resembling a smile.

'All set for the concert tomorrow night, Jenny? Mrs Kingston and I are greatly looking forward to it,' Derek bellowed, running his thumbs up and down the too-tight straps of his braces.

'Yeah, about that. Something's come up and I'm not sure I'll be able to make it tomorrow,' I lied, turning my bottom lip downwards in a fake picture of disappointment. Jacob's brilliant white Veja came down purposefully on my own battered Converse. I ignored him.

'What do you mean, you're not going to make it?' Derek huffed, beads of perspiration already gathering on his forehead. 'I've reserved the front page for a write-up, Jenny, I don't need you letting the side down.'

'I've asked Sally to cover it for me,' I said quickly, making a mental note to fire off an email to Sally ASAP as Jacob pressed down harder on my toe. Derek shook his head so fast he looked like he was malfunctioning, a strand of his greased-back hair breaking free from its normally impenetrable Brylcreem shell.

'No, that won't work. That won't work at all. Sally's off work for the foreseeable – doctor signed her off with *stress*,' he tutted, waggling his fingers in little air quotes as though mental health were a made-up concept. A dog-ate-my-homework-style excuse. 'No, you'll have to go, Jenny; the show must go on, as they say.' He chortled, an awkward silence as he waited for one of us to commend him on his play on words. When we failed to oblige, he slicked the rogue strand of hair back against his head with the palm of his hand, clearing his throat loudly. 'Yes, well, that's settled then. I will see you *both* there tomorrow. No excuses,' he added firmly, when I opened my mouth to argue.

'No excuses,' Jacob mouthed silently at me as Derek waddled off to terrorise some other employee. I ripped a page out of my notebook, screwed it into a tiny ball and lobbed it at Jacob's head.

'It's quite the turnout, isn't it?' Mum remarked, her eyes sparkling almost as much as her green sequin jumpsuit as we joined the queue of people snaking their way round the car park towards the community centre.

'Mhmm,' I managed, my voice shaky. My brain was incapable of forming words right now, of thinking about anything except Luca. What I'd say when I saw him. What he'd say when he saw me. Oh God, what if he didn't say anything at all? Or worse, gave me a tight smile and a firm handshake as though I were just like everyone else here tonight? I stood on my tiptoes, bobbing this way and that to try and catch a glimpse of the front of the queue, but there were too many people, my view obstructed by the back of Terry's head several inches above everyone else's.

'You all right?' Jacob murmured next to me, hoisting his camera bag further up one shoulder as the queue inched forwards.

'Fine,' I said quickly. Too quickly. Jacob's fingers found mine, giving them a squeeze that said *I'm here*. I smiled at him, message gratefully received, albeit doing next to nothing to still my rapidly beating heart.

As soon as I saw him, it felt like someone had tied a ten-tonne weight around my heart and thrown it overboard, my fingers tightening so hard in Jacob's that I heard him suck his breath in sharply between his teeth. There he was. Stood on the cracked top step of the community centre dressed all in black. Black shirt unbuttoned just enough to reveal a hint of olive skin, black trousers, black hair in its normal unruly tangle that on anyone else would look scruffy but on him, looked just right. Perfect, in fact.

Luca's eyes flickered down the line, a brief nod or smile for someone he recognised, before catching on mine. His smile dropped, like a storm cloud passing in front of the sun, and my chest stung in response. I watched as a thousand emotions passed across his face, rippling the muscles along his jawline. Surprise, as if he wasn't 100% sure I would come tonight. Betrayal. Anger. Pain. That last one made me look down at my feet for a second, shame and regret flooding over me as I was hit with the memory of him stood in that doorway, the remnants of whatever had been between us lying broken at his feet. By the time I looked up again, Luca had turned sharply on his heel, muttering something in Ivan's ear. Ivan's eyes found me in the queue; he gave a brisk nod of understanding and then Luca was gone, ducking inside the hall just as we reached the stone steps.

'Aha, the woman that made it all happen,' Ivan announced grandly, holding both arms open wide and pulling me in for a hug.

'Hardly,' I mumbled into the bobbly knit of his cardigan, my cheeks flushed with embarrassment.

'Luca just had to . . .' Ivan threw his thumb vaguely over one shoulder, eyes rolling heavenward as though searching for a plausible end to that sentence. Clearly coming up short, he turned to greet my mum. 'And this must be the infamous Ms Thompson?'

'Oh gosh, what's she been telling you?' I heard Mum titter behind me as Jacob and I stepped inside.

'I'm sorry, have we come to the right place?' Jacob let out a low whistle, his head performing a slow one-eighty from shoulder to shoulder as he gawked at our surroundings. The hall was packed. Neat rows of mismatched chairs on either side of a makeshift aisle were already filling up, the air thick with a heady cocktail of one too many perfumes which, while a little overwhelming in such a small space, did a good job of hiding the damp smell. Rainbow-coloured bunting crisscrossed from one side of the hall to the other, the lights turned down low enough to reveal a canopy of a thousand glow-in-the-dark stars stuck to the roof above us.

'And they say you can't polish a turd. Well, never have I seen a more beautiful, sparkly turd in all my life!' Jacob declared, the shutter of his camera firing like a machine gun. He was right. It was beautiful.

'And to think they want to close this place down,' someone tutted to my right. I turned to see a woman with a 1960s hairdo that looked highly flammable and a practical button-down shirt dress. From the framed photograph on Derek's desk, I recognised her to be his wife. Derek was stood beside her sporting the most hideous brown suit and yellow shirt combination that I had ever seen, clutching a paper plate piled high with beige food.

'Yes, terrible. Truly terrible,' he agreed, doing an uncanny impression of a turkey with the skin under his chin as he shook his head so vigorously that a bit of whatever he'd just stuffed into his mouth flew through the air, landing on the back of a poor unsuspecting passer-by. 'When I heard that their funding had been cut, I told my team to drop everything. This was the number one priority.' *Number one priority, my arse.*

I pressed my lips tightly together as I pulled my notebook out of my bag, feeling a familiar jolt of electricity as I ran my fingers over the blank page. The thrill I always got whenever I started a new story, of not knowing where it might take me. But there was only one ending that I was interested in tonight.

Even when I wasn't looking at him, I knew where Luca was at all times. Could feel his presence as he moved about the hall, smiling and mingling with everyone but me. His lashes splayed across his cheeks, his eyes catching mine over the shoulder of a woman in a cherry-red kimono, as if he could feel it too. This maddening, undeniable pull between us, as though both our hearts were tied to either end of a fishing line. A frown burrowed itself into his forehead and he looked away again.

'So stubborn,' I muttered angrily to myself, cursing Luca's refusal to meet me halfway.

'Sounds like someone else I know.' Jacob lifted his camera away from his face for a second to give me a knowing look.

I scowled at him, clicking the top of my pen up and down, up and down, as I watched the kimono-wearing woman turn and hurry over to where two young boys were passing a can of Coke back and forth between them with the saucer-eyed, lip-licking look of two children who'd already consumed far too much sugar.

'Well, go on then,' Jacob urged, giving me a firm shove in the square of my back that sent me stumbling forwards. Luca's jaw tensed as he saw me approaching, turning in a wild, desperate circle before tagging onto a group of people to his right.

'So sorry to interrupt, but do you mind if I borrow this one for a second?' My hand clamped down on Luca's forearm, his whole body going rigid at my touch.

'I'm actually in the middle of something,' Luca said tightly, still refusing to address me directly. The woman to his left peered up at him, with clearly no idea who he was.

'Just one second,' I repeated, teeth clenched as I dragged him away from the group, heart pounding from the effort. Or maybe it was the feeling of his skin against mine. Warm and smooth and oh so familiar.

'What?' he said briskly, snatching his arm free.

'I thought we should talk.'

'About what?'

I sighed. So, he was playing the let's-pretend-it-never-happened card. Fair enough. My own version was so dog-eared and tattered from overuse that it was barely discernible these days.

'About us.'

'Us?'

It was said quickly, but I still felt the kick. The mocking undertone that kids used to tease their friends who still believed in Father Christmas. A man in a pink shirt walked past, clapping Luca on the back in greeting. Luca's face broke into a smile, that gorgeous, crooked smile that still turned my insides to liquid, the one I used to be able to draw from him so easily. God, what I'd give for him to smile at me like that again. But it vanished as soon as the man went to find his seat, his face hardening when he turned back to me.

'Yes, you and me,' I pressed gently.

Luca sighed. 'There is no you and me, Jenny. There never was. I realise that now.'

'That's just not true.' I took a small step forward, my hand reaching for his arm, but he recoiled, colliding with a chair in his haste to keep that physical boundary between us. My hand dropped uselessly by my side, the ache that had taken root since I saw Luca stood in the hospital doorway, fingers clenched around that cellophane-wrapped bouquet, burying an inch deeper into my chest. 'I was going to tell you Luca, truly I *was*.'

'No, you weren't.' He shook his head with the pained conviction of someone who'd been here before. Who'd lived through it once and vowed to never do so again. The unspoken comparison to Rachel made me wince.

'I wanted to. I just . . .' My voice trailed off, a fierce, desperate need to correct this misplaced belief he had about himself suddenly more important than finishing that sentence. 'It was never a question of you not being enough, Luca. You are enough, I want you to know that. I *need* you to know that.'

Luca scoffed, scuffing his shoe against the floor. 'Could have fooled me.'

He turned to leave but I grabbed his hand, afraid of what it might mean to watch him walk away from this thing we'd both been cradling so carefully between us. This maddening, beautiful, petrifying thing, which I realised in that moment I didn't want to end.

'Luca, *please*,' I begged, my grip tightening around his wrist. I didn't know it was possible to miss a person so much when they were standing right in front of you. But this hard-faced, stony-eyed man looking back at me was not the Luca that I knew. I missed that Luca. The one who annoyed me at least fifteen times a day. Who used to smile whenever he saw me, his eyes sparking with something hot and fiery. The one I could feel slipping away from me.

'I can't do this again, Jenny,' he hissed fiercely, his eyes like two flames when they finally met mine. Two dwindling flames on the verge of being snuffed out. 'I can't open my heart to someone, trust them with the deepest, darkest parts of myself, only to learn that their heart belongs to someone else.' His voice was frayed, painful. A bitter cocktail of regret and guilt burnt the back of my throat as I watched Luca's fingers rake his hair back from his face. God, that beautiful, perfect face. It looked broken, hardened in places it shouldn't be. 'I have to protect myself, Jenny, and I'm not about to stand here and beg you to pick me, because that's not fair. To you. To me. To any of us.'

My stomach bottomed out, anger pumping red hot through my veins. Anger at everyone that had ever left him. Anger at anyone who'd made him feel like he wasn't good enough. Myself included. I wanted to tell him that he was worthy and deserving and that I for one couldn't imagine my life without him. But when I opened my mouth, no sound came out. Luca nodded, my silence all the confirmation he needed. I watched him walk away, his stride quick and decisive. A jolt went through me when he didn't turn back, my fingers outstretched as if trying to delay the moment of separation for as long as possible. I felt it then. My heart cracking and something inside of me unexpectedly shattering. Even though I thought there was nothing left to break.

'One. Two. One. Two. Testing. One, two, three.' Ivan's heavy breathing echoed down the microphone he was holding in one hand, the other shoved deep into the pocket of his cardigan of choice for the evening. Black with tiny gold stars scattered down the back.

'Ladies and gentleman, if you could please take your seats, the show will begin in five minutes.'

Fresh tears stung my eyes, and I blinked them away. I walked quickly over to the empty seat on the end of the row beside Mum, trying to ignore the searing pain in my heart. The very thing I'd been trying to avoid by keeping Luca at arm's length, and yet here I was, aching in places I'd forgotten even existed.

'All OK, love?' Mum's tone was purposefully light in a way that told me she knew everything was categorically *not* OK.

'Fine,' I whispered, digging my fingernails into the soft flesh of my palms in a bid to feel something, anything but the crippling pain in my chest. An old wound ripping open at the seams. I could feel Mum's eyes on me as I stared into space, unable to do anything but keep looking at the damp patch on the floor.

'Jenny, love?'

I didn't move. It was like my whole body was immobilised, finally broken beyond repair. I smelt Mum's hairspray as she leaned in closer, that retro floral scent of L'Oréal's Elnett that instantly transported me back to when I was little, bare feet kicking off the end of Mum's bed as I'd watch her getting ready, the hairspray tickling the back of my throat.

'Jenny, is it Joe? Is he here right now?'

The sound of Joe's name prompted something inside me to snap and my head spun round so fast I felt the tip of her nose brush against mine.

'No, Mum,' I hissed angrily, having to work to keep my voice from getting any louder. 'Joe's gone, all right? I've not seen him since my accident and it's becoming increasingly clear that I'm never going to see him again, OK? Are you happy?'

Mum's eyes crinkled at the edges, wincing at the sharp sting of my voice. I sighed, pulling the programme out from where it was bunched beneath me, pretending to read.

'You know,' Mum said slowly, as my fingertips scrunched at the edge of the programme, 'when someone or something we love dies, it feels like the whole world has stopped, frozen at that precise moment because the thought of life carrying on seems impossible. But no ice ever freezes so thick that it can never thaw, Jenny, and quite often that thawing can reveal hidden beauty beneath.' She paused, clearly hoping that I'd ask what she meant. What possible beauty could have come out of losing the very person that made my world turn? When I refused to play the game, she continued. 'Like the reminder that life's short, Jenny. Too short to take any of it for granted, and that we have a duty to make the most of every precious second, because every single one is a gift. By my calculations there's still—' she paused, each of her fingers touching her thumb in turn '—189 days left of the year. 50, 60, maybe even 70 odd years left on this planet for you, if you're lucky.'

'What are you saying?' I huffed impatiently.

'I'm saying you've still got time, sweetheart. Time to take a first step, time for doors to close and others to open. Time to say "goodbye" and "I love you". My point is there's still time,' she repeated, her fingers squeezing mine with such urgency I felt my eyes prickle with tears. 'There's no correct timeline for life, my darling. You do things at your own rhythm, in the order that *you* choose. Don't let what anyone else is doing dictate your next step or make you feel like a failure just because you're taking a different path. You're never too young, or too old, or too late. Happiness can still be found even in the darkest of times, you've just got to be willing to let it in.' She inclined her peroxide-blonde head over to where Luca was crouched beside the bench of children, simultaneously tying Kiki's shoelaces and pulling a silly face to crack a smile from an anxious-looking Andrea. A drop of water plopped onto the programme in my lap, blur-ring the words to nothing. I looked up, frowning at the roof before realising that it was me, big, silent tears roll-ing down my cheeks and into my lap.

I took a slow, steadying breath. 'I don't know, Mum,' I sighed wearily, twirling my engagement ring round and round my finger. 'I've made such a mess of things and I think it's too late to fix it.'

'It's never too late, sweetheart,' Mum said wisely, pat-ting my knee as the lights went down. 'Have you been to Joe's exhibition yet?' she whispered in the dark as the children marched single file onto the stage to rapturous applause. I frowned, wondering what that had to do with anything.

'You know I haven't. So, you can stop passive-aggressively leaving the flyer all over the house for me to find,' I huffed, annoyed she'd brought it up – although not as annoyed as I'd been on finding the flyer inside the fridge when I'd gone in search of orange juice that morning.

'It's the final night tomorrow. Your last chance to see it before it closes,' she pressed, a teasing singsong to her voice that made my jaw clench. She managed two seconds. Two seconds during the dying-off applause before she leaned in once more. 'Letting go is not forgetting, sweetheart. It just means that you find a way to survive without them, of remembering them without pain. I think you should go and see it.'

'OK!' I hissed through gritted teeth, stabbing the clicker of my pen with excessive force against my notepad. 'If I say I'll think about it, will you drop it?'

Mum sat back with a little humph of satisfaction, her lips pressed tightly together as though there were something else she was desperate to say. But then everything around me fell silent. Except for the beautiful, almost angelic sound of Kiki in her sparkly velvet dress standing centre stage, singing the opening lines of 'This Is Me' from The Greatest Showman. Little Kiki who'd barely uttered a single word since her mother died a year ago, her unwavering voice so full of strength and hope that it filled the entire hall, bursting through the holes in the leaky roof and spilling out into the night sky. It filled me too, touching every fibre of my being from my head right down to my toes, a pressure building inside of me like a balloon ready to take flight. Ready to soar.

19

'I can't do this.'

I was huddled in the doorway of a little antiques shop in The Lanes, counting the checkerboard black and white tiles beneath my feet to stop myself from hyperventilating.

'Jennifer Thompson,' Mum said firmly, her voice crackling in my ear down the phone. '*You* are the strongest person that I know. *You* can do anything.'

I managed a weak smile. 'It's just—'

'Do you want me to go with you? I could be down there in ten minutes?' I heard the faint jangle of her car keys amidst the raucous pub crowd and my heart swelled at the thought of her dropping everything just to be here with me. I took a deep, unsteady breath in through my nose.

'Thanks, but I think this is something I need to do on my own.'

'OK, love. Call me after? Let me know how it goes?' Her voice had that slightly giddy high-pitched tone of excited anticipation, as if she knew something I didn't.

I nodded, before realising that Mum couldn't see me.

'OK,' I muttered, grasping the phone tightly against my chest long after I'd ended the call.

The Lanes art gallery was abuzz with activity, light and laughter spilling out onto the cobbled street whenever the door opened, an endless stream of silk scarves and crisply pressed trousers coming and going. It took a few deep breaths before I could pluck up the courage to emerge from the shadow of the doorway, my ankles wobbling unsteadily as I crossed the street. A man in a smart black suit was manning the door. He looked up as I approached, eyes widening in recognition, even though I'd never met him before. He held the door open for me.

'Welcome to the Joseph Carter exhibition.' He smiled warmly, handing me a glossy pamphlet with Joe's face on the front cover. There he was, in glorious black-and-white. My Joe. I traced my fingers over the lines of his face, a familiar ache blooming in the pit of my stomach that made me just want to turn and run. I nodded dumbly, one foot still on the street, the other on the kerb, as though my feet were still deciding which way I should go.

'You've come just in time, it's the final day of the exhibition. Last chance to see it in all its glory.' The doorman's words were enough to propel me up the steps and through the door before I could change my mind.

It was busy inside, the air warm and alive with the buzz of conversation, bubbles chattering just as excitedly to each other in the long, thin-stemmed glasses that everyone seemed to be holding. I grabbed one from a passing tray, the waiter throwing me a judgemental look as I downed it in one, swapping my empty glass for another full one before he could move on. I joined a sort of unofficial queue, a woman dressed in all black shepherding me along behind a gentleman in a green corduroy suit. I was grateful to have been given some sort of direction, a set path to follow. The woman held my gaze for a second longer than normal, something akin to recognition passing across her face before she shifted her attention to the person behind me.

'Fantastic,' the man in green marvelled as we stood in front of the first photograph. It was a black-and-white portrait of an elderly couple. They were sat on one of the wrought-iron benches that lined the promenade, a tartan blanket stretched across both their shoulders as if they were a single entity. A package deal. The woman's shoes didn't quite meet the floor, the tips of her toes just scraping the concrete as she rested her head on the man's shoulder with the ease of someone who'd been doing it for a lifetime. Joe had chosen to take the photograph from behind, their stooped backs facing the camera, and I could see why. As an onlooker, you were treated to the very same view that the couple were enjoying, the vast expanse of ocean beyond the railings stretching as far as the eye could see, a sea of infinite patterns and colours.

'Just fantastic,' the man repeated before moving on to the next photograph, and I felt an overwhelming surge of pride. I had to tighten my grip on my champagne flute to stop myself from tapping him on the shoulder and saying *Joe took these. Yes, my Joe. Isn't he incredible?*

The next photograph was also black-and-white. A young girl wearing wellies that looked about two sizes too big, her face shining with pure, untarnished joy as Joe managed to capture the exact moment she landed in a giant puddle, water fanning around her like the hem of a skirt. I could almost hear the squeal of delight that her tiny O-shaped mouth must have made, my own mouth shaping itself into an involuntary smile. I walked slowly along, following the line of people around the room as we moved from photograph to photograph, each invoking a different emotion to the last.

A small crowd had gathered around the next installation, which had been suspended from the ceiling, giving it pride of place in the very centre of the gallery. I watched the backs of people's heads turn this way and that, pointing things out to the person next to them, but there were too many people for me to even glimpse a corner of it. And so I waited, sipping my champagne and experiencing it through everyone's facial expressions. People were smiling. Their shoulders shaking with laughter. Their brows creased thoughtfully. That man looked like he had tears in his eyes. And that woman – well, she was looking right at . . . me? I frowned, peering over my own shoulder, but there was no one behind me. She was two rows in front, so the fact she was looking in the opposite direction to everyone else wasn't exactly subtle. She whispered something to the woman stood next to her who also turned and glanced my way, something about what she saw prompting her to nod in agreement. I felt my cheeks flush and for some inexplicable reason I automatically looked down at my skirt, my free hand scrabbling blindly at the back to check it wasn't tucked into my knickers. It was not.

I smiled down at my Converse, the idea of that happening, of the world coming full circle and recreating the moment I first met Joe, tonight of all nights, enough to draw a bubble of laughter from my lips. By the time I looked up again, a gap had appeared in the crowd, and the image that greeted me made me freeze. It was the only photograph in full colour, the vibrant blues and yellows and reds almost blinding in their intensity amidst a room of black and white. But that wasn't what caused all the breath to leave my body.

It was me. The photograph was me. Or rather a version of myself that was so far from who I was today, I almost didn't recognise her. I was wearing my favourite blue dress, the one reserved for special occasions, with its tight fitted bodice and tulle skirt that stopped several inches above the ankle. My head was tipped backwards in frozen laughter, my arms stretched out almost as wide as the skirt of my dress, which formed a blurred ring around my shins. Rain was falling all around me, droplets glittering against the bare skin of my arms as I turned my head up towards the sky, welcoming the raindrops as they bounced around my bare feet. The memory was hazy to begin with, like looking through a fogged-up window, but then the edges sharpened, and I was jolted right back to that day.

It was a Saturday. A perfect summer's evening. July, I think. Joe and I were on our way back from a wedding, whose I don't remember. Clearly that detail was irrelevant. It was such a warm evening that we'd decided to walk home, Joe with his tuxedo jacket slung over one shoulder, me with my heels dangling from two fingers. We were talking about everything and nothing. Whose turn it was to make the hot chocolates that evening and whether we'd ever consider living abroad (after a full list of pros and cons, we settled on no, we'd miss our friends and family too much). Somehow, we then got onto the topic of who we thought would die first.

'Definitely me,' I proclaimed without hesitating. 'My love for ice cream coupled with your quite frankly ludicrous love affair with cycling means I'm probably already double your metabolic age.'

Joe laughed, loosening his bowtie so it hung around his collar. 'I always wanted to date an older woman.' He grinned, wiggling his eyebrows teasingly. I pushed him playfully away, but he grabbed hold of my hand, hooking his arm around my waist, not letting me go. 'Well, what with your sociopathic obsession with true crime podcasts, I'm going to say me.'

'I do know about ten different ways I could murder you and get away with it,' I agreed, my voice deadpan.

'I don't doubt it.' Joe chuckled, his fingers tickling my ribs until I squealed. We walked in silence for a while, our steps perfectly in sync. The sun had almost set, its pinky-orange hue flickering across the horizon, like someone had torn a rip in the otherwise ink-blue sky.

'If I did kick the bucket first though, I'd want you to find someone else.'

'You mean break my period of perpetual mourning?' I cried, my free hand flying dramatically to my chest in mock horror.

'I'm serious.' An edge to Joe's voice made me look up and I saw that he was. Serious. His eyes wide and imploring as they stared down at me, as if he was looking right into my soul, his jaw jutting out in that way it did whenever he was talking about something important. 'I'd want you to move on, Jenny. To find happiness again. I'd hate to think that I was ever responsible for holding you back, for pressing pause on your life.'

I stopped walking, the concrete warm beneath my feet as I turned, staring up at the man I loved. The man that was standing in front of me telling me he wanted nothing more than for me to be happy, even if that happiness was with someone else. I wound my wrists around his neck, balancing on my tiptoes to reach.

'Well, you have set somewhat of a high bar, Mr Carter—'

'That is true, I pity the poor sucker that's got to follow this.' A smug grin teased his mouth upwards, the seriousness of the conversation disappearing as quickly as it first began.

'—but I promise to try,' I whispered, my eyes locking with his before I sealed my vow with a kiss.

That's when the rain had started. Lightly at first, a fine mist that you could barely feel. But then the heavens opened, steam swirling around my toes as the raindrops pummelled the warm concrete, soaking us in an instant. I shrieked, running a few short steps to shelter under a nearby tree, but when I turned back around, Joe hadn't moved. He was wet through, his white dress shirt almost translucent as it stuck to him like a second skin. But he was grinning, face tilted upwards as he welcomed the raindrops chasing one another down his cheeks. He held out a hand.

'Come dance with me.'

'You're crazy!' I shouted through the downpour, still huddled under the safety of the tree.

'Maybe.' He laughed. 'But life's too short to wait for the rain to pass, Jenny.'

His words echoed round my head now, demanding to be heard as I remembered how I'd reached out, letting him pull me tight against his body. Our hips moved as one, a single shadow swaying back and forth on the pavement in the final drops of sunlight. Joe spun me round, laughter and rainwater ricocheting all around us. I remembered the flash of Joe's camera, the click of the shutter echoing in my ears as he took a step back and captured that moment. Like he knew on some level that I'd need to see it one day.

A single tear rolled down my cheek as I read the title of the piece, a single word in simple font on the plaque beneath.

Life.

A flash of navy caught my eye, dragging me back to the present day. There it was again. A familiar head of sandy-brown hair weaving its way through the crowd, that distinctive double crown I'd recognise anywhere. It was him. My heart threatened to leap straight out of my mouth as I jostled my way through the throngs of people, desperate to catch another glimpse. My elbow collided roughly with someone as I went, but I ignored the pointed tuts and sound of breaking glass tinkling behind me. The white walls of the gallery blurred as I spun around, frantically trying to spot him amidst the happy, oblivious strangers.

And then there he was. Stood by the open door, hands buried in the pockets of his jeans, looking straight at me.

His unseasonably thick woollen jumper and beaten-up Chelsea boots looked out of place amidst a sea of crisp white shirts and floaty summer dresses. He gave a small, private smile, as though he'd just had the exact same thought, and then ducked through the door, disappearing into the street.

'Joe!' I yelled, without caring who heard me. Not that there was much chance of that. My voice was swallowed up by the buzz of chatter, everyone talking a little too loudly thanks to the free champagne still being circulated on tiny silver trays.

'Excuse me!' I yelled, not caring who or what I collided with as I elbowed my way towards the exit. I lunged for the door, stumbling down the steps and out onto the street, my upper lip beaded with sweat as I looked first left and then right, just in time to catch sight of Joe turning down a side street.

'Joe, wait!' I called desperately. But he didn't stop. He kept walking, disappearing from view. I was crying now, running as fast as my legs would carry me. I couldn't let him get away. I just couldn't. I skidded round the corner, but Joe was still striding purposefully in the opposite direction, as if he had some place more important to be.

'Just *WAIT!*'

My voice echoed down the empty street, rebounding off dustbins and dark shopfronts. Joe stopped suddenly, his chin falling to his chest, before turning slowly beneath the soft glow of the streetlight.

'Why . . . won't . . . you . . . just . . . *wait?*' I panted angrily, doubling over to catch my breath.

'Wait for what?' he asked simply.

'For *me*, Joe!' My voice cracked and I swayed unsteadily on my feet, my knees threatening to give way. 'Don't leave me,' I whimpered, my voice now nothing more than a whisper.

Joe looked up at the night sky, his chin angled towards the stars as he blinked quickly, furiously behind his glasses. And then he was marching towards me, closing the gap between us in six long strides until we were mere centimetres apart.

'Jenny, look at me,' he said fiercely. I lifted my head, craning it upwards at a familiar angle to stare into his cornflower-blue eyes that were almost electric behind his tortoiseshell frames. 'I will *never* leave you. *Never*,' he repeated slowly, closing his eyes as though the very idea was too painful to harbour even for a moment. 'I will look for you in every lifetime, Jenny Thompson, in this world and the next, and I will love you there. But you need to stop running from *this* life. You're constantly running – from your emotions, from your friends, from any possible chance of something good, of something *great*.' He didn't say Luca's name. He didn't have to. The meaning was clear.

'It wasn't enough time,' I sobbed. 'You and me, we didn't get enough time.'

Joe's eyes crinkled at the edges. 'No amount of time ever would be.'

I could feel the tears running hot and silent down my cheeks. Joe's fingers twitched by his side as though he was fighting the urge to reach out and wipe them away. My shoulders slumped inwards, the hollow part in my chest aching like it had never ached before. I nodded weakly, my throat too thick to allow any words through. My gaze fell to the pavement, counting each cobblestone in turn as I waited for my breathing to slow, working up the courage to confront the very thing that I'd been running from for so long. I reached fifty-six before I could speak.

'I don't know what this feeling is.' My voice was small, afraid. An image of Luca growing stronger and more defined inside my head. Those liquid chocolate eyes. That black mass of hair, the curls at the edges just begging to be twisted through someone's fingertips. Those giant hands, permanently ink-stained from scrawling lyrics about heartbreak and new beginnings on the back of used envelopes and takeaway menus.

'It's love,' Joe said gently, his smile unwavering as he coaxed my gaze back up. 'Or the beginnings of it, at least. So, what are you doing still talking to me?'

My teeth ground together, pain ricocheting through my jaw, but it was only when another kind of pain found its way to my heart that I dared to breathe. Dared to speak.

'I'm scared,' I whispered, the admission rushing from my mouth in a single exhale.

'Scared of what?'

'Everything!' I blurted out, wincing as the alleyway repeated my answer back to me. I was scared of fucking everything. Of what might happen if I let Luca in, my already-punctured heart just one blow away from shattering into a million irreparable pieces. Of what would happen if I didn't. Scared of turning the page and starting again when I thought I'd be twenty chapters deep at this point in my life. But most of all, scared of losing Joe.

'I miss you so much,' I sobbed, the tears coming thick and fast now. I wanted nothing more than to reach out and bury my face in the scratchy wool of his jumper, to feel the warmth of his body against mine.

'I know.' Joe smiled simply, his dimples cutting into his cheeks. 'And I miss you more than you could possibly imagine. But it's OK to be scared. Fear is good. Fear means you've still got things in your life you're not willing to lose.' His words hit somewhere deep inside of me, my pulse quickening at the thought of losing Luca. 'Don't be afraid to love, Jenny. Love hard. Scream it from the flipping rooftops, because it's what makes the ride worthwhile. You're never going to lose me, Jenny, I'll always be here.' His hand hovered over my heart, my skin tingling beneath his palm as I let his words sink in. I don't know how long we stood there in the dim glow of the streetlight, the air silent and still as though the world had stopped spinning, allowing us this moment for as long as possible.

My breath hitched at the back of my throat as Joe took a single step backwards, and my heart gave an almighty thump for what was about to happen. Because how do you look at the person you love and tell yourself it's time to let them go? Joe took another step back and then another, his boots eerily silent against the cobblestones as he moved further and further away from me, his eyes never leaving my face. I faltered, my right foot stumbling forwards to try and lessen the gap between us.

'I'll always be here,' Joe repeated calmly, raising his hand to his heart with a reassuring smile. I mirrored him, my heart pounding beneath my palm as I held it to my chest, tears flooding down my cheeks. And then he turned and disappeared into the night, the darkness swallowing him whole. I knew that would be the last time I'd see him. And although the constant, dull ache that had been there ever since Joe's death intensified somewhat, I did not crumble.

I knew what I had to do. What I wanted to do. I just prayed I wasn't already too late.

'Come on,' I growled at the ancient row of buzzers, jabbing my finger at each one in turn in the hope that someone, anyone, would answer.

'Yes?' crackled a voice through the speaker. It was female. Old. That distinctive air of permanent irritation I recognised instantly.

I grimaced. 'Hi, Mrs Norris, it's Jenny. Jenny Thompson.'

'Jenny Thompson?' She said the words impossibly slowly, pronouncing each syllable with the speed of a snail.

'Yes, from number 4. Can you buzz me in, please?'

'I thought you moved out?'

I bit my tongue, bashing my head repeatedly against the stone wall. The woman is convinced it's still 1942, and yet she remembers that tiny, insignificant detail?

'Well yes, I did move out, but—'

'*Such* an inconvenience,' she drawled, a dramatic sigh wheezing through the intercom. As though my whole world being turned upside down was incredibly tiresome – for her. 'You know, as the building's longest resident, I would have appreciated some notice, Jennifer.

The new chap up there has people coming and going at all hours. *Music students* apparently,' she scoffed, somehow making the words sound dirty. 'Honestly, does he think I was born yesterday?'

'Can you just buzz me in, please?' I shouted, losing what dwindling patience I had left. She was ruining my end-of-the-movie-running-through-the-airport-to-stop-the-guy-getting-on-the-plane moment.

'Young people these days, no manners,' Mrs Norris tutted, but the door buzzed open a few seconds later.

'Thank you!' I yelled into the speaker, wrenching the door open and taking the stairs two at a time. By the time I reached the top floor I was sweating profusely, my top sticking to my body in odd places, but I didn't care. I rapped my knuckles sharply on the door, my heart in my mouth.

Nothing.

I knocked again, louder this time.

Still nothing. Fuck. This was the equivalent of turning up at the airport to find you'd not only missed the guy, but that the plane had already taken off! Bloody Hollywood and their making you think that big, grand gestures always end with a foot-popping kiss. My hand hammered repeatedly against the door until my palm burned.

'Luca, it's me. Please open the door,' I pleaded. I knew he was in. I'd seen the lights on in his flat from the road. But the unopened door spoke volumes in the silence of the landing, a big, loud HE DOESN'T WANT TO SEE YOU echoing round my head. I leaned my forehead against the door for a second, my hand flopping to my side in defeat. I turned, eyeing the tired, worn stair-case with a sigh. But my sinking heart did a little leap, fluttering to life when I heard soft approaching foot-steps from inside the flat. I screwed my eyes tightly shut, trying to steady my breathing as I silently mouthed the words I'd been practising on the journey over. I heard the door click open, the hairs on my arms standing on end as though I was being drawn towards him by some invisible force.

'Look, I know you're mad at me and you have every right to be,' I said quickly, tripping over the words in my haste to get them out before Luca could close the door in my face. My eyes were still closed, clamped firmly shut until I'd said what I'd come here to say, because I knew that one look into Luca's eyes and my brain would be scrambled. 'I was scared. Scared of starting again, scared of losing someone who's been a part of my life for as long as I can remember, scared of what I've felt every day since I met you – OK, maybe not the first day, you were pretty annoying back then, still are actually – that's not the point.' I frowned, shaking my head. 'The point is, you've been kind and loving and patient whilst I try and heal from all the things you didn't break. And the thing I'm most scared of is walking away from you today and never feeling again for the rest of my life how I feel when I'm with you. So, I choose you, Luca. I can't lose you. I just can't. And I'm sorry I fought that for so long. But you make me feel like there's everything to live for, and I've not felt like that in a really, really long time. I don't know what the future holds, and I've got no fucking idea where I want to be in 10 years' time. But wherever I am, whatever I'm doing, I know I'll be happy as long as I'm with you.'

'Sorry, *who* are you?'

My eyes snapped open, the unfamiliar female voice causing the breath I didn't realise I'd been holding to rush out in a single, loud sigh. A woman's face was just about visible behind the door: tiny button nose, big blue eyes, even bigger lashes. A pink chrome-manicured hand gripped the side of the door as she peered around it, as if she was afraid I might barge my way in.

I blinked, my cheeks warm at the thought of having just poured my heart out to this complete stranger.

'I'm Jenny,' I said, finally finding my voice. 'I'm, umm . . . a friend of Luca's.'

'A *friend*?' The woman's eyes travelled disdainfully down to my feet and back up again. 'Luca's never mentioned you,' she said dismissively, her tone almost accusing. Like she thought I was making it up. I smiled tightly.

'Well, he didn't know I was coming, kind of an impromptu visit, so—' I expected her to open the door, invite me in. But her welcome was about as frosty as her stare. I leaned this way and that, trying to see around her into the tiny slit of the flat that was visible behind the half-closed door. 'Is Luca home? I really need to talk to him.'

The woman's eyes narrowed a fraction, her lips pursed as though she were contemplating something important, like a chess player determining their next move. And then the frostiness was gone, a giant, beaming smile lighting up her face.

'Sorry, how rude of me. I've not even introduced myself,' she scolded herself, flashing her pearly whites as she held the door open. 'I'm Rachel. Luca's fiancée.'

I froze, my whole body numb. Rachel was still talking, her lips moving animatedly, but I was too focused on what she was wearing to hear a word she had to say. Her bare feet peeped out from Luca's oversized grey jogging bottoms that hung low and loose around her hips, the drawstring tied in a double bow to keep them up. That familiar white t-shirt that I'd last seen on Luca's bedroom floor, because that's where I'd thrown it after peeling it from his body, swamped her tiny frame. But it was the ring that sparkled on the third finger of her left hand that stopped my heart in my chest.

'Luca's just in the shower. Things got a bit—' Rachel paused for a fraction too long for it not to be intentional, purposefully waiting until I met her gaze before she finished '—dirty.' A sharp pain shot through my chest. 'I'll tell him you stopped by, OK?'

But it was the kind of question that didn't wait for an answer, the door slamming shut in my face. The brass number 4 and flaky red paint blurred at the edges as my eyes stung with tears. Tears of regret and disappointment and jealousy and pain. I waited until I felt my legs could support me again, and then I began the long, slow journey back down the staircase. Away from the flat. Away from Luca. Away from all of it.

20

Three weeks later

There were flowers everywhere. Two milk churns overflowing with them at the entrance to the church car park. A meandering path of delphiniums and eucalyptus standing to attention along the winding gravel pathway. Ivy draped artfully over a rustic pallet sign that read *Matt & Alyssa's Wedding* in careful, hand-painted script.

'God, I love weddings,' Jacob declared, taking a long breath in through his nose before bending to fix his tie in the reflection of a parked car.

'I'll see you in there, love, I'm going to try and find your brother before it all kicks off,' Mum said, patting her intricate-looking updo with one hand before heading up the path towards the church. I glanced around, marvelling at a woman tottering across the car park under the largest, most ridiculous hat that I had ever seen, complete with full-size peacock feathers. A man was trailing behind her, one trouser leg tucked into his sock, a tatty, well-thumbed copy of Moby Dick sticking out of his jacket pocket.

'Come on, Barry,' snapped a familiar nasal voice. 'Would it kill you to go any faster?'

'Bet that's not the only time she's said that to him.' Jacob sniggered, winking mischievously at me in the reflection of the car window. I rolled my eyes, throwing Kristina a little wave and poor Barry a consolatory smile as they passed us. My heart bloomed as I spotted a head of unruly black hair just ahead of them, the half-inch of exposed skin just visible above the white shirt collar a familiar shade of olive. But it withered again a second later when the stranger turned to greet Kristina, their face not the one I was hoping to see.

He wasn't coming. Of course, he wasn't coming. Yes, we'd made a stupid pact two months ago about him being my plus one, but that was before. It had been three weeks. Three long weeks since I'd last seen or spoken to Luca and still, I was no closer to forgetting about him.

'You're looking for him, aren't you?'

I blinked, my shoes grinding against the gravel as I turned to see Jacob straightened up, tie knotted to perfection, face knotted with concern.

'What? Of course not,' I lied, shaking my head rather aggressively as though by doing so I might dispel any thoughts of Luca from either ear. 'Besides,' I continued, taking a deep breath, 'I've already got two of the best dates anyone could wish for, you and—'

'*I'm here!*'

We both turned to see Alice somehow simultaneously exiting an Uber, applying lipstick, and shimmying a pair of blue hospital scrubs off from underneath her dress. She looked remarkable full stop, let alone for someone who'd just finished a twelve-hour shift. Her hair was pinned neatly behind one ear, her green eyes shimmering beneath silver eyeshadow, the fringed hem of her flapper dress fanning dramatically outwards as she skipped lightly towards us.

'Umm, I think you've forgotten something.' Jacob looked physically ill staring at Alice's feet, which were still encased in her hospital Reeboks.

'Right, hold this.' Alice shoved her Tesco's carrier bag at Jacob, who balked at it with the same level of disdain Anna Wintour would grant an all-black outfit, as she kicked off her trainers, flung them into the bag and produced two gold slingbacks.

'Happy?'

'I'm wearing a £750 Hugo Boss suit and holding a Tesco bag that smells of egg mayo, what do you think?'

I smiled affectionately at my best friends as they bickered over who would hold the bag (Alice eventually relenting when Jacob threatened to dump it in a bush), looping one arm through each of theirs as we ascended the steps to the church.

'There's something kind of beautiful about having lifelong friends,' I sighed gratefully. 'You know, the ones that have witnessed every possible version of you and loved them all.'

'Well, I wouldn't say I loved the whole "not washing for five days" version of you,' Alice noted with a judgemental lift of her eyebrow. I nudged her in the ribs.

'You know what I mean.'

Alice grinned up at me, resting her pixie crop on my shoulder.

'I for one am very much here for the badass bitch version of you from last week who told Derek where he could shove his story about the man who got his Tesco Clubcard tattooed on his forearm because he kept forgetting it.' Jacob chuckled before raising a finger sharply in the air. 'Although I want it on the record that I still haven't forgiven you for handing in your notice and abandoning me. Who's going to shamelessly mock our co-workers with me now?'

I smiled up at him, giving his arm a reassuring squeeze. 'Well, this whole being unemployed business is proving very hectic so far, but I'm sure I could move things around in my diary and meet you for lunch.'

The truth was, I'd been waiting for the regret to hit from the second I'd waltzed up to Derek and handed in my notice last week. That stomach-twisting fear at the realisation that I was an unemployed 30-year-old woman living in her mum's spare room with zero plans for what I wanted to do with my life. But actually, that wasn't exactly true. I *did* know with 100% certainty that I did not want to spend the rest of my life reporting on phallic-shaped vegetables or delinquent seagulls. And after everything that had happened this past year, I'd realised that turning 30, or any age really, meant nothing. Yes, it's a nice round number with a zero at the end and, sure, a certain finality to it – the end of another decade – but we often forget that it marks the beginning of something, too. A new chapter. A chance to start over. And that was precisely what I was in the market for.

'Your mum mentioned that you finally cashed Joe's life insurance cheque,' Alice noted, her head bobbing in approval.

'Yeah, well, I thought it was probably time.' I shrugged with a small smile. 'Plus, Mum almost had a heart attack the other day when she sucked it up with the hoover, so it was more for her continued sanity than anything.'

'And here I was about to take pity on the unemployed and offer to buy you lunch! The Tesco meal deals are most definitely on you next time, and fair warning, I'm going Tesco Finest.' Jacob grinned, resting his head on my shoulder and giving me a tight squeeze. I took a deep breath, wondering if I should tell them or not.

'Actually, I might have already—'

But Jacob spun around sharply, the panicked expression on his face cutting me off.

'*Shitballs!* Pretend you're talking to me,' he barked.

'We *are* talking to you.' I frowned.

'Unfortunately.'

Jacob ignored his sister's sassy aside and sneaked a peek over his left shoulder. Alice followed his gaze, her eyes zeroing in on a man in a burgundy velvet jacket and black dress pants.

'Isn't that—?'

'Yes!' Jacob whimpered before Alice could finish her sentence.

'Didn't you and he—?'

'Mhmm.'

'In the bushes at Hove Park?'

'It was actually under a very majestic elm tree at midnight,' Jacob corrected her, lifting his chin a fraction higher but then immediately ducking back down to hide from view.

'Oh, how romantic. You're practically a modern-day Cinderella,' Alice drawled, rolling her eyes at a crouching Jacob, who seemed to have forgotten he was wearing slip-on loafers and was busy pretending to tie some imaginary shoelaces. 'You do know that with your record, it's statistically very likely that one of your former lovers will be within 50 metres of you at all times? I don't know why it's a surprise every time we bump into one.'

'It is not *every* time,' Jacob pouted, grabbing an order of service from the stack by the door and holding it an inch from his face as we entered the church, much to mine and Alice's amusement.

We found our seats in the second row from the front just before the music started, a single violinist playing Christina Perri's 'A Thousand Years'. A hush fell over the room, a hundred heads turning to catch a first glimpse of Alyssa as she walked arm in arm down the aisle with her dad. But I remained facing forwards. Not because I was sad or jealous, or wishing deep down that it was me in that white dress as my fingers circled the band of soft skin where my ring used to sit – the ring that was now safely tucked away in the shoebox under my bed along with a thousand other memories just waiting to be relived when the time was right – but because I was busy watching my brother. There's something magical about the moment a groom first sees his bride. That wide-eyed look of pure adoration, head jerking backwards in disbelief as if he can't believe his luck, that will make even the most cynical of unbelievers yearn for what he's feeling in that exact moment. True, complicated, worth-fighting-for love.

We walked the short distance from the church to the reception venue, a merry trail of fascinator-topped blowouts and rose petal-sprinkled shoulders snaking their way across the public footpath to Devils Dyke Farm, where a cavernous stretch tent sat overlooking the rolling fields, the sea a glistening strip of blue in the distance. Delicate flowers in mismatched bud vases nodded in the warm afternoon breeze, arranged down the centre of three long rows of tables covered in white tablecloths. A vast square of dance floor lay invitingly in front of the stage, where an acoustic guitar waited patiently in a metal stand. That leather strap, the one you could tell was once a deep red but which was now more of a lifeless salmon colour, looked just like—

'OK, looks like the canapes are coming from somewhere over there,' Jacob deduced quickly, doing his best flight attendant emergency exit hand gesture towards the back where waiters were appearing, carrying black slates piled high with impossibly tiny food. 'If we linger by the bar, we'll get first dibs when they bring them out.'

'You had me at bar,' Alice said, following Jacob willingly through the throng of guests. I was two glasses of champagne and four mini burgers deep when Jacob erupted into a spluttering, red-faced mess beside me.

'Oh. My. God!' he wheezed, smacking Alice repeatedly with the back of his hand and prompting me to slosh champagne down my front.

'What now?' Alice asked lazily. 'Don't tell me you've spotted another of your ill-fated lovers? One is a coincidence. Two is a cry for an intervention.' Jacob's eyeballs bulged at something behind me and Alice turned to look, but I was too busy dabbing at my fizzing cleavage to notice.

'*Shit!*' Alice muttered, spinning back around with a frantic look in her eyes. 'Did you know about this?'

she hissed at Jacob who just shook his head, hijacking another glass of champagne from a passing waiter and thrusting it into my hand.

'You're going to need this,' he warned, wincing.

My own eyes narrowed. 'OK, can someone tell me what's going on? You two are acting even weirder than normal.' I lifted myself onto my tiptoes, trying to see past them. Alice lunged towards me, grabbing both my shoulders and spinning me around so I was facing the other way, my back to the dance floor.

'OK, if I tell you something, will you promise not to freak out?' she asked with that deliberate, slow calmness that instantly makes anyone the opposite of calm.

'I'm already freaking out! What's got into you two?'

'Ladies and gentleman, it's my immense honour to introduce you to Mr and Mrs Thompson.'

My heart slammed against my chest when I heard his voice, raw and husky as it echoed into the microphone. People waved their napkins in the air around me, glasses held aloft in salute of Matt and Alyssa sparkling beneath the fairy lights as the couple began their first dance as husband and wife. But once again, my focus was elsewhere. On the man in the black suit, his tie already missing or never having made it in the first place, guitar slung over one shoulder as he began a rendition of John Legend's 'All of Me'.

I knew I missed Luca. I'd thought about him every minute of every day for the past three weeks. But seeing him standing on that stage, all tousle-haired and clean-shaven, singing about a bond between two people that I'd made damn sure we'd never get the chance to explore,

313

my entire body felt on the verge of coming apart. Around me, couples started pairing off, women dragging unenthusiastic men away from their beers to join Matt and Alyssa on the dance floor. Jacob touched my arm, said something I didn't quite hear, but I just shook my head, forcing a smile and shooing them towards the mass of swaying bodies. I watched as Luca's gaze roamed the tent, scanning, searching for something.

'He's certainly not looking for you,' I muttered into my champagne glass, downing the contents in one to try to calm my breathing. I turned away, the sight of him in that crisp white shirt, the same one I'd peeled off him that night in the hallway, almost too much to bear. 'He chose Rachel,' I reminded myself firmly, my own words like a dagger to the gut.

Even though my gaze was fixed firmly on the ground, I *felt* the exact moment Luca's eyes found me in the crowd. Something inside of me melted, every fine hair on my arms standing to attention, as though I was being pulled towards him by some undeniable force. I tried not to look up. I *really* tried. But it was like asking someone not to breathe. And so, I lifted my head, lost myself in those walnut-brown eyes for what I promised myself would be the final time. I knew instantly that I shouldn't have looked. The way he was staring at me, as if I was the only person in the room, his eyes boring deep into the fractured parts of myself that I'd tried so long to hide as he sang about all of him loving all of me.

I turned, muttering apologies as I pushed my way through the crowd, suddenly needing to be anywhere but here. I didn't stop when I exited the tent, kicking off my shoes and breaking into a run across the field, the hem of my dress trailing behind me as I tried to outrun the ache in my chest. It felt like a bowling ball had landed in my stomach. That sudden drop, the familiar crushing weight of feeling like I'd just lost something good. Maybe even something great. I ran until I couldn't run anymore, my hands anchored against the wooden fence that bordered the field, my breath sharp and hot in my throat.

'You know, if I didn't know any better, I'd say you were avoiding me.'

My eyes fluttered closed, the smell of his aftershave on the early evening air all it took to make my heart tighten with longing. I turned slowly, bracing myself to meet his gaze, but nothing prepared me for that hint of a smile. The one that made me feel like I'd stepped straight into the sunlight as he stood leaning against a tree a few metres away, visibly panting as though he'd jumped straight off that stage and sprinted after me.

'Of course not,' I lied. 'I didn't even know you were going to be here tonight.'

Luca ran a hand down his face, pushing off from the tree and taking a step towards me. 'Alyssa asked me to perform their first dance after hearing me sing at the bar on her hen do. I presumed you knew.'

'No, I didn't,' I breathed shakily. 'I'm surprised you came, after . . .' My voice trailed off to nothing.

'She asked me before everything that happened, so—' There was a distinct, *otherwise I wouldn't be here* subtext that made me wince. We stood in silence for a while, the night air crackling between us, charged with everything unsaid.

'Are you here alone?' I was going for casual, polite small talk, but my voice came out strangely high-pitched. The molten ring of gold around Luca's irises sparked as he took another step across the grass.

'Yes, Thompson. I'm here alone.'

Hmm, Rachel must have stayed at home. Can't say I blamed her.

Luca hesitated. 'You?'

'No.'

Something strange happened to his face. His mouth became pinched, his jaw frozen at an unnaturally hard angle.

'Oh, right.' He halted, shoving his hands deep in his pockets as the toe of his shoe butted against the gnarled roots of the tree. If I didn't know any better, I'd swear he was jealous.

'I came with Alice and Jacob,' I clarified, scrunching my bare feet into the soft grass, the blades tickling between my toes. I couldn't tell if that hopeful lift of his brow was wishful thinking on my part, or if he was genuinely relieved that I hadn't brought a date. Ergh, who was I kidding, of course it was the former. He was with Rachel. Luca's hand raked through his hair, brushing all but one strand out of his face as he took two more strides towards me.

'I wanted to thank you.'

His words threw me off guard. 'Thank me? For what?'

'For the article you wrote about the concert. It was – beautiful.'

I shifted against the fencepost, the skirt of my dress catching against a stray splinter. 'It was a beautiful event.'

Luca nodded, biting down on his bottom lip. 'Yeah, you know, it's the strangest thing. We received an anonymous donation a week ago, enough money that we don't need to worry about closing any time soon. We might even look at expanding.' His head tipped knowingly to one side. Those eyes, those big, perfect eyes searching my face as his hand came to rest on the fencepost beside me. The bank had assured me that the transfer would be anonymous. No way for Luca to trace it back to me, which was important, as I wasn't sure he'd accept it if he knew it had come from me.

'That's amazing.' I feigned surprise, not trusting myself to look at him for fear he'd see straight through me.

'Mhmm, amazing,' he echoed, a knowing edge to his voice that made me look up. The closeness of him made my breath catch in my throat and I knew he'd heard it too. I needed to get out of there, but I also didn't want it to end.

'It's a shame Rachel couldn't make it,' I said quickly, going to take a step backwards to try to put some more distance between us but forgetting about the fence. This, us standing so close that his trousers brushed the front of my legs, was making my fingers itch to pull him flush against me and nestle my mouth in the crook where his neck met his shoulder.

Luca frowned. 'Why would she?'

'I get it might be a bit awkward, but I hope she didn't not come because of me.'

Luca cocked his head to one side, a dazed look on his face as if he'd just woken up. Anger bubbled up inside of me. Was he really going to make me say it? Was he really going to be that guy?

'Rachel? Your *fiancée*?'

'Rachel's not my fiancée.' Luca looked more confused than ever.

I huffed, losing patience. 'You can drop the act, Luca, I know.'

'Well, please enlighten me, because apparently you know more about my personal life than I do.'

'I came by the flat the night after the concert. Rachel answered the door. Wearing your clothes. And an *engagement ring*,' I added pointedly when Luca just continued staring at me blankly before understanding finally dawned on his face.

'Rachel was at my flat that night.' My heart sank, even though I already knew that fact to be true. 'She showed up out of the blue telling me how she'd been *working on herself*—' Luca's eyes rolled a full three-sixty, his fingers wagging in lazy air quotes '—and after inviting herself in, she basically spoke *at me* for a full thirty minutes before announcing she thought we should get back together.'

I swallowed, the lump in my throat as solid as a rock. 'Well, I'm happy for you,' I said tightly, twisting my mouth into something I hoped resembled a smile.

Luca's eyebrows inched upwards. 'You don't honestly think I said yes, do you?'

I risked a glance at him. His eyes were serious, unblinking.

'I don't understand,' I whispered. But I think some part of me did understand. Or rather, it hoped it did. And that hope burned like a kindling flame in a rainstorm, flickering but refusing to go out. 'She was wearing your clothes.'

'After she opened my most expensive bottle of red wine, she then proceeded to spill an entire glass down herself. Personally, I think it was just a poorly executed excuse to take her clothes off – not that she's ever needed one before – so I gave her some old clothes to wear whilst I washed her dress.'

'And the ring?'

'It's her engagement ring from the guy that she cheated on me with.' Luca shrugged. 'Turns out they'd had a big fight earlier that day, which makes the whole timing of her showing up at my flat *very* Rachel.'

I frowned, slowly rearranging the pieces in my head to reveal a completely different picture. One that made my heart soar in my chest. 'Wait, so she's still with the other guy?'

'As far as I'm aware.'

'But she introduced herself as your fiancée.'

Luca's head flip-flopped from one side to the other. 'Yeah, well, that sounds like something Rachel would do. She was probably jealous, trying to stake a claim or whatever.'

'Jealous? Of what?'

'Of you, Jenny.'

I snorted, rolling my eyes. 'What could she possibly have to be jealous about?'

Luca's brows stitched together, his mouth pursing in disbelief. A mouth so impossibly soft compared to the sharp lines that made up the rest of his face. 'You really don't see it, do you?'

'See what?'

'How amazing you are.'

All the breath rushed out of me, the seesaw in my chest going back and forth with the speed of a steam engine's pistons. The world seemed to grind to a halt for a second, the distant sound of the DJ fading to nothing, the hem of my dress stilling around my ankles in the warm breeze. It was just us. Me and Luca. And the million questions ping-ponging round my head.

'What—'

But Luca held up a hand, cutting me off.

'My turn to ask a question,' he said, his tongue running briefly over his bottom lip. 'Why did *you* come to the flat that night?'

'I . . .' I hesitated, floundering for an excuse, something, anything but the truth. *You mustn't tell him how you feel, you mustn't let him in*, some part of my brain whispered. *We did that once before, remember, and it almost broke us.* But I'd come a long way this year and while, for a second, it felt too frightening to say the words I wanted to out loud, I knew better than to listen to that voice anymore.

'I came to tell you that I don't have the strength to stay away from you anymore,' I said, looking him right in the eyes. 'You made it impossible for me not to fall for you, even though I promised myself that I'd never, ever do so again. But then I met you and you made the fall feel like I was flying. So, I can't lose you, Luca. I just can't. And that's your fault, with your floppy hair and your sexy serenades and your kind, impossibly giving soul. I mean, seriously, pick a lane already!'

Luca pressed his lips into a tight line but otherwise didn't interrupt me.

'I came to tell you that I'm sorry. You were more honest than I ever was, even with myself – especially with myself – and I did the very thing you feared the most. I let you down, and I'm sorry. But it was never a choice between you and Joe, Luca, and it pains me so much that I ever made you feel like it was. Joe will always be a part of me, but he makes up the chapters of my past, and now I'm ready to turn the page and find out what happens next. Something was going on up there the day I met you,' I said, glancing briefly up at the stars above us. 'I like to think that Joe had a little something to do with it. He always knew what I needed even before I did.' I smiled fondly as a particularly bright star winked back at me, twinkling in agreement against the midnight blue sky. Luca's face was completely still, his angular cheekbones painting a beautiful canvas of light and shade across his face, as though they'd been sculpted specifically to be viewed under the light of the moon. By the woman trying to win his heart.

'I'm not perfect,' I sniffed, lifting my arms and letting them fall hopelessly by my sides. 'In fact, I'm a bit of a mess. I'm 30 years old. My credit score's non-existent. I still live with my mother and, as of very recently, I am unemployed. For the first time in my life, I've got no plan – I don't even know if I want to get married, or have kids, or settle down, or whatever the hell else society says you should be doing at my age. But I do know that I can't imagine waking up to one more sunrise and not have your face be the first thing that I see.' The truth rolled off my tongue so easily. There was no forcing it past a lump in my throat, or screwing my eyes shut to say it. It simply flowed out of me like a breath, just another star floating bright in the sky above us. Luca was silent. Frozen. Part of me might have questioned if he was still alive, if it weren't for his chest rising and falling double time beneath the thin cotton of his shirt. *Shit.* This was it, wasn't it? This was the reason I'd been so scared to tell him the truth, to open myself up to the pain.

'That's it.' I sniffed again, wrapping my arms tightly around myself, as if by doing so, I might somehow be able to hold the fractured pieces of my heart together. I was crying now, big, fat tears running down my cheeks and dripping from my chin, sparkling amongst the dew in the grass below. 'That's all I've got. I mean, I think my speech was better the first time, and I don't think that fourth glass of champagne did me any favours, but—'

'Jenny.'

The fingers of his right hand caught my chin, coaxing it softly upwards until our eyes met.

'You *are* perfect, Jenny Thompson,' he declared feverishly, tucking a wayward curl behind my left ear. I leaned into his touch. I couldn't help it. 'I don't think you realise how beautiful you are, and I'm not talking about the way you look tonight – although *Christ*, you look so fucking hot.' His eyes roamed hungrily over my dress, the delicate spaghetti straps, the corset-style bodice, the full lace skirt, before settling once more on my face. 'I mean *all* of you. The broken parts, and the bruised parts, and the parts that you're still afraid to show me. But guess what? I've got those too, we all do. I was so busy looking for all the warning signs, pinpointing any little similarity between us and the failed relationships in my past, that I overlooked all the good. And seeing Rachel again after so long just confirmed how different you really are. We might be messy and complicated, but so is life, Jenny, and unlike other people, you didn't run at the first sign of trouble. You stayed and fought for me, or at least, you tried to, even when I was intent on pushing you away. When we first met you weren't ready to let go of the past and I guess, in a way, I was guilty of the same thing. But I've realised – maybe with a little help from Jasmine and her *101 Reasons You're an Idiot & You Should Be with Jenny* PowerPoint presentation that she made me sit through last week – that I need to let go of that giant chip on my shoulder. The one that constantly tells me I'm not good enough – for my dad, for Rachel. For you.'

My bottom lip trembled, and I blinked away the tears that were blurring the face of the man who'd just taken my hand in his.

'I've not been able to stop thinking about you since the second we met, so I don't know what else to do other than take a leap of faith and just pray that you'll leap with me.' And in that moment his face filled with everything that for so long I'd dared not look for. Certainty. Tenderness. Maybe not quite love, not yet anyway, but something damn similar.

And so I leapt, without hesitation, without overthinking, without anything but the overwhelming need to hold him, to call him mine. I flung my arms around his neck, not wanting one more second of separation to pass between us, and pressed my lips to his. That night we spent together we must have kissed a thousand times. But not one of them felt like this, neither of us holding any part of ourselves back. His arms snaked their way around me, feverish hands roaming over my hips, the small of my back, beneath the hem of my dress. He walked us slowly backwards, not allowing even a whisper of breeze between us, until his hips pinned me back against the wooden fence.

'Do you think my heart will ever stop trying to jump out of my chest whenever you touch me?' I asked breathlessly, burying my face against his neck to stifle the sounds he was drawing out of me. He paused the slow, delicious journey his mouth was making down the side of my neck.

'I sincerely hope not,' he whispered against my mouth and I wished I could swallow his words, let them take root inside of me, their branches growing and twisting around every single part of me. I kissed him again. Slowly this time, framing his face with my hands. The kind of kiss two people might have who are only just starting to believe they have all the time in the world together.

'So, tell me more about this PowerPoint?'

The corner of Luca's mouth hitched as he drew me tightly against him, linking our fingers together as we walked hand in hand across the field, two sets of footprints trailing after us. 'It was *long*. There were Venn diagrams and Photoshopped pictures of the two of us under the Eiffel Tower.'

'And 101 reasons why we should be together?'

'And 101 reasons why we should be together,' Luca confirmed with a laugh. 'Jasmine doesn't do things by halves.'

'Well, I look forward to hearing every single one over dessert.'

Luca stopped abruptly, pulling me backwards until I landed against his chest, my lips mere inches from his. 'Dessert before main course? Miss Thompson, you really are quite scandalous.'

I shrugged. 'This guy I know introduced me to it.'

'Sounds like a keeper.'

I smiled up at him, watching his eyes sparkle in the moonlight.

'You have no idea.'

Acknowledgements

My first thank you goes to my absolute powerhouse of an agent, Sarah Hornsley, who I firmly believe was in fact Superwoman in a past life. Thank you for seeing something in me from day one – I'll never forget that first email I got from you that changed everything. Thank you for never giving up on me, for picking me up and dusting me off when things didn't go to plan, and for always being game for a glass of wine at lunch!

Working in publishing, I know it takes a village to publish a book and what a gorgeous village I've stumbled upon. Thank you to Sam Humphreys for taking a chance on me and giving Jenny, Joe and Luca a shot before anyone else – there aren't enough words to express my gratitude so just, thank you! To Melissa, Leonie, Jenny, and the whole team at Bonnier for your tireless work and support to bring *The Man I Loved Before* out into the world.

Mum, Dad, I guess now's when I should probably thank you for making us that crazy family who didn't have a TV growing up. Whilst I might have lamented about missing out on *Sabrina the Teenage Witch* and *Cartoon Network*, it sparked my love of books at an early age and set me on this wonderful path. Rob, James, thanks for being the best big brothers a girl could ask for – you inspire me every day with your work ethic and dedication and allowed this bookworm to believe that maybe, just maybe, she might be able to achieve the impossible.

Thank you to my loveable lump of a golden retriever, Milo, who gives me a reason to step away from the laptop every day and get outside. If he knew how many book ideas were cooked up and plot holes fixed on our dog walks, he'd most likely insist on a cut of the royalties, so I'll be keeping that one to myself!

A HUGE thank you to every reader who's picked up this book. I'm a book lover first and foremost, so I'm immeasurably honoured that you've chosen to spend time with Jenny, Joe and Luca. I hope you laugh as much (and cry a little less!) as I did when writing them.

And lastly, a special thanks to my husband, Marc. Thank you for your unwavering support and encouragement of my dream-chasing; for your gracious acceptance whenever you ask what our plans are at the weekend, and I say writing; for putting up with the glare of my laptop screen in bed; for your patience and kindness and showing me every day what true love really is. The first and last page of this book are dedicated to you, my love, for you are my beginning and my end.